WITCHIN' AROUND THE CLOCK

A WICKED WITCHES OF THE MIDWEST MYSTERY
BOOK FIFTEEN

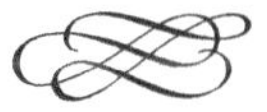

AMANDA M. LEE

WINCHESTER SHAW PUBLICATIONS

❀ Created with Vellum

PROLOGUE

15 YEARS AGO

"It's time to talk about where babies come from," my mother announced.

My mouth dropped open as stunned disbelief washed over me. I understood when we were called to the dining room that it wasn't going to be a pleasant conversation. I expected punishment for what we did to the Baker boys — perverts, every single one of them — and maybe even a lecture on how we needed to be careful when it came to dropping the sort of curses that needed medical attention. I didn't believe that itchy fingers and sweaty genitals were the sort of things that would draw attention to us, but my mother and aunts thought otherwise.

I, Bay Winchester, was prepared to be yelled at by the elders. I figured it was possible a grounding would be thrown in. If my mother and aunts were feeling particularly vindictive, there was always the chance we would be sentenced to spend time with Aunt Tillie. Of course, she taught us the sweaty genitals spell, so she could be in trouble, too. It was unlike her to miss a good punishment session ... and yet she was nowhere to be found.

"I don't want to talk about where babies come from," I countered, rubbing my sweaty palms over my knit shorts as I tried to put my thoughts in order. "I'm good ... thank you."

"None of us want to talk about where babies come from." My cousin Thistle, her eyes full of mayhem and contempt, looked as if she would rather throw herself off a bridge than continue this conversation. I couldn't blame her. "If you're trying to kill us, this is a great way to do the deed."

My mother wasn't the sort to back down. She recognized Thistle was in a combative mood — that was her perpetual state these days — and looked more resigned than miffed. That was a telling detail ... that Thistle somehow missed.

"We already know where babies come from anyway," Thistle continued, her arms folded over her chest. "We don't need a repeat of that information."

Mom was calm. I had to give her credit. Her natural instinct would be to scream and run. She was holding it together. "Okay. I'll play." Her gaze never faltered. "Where do babies come from, Thistle?"

Instead of answering, Thistle rolled her eyes. That allowed my other cousin, Clove, the opportunity to shoot her hand into the air.

Thistle shot Clove a withering look. "Oh, stop being a suck-up," she growled. "This isn't like licking the beater, Clove. You don't want to answer this question. It's a trap."

Clove, who liked being the center of attention, didn't back down. "I know where babies come from." The grin she shot her mother was mischievous. Unlike my mother, Marnie remained hidden at the edge of the group. She clearly wasn't as keen as her sister to bless us with the sex talk.

Mom nodded perfunctorily at Clove. "Where do babies come from?"

"The stork," Thistle bellowed before Clove could respond. "They come from the stork. Are we done here?"

"No." Mom rested her hip against the counter and focused her full attention on my temperamental cousin. "We got a call from Terry this afternoon. Do you know what he told us?"

Terry Davenport was a local police officer who stepped in and served as a father figure when we started getting out of line. We'd been unnaturally close for years, ever since I informed him his dead mother was still watching over him — I can see and talk to ghosts — and he decided to make sure I got in only half the trouble I really wanted to take on.

Clove's hand shot in the air again. "I have a guess."

"I am going to break your arm if you don't stop doing that," Thistle warned.

"Knock it off." Thistle's mother, Twila, flicked her daughter's ear as she passed behind her. "Making threats won't delay the inevitable. This is happening whether you like it or not."

I pursed my lips as I focused on Twila's clown-red hair. She only lacked the makeup to look like an actual clown and make this horrifying experience truly complete.

"We know where babies come from!" Thistle was beside herself. "We don't need a repeat conversation. You told us where babies come from when we were eight and we're still traumatized."

Wasn't that the truth? I shuddered at the memory. "You even had that book with the photos."

"Yes, well, now we have a video," Mom countered. "We thought, instead of just talking at you, we would sit down and discuss things with you while watching a miracle. Doesn't that sound nice?"

Even Clove was suddenly leery at mention of a video. "You want to make us watch a video of a baby being born?"

Mom bobbed her head. "That's exactly what we want. We think it's time, given what happened at the lake yesterday, that we make absolutely sure that you're aware of what you're dealing with."

At the lake? Now I was confused. "Listen, what happened at the lake yesterday was ... a necessary evil. There's no reason to punish us with this freaking torture. We won't do it again."

"Speak for yourself." Thistle's gaze was dark. "I have every intention of doing it again if those turd fondlers don't get it in their heads that we don't want to play certain games with them."

Mom tilted her head, considering. "Wait ... I think I'm behind. What do you believe happened at the lake yesterday?"

Oh, well, that was interesting. She didn't even know the true extent of what she was dealing with. That begged a certain question ... and I wanted answers. "What do you think happened at the lake yesterday?"

"I asked first."

"Don't answer that," Thistle barked, her eyes on fire. "It's a trick question. She wants you to own up to something so she can punish you. If we keep our mouths shut, we'll never get punished again."

"That's a lovely thought, Thistle," Twila drawled. "But it's not even remotely true. We already know what you did, and you're definitely going to be punished for it."

Even though Twila unleashed the words with conviction, there was doubt lurking in the depths of her eyes. This situation was quickly spiraling, but it wasn't yet altogether lost. The hope I'd begun hoarding like gold fled just as easily as it appeared when Aunt Tillie, my persnickety great-aunt, appeared in the doorway.

"What's going on?" Aunt Tillie was the suspicious sort and she clearly sensed trouble. Her gaze bounced between Thistle, Clove and me before shifting to her nieces. "What did I miss? Did they do something? You know I don't like missing out on punishments. Why didn't you call me?"

Mom made a face. "We're not punishing them."

"You're not?" I was relieved ... and yet still terrified.

Aunt Tillie looked disappointed. "Why aren't you punishing them? They always deserve punishment. After what they did yesterday ... ." She trailed off, uncertain.

"That's right, old lady," Thistle hissed under her breath. "Figure it out. If we get in trouble for what happened at the lake yesterday, you're going down with us."

If Thistle meant to keep our mothers from overhearing her, she did a rotten job of it. She has one of those voices that carries. To be fair, all our voices carry. Quiet isn't a word you could use to describe the Winchester house. We were all big mouths and there was no getting around it.

"Don't make me put you on my list," Aunt Tillie warned Thistle.

They were often at loggerheads because they enjoyed fighting with one another. It looked as if the antics were going to start early today.

"I'm not afraid to be on your list."

"Then you're dumber than you look."

Mom cleared her throat to get our attention. She looked frustrated. "This is a serious topic," she insisted. "Terry was quite upset when we talked yesterday. He said there was sexual contact between you and the Baker boys."

Oh, well, this conversation was happening whether we wanted to engage or not. This was just ... the worst. I mean, the absolute worst. I wanted to find a hole to crawl in and die.

"You had sexual contact with the Baker boys?" Aunt Tillie's eyebrows flew up her forehead. "Are you idiots? That wasn't the plan. You were supposed to teach them a lesson, not give them a thrill. Did I teach you nothing?"

Thistle made a rude gesture with her hand. "Shut it!" She obviously didn't want the story getting out. I had a feeling it was far too late to stop that from happening.

"Wait ... I'm starting to feel as if we're missing part of the story," Mom lamented. "What happened yesterday?"

"What do you think happened yesterday?" I challenged.

Mom's eyes narrowed. "That's not going to work on me, Bay. Aunt Tillie might've taught you that trick, but I'm not simply going to forget my original question."

That was a bummer. "How do you know that's what I was doing?"

"I'm not an idiot." Mom's gaze bounced from face to face before landing on Aunt Tillie. "You're technically the adult in this group — although you would never know it — and I believe that means you should explain things."

I wasn't sure that was better. I didn't want to watch a birthing video, so I was ready to try anything. "Yeah. You explain it to them."

"I think that's a fabulous idea," Thistle drawled, evil intent etched across her features. "You tell them what's going on."

"Doesn't anyone want to hear me explain where babies come from?" Clove asked with a pout.

"No!" Everyone in the room barked at the same time.

"Well, then why even ask? That's just mean."

Mom ignored Clove's outburst and focused on Aunt Tillie. "Talk ... or I'll make sure that still you've got hidden in the woods is discovered by some poor, unsuspecting law enforcement official. Is that what you want?"

Aunt Tillie's gaze darkened to the point where her eyes looked like black holes of death. "You're definitely on my list."

"I don't care." Mom was firm. "I want to know what happened at the lake yesterday. Terry said the Baker boys walked into a cave with the girls and then ran out screaming a few minutes later ... and they weren't wearing any swim trunks."

It took everything I had not to laugh at the memory. Even though I knew we were in trouble, that we were being threatened with a potentially heinous punishment for something we didn't do, I wouldn't be sorry for what happened to the Baker boys. They had it coming ... and then some.

"And you think the girls did something with the Baker boys that made them drop their shorts?" Aunt Tillie asked. "You should have more faith in them."

"Yeah," Thistle muttered. "You should definitely have more faith in us."

Aunt Tillie, never moving her eyes from Mom's face, cuffed the back of Thistle's head.. "I can guarantee that what you think happened didn't happen. I mean ... who told you that load of malarkey anyway?"

"Terry."

Aunt Tillie rolled her eyes. "Oh, well, Terry. I should've known."

I felt the need to stand up for him. He'd been a good and loyal friend through the years — well, when he wasn't trying to get us into trouble, that is — and I didn't want to hear him unfairly maligned. "He's just confused. He didn't mean to get us in trouble."

"You always stand up for him," Aunt Tillie groused. "He's still 'The Man.' You need to remember that. As for what went on with the Baker boys, it wasn't a big deal. They got what was coming to them."

Mom's forehead wrinkled. "They were owed sex? I don't understand."

"Oh, geez." Thistle slapped her hand to her forehead. "There was no sex. Stop saying that word."

"I thought we were talking about babies," Clove complained. "I would rather talk about babies than sex."

"Where do you think you're going to get those babies, kvetch?" Aunt Tillie shot back, shaking her head. "Maybe you should watch whatever torture video they've prepared for you."

"Just her," Thistle argued. "I don't want to watch it."

"You're watching it," Mom insisted. "We don't want any accidental grandbabies showing up. It's time we had this conversation."

"We know where babies come from." I was shrill as I gripped my hands into fists. My fight-or-flight response was kicking into high gear. "We don't need to watch a video on it."

"Apparently you do, because the Baker boys were naked in front of you."

"They weren't naked because we had sex with them," Thistle snapped. "They were naked because Aunt Tillie taught us how to cast a genital sweating curse and we unleashed it on them because they're dirty perverts who keep grabbing our butts. We're not sorry either. They had it coming."

Whatever Mom was expecting, that wasn't it. Her eyebrows drew together as she lobbed confused looks in Twila and Marnie's directions. "I don't ... are you saying you didn't have sex with the Baker boys?"

I was horrified at the prospect. "Of course not. We wouldn't touch them with Aunt Tillie's poking stick. You know the one she made to poke Mrs. Little through the window of her store when she's bored? We wouldn't use that."

"Definitely not," Thistle agreed. "They're gross ... which is why we paid them back."

"Oh." Mom looked momentarily placated. "I guess ... well ... I don't know what to say. What have those boys been saying to you?"

Thistle shrugged. "The normal stuff. We told them we didn't like it, but they didn't listen and then made it worse by grabbing us, so we paid them back."

"By making their genitals sweat?" Mom remained confused as she focused on Aunt Tillie. "How did you even know to ask your aunt for that curse?"

"Oh, we didn't ask," I replied. "She volunteered when she heard us plotting against them. We didn't know the curse was a thing either, but it sounded fun ... and like a fair punishment."

"And the entire punishment is making their genitals sweat?" Mom asked.

"Actually, it's more that they feel as if they're on fire," Aunt Tillie corrected blandly. She was clearly losing interest in the conversation. "It's a karma spell. I thought it was appropriate."

"Yeah, but ... ." Mom trailed off, took a moment to think, and then regrouped. "You know what? I happen to agree with you just this once. I think the karma spell was an inspired touch, and I'm relieved none of you had sex with the Baker boys."

"Stop saying the word 'sex,'" Thistle ordered. "We don't want to hear that word come out of your mouth. Any of your mouths really. It's terrifying."

"It's a normal part of growing up," Mom countered. "Apparently, it's not on the agenda for today, though. You may go."

This was too easy. "Just like that?" I was understandably dubious.

"Just like that." Mom's smile was serene. "We'll revisit the baby video at a later date."

"That was a nasty threat," Thistle muttered.

"Oh, but I want to watch the video now," Clove pouted.

"Then you'll be watching it alone," I shot back.

"The video can wait for another time." Mom had relaxed into a relieved smile. "As for the Baker boys, I don't feel sorry for them. Just don't have sex with them. You'll live to regret it if you do."

"Don't worry. We understand about sex. There's nothing you have to teach us that we don't already know."

"Is that a fact?" Mom's features lit with intrigue. "Why don't you tell us exactly what you know?"

Wait ... this conversation had taken another turn. How did that even happen?

"You just couldn't let it go, could you?" Thistle complained. "You had one job. All you had to do was walk away without opening your mouth. You couldn't manage it."

That was rich coming from her. "It's not my fault."

"You always say that."

"This time it's true."

"Yeah, yeah, yeah."

ONE

PRESENT DAY

"I could've lived my entire life without knowing there was such a thing as a mucus plug," Thistle announced, her blue hair standing on end thanks to the constant swiping of her hands. She looked as if she'd accidentally stuck her finger in a light socket.

I nodded in agreement as I made a face. Clove sat between us, a pregnancy book — complete with photos — open on her lap. She'd brought the book to work because she needed help dealing with everything inside of it. Thistle didn't want to have to undergo the ordeal alone, so she'd called me away from The Whistler, the newspaper I own and operate in Hemlock Cove, to help her deal with Clove's mini-meltdown.

I was starting to regret picking up the call.

"Listen to this," I complained as I took the book from Clove. "A mucus plug accumulates in the cervix during pregnancy and is dislodged right before giving birth. It might be clear or bloody."

"Ugh!" Thistle made a disgusted face. "It's as if whoever made up this process had to make it as horrible as possible."

I wasn't much into conspiracy theories, but I had to agree with her. "You just know it was a man."

"Definitely."

For her part, Clove wasn't amused with our antics in the least. "Focus on me!" She snapped her fingers between our faces and grimly reclaimed the book. "I didn't bring this book here so you could read it and terrify me. I need your help."

Even though messing with Clove was something of a hobby for the entire family — snark and sarcasm reign in the Winchester household, after all — I couldn't hold out in the face of her misery.

"It'll be okay," I reassured her, grasping for the right words. "You're going to make a great mother."

The expression Clove made would've been funny under different circumstances. "Don't be ridiculous. Of course I'll be a good mother. I was born to be a good mother. It's this birth stuff I don't get. Why can't babies just kind of crawl out without hurting you or anything?"

Thistle made a horrified face. "Crawl out? What kind of mutant baby are you expecting?"

Clove ignored her and tapped the book. "Focus!"

Several weeks ago, she'd announced she was pregnant ... but only to Thistle and me. Not only was she going to have a baby, but she was also much farther along than we were comfortable with. She was showing, although the clothes she selected did a good job of hiding that fact. She'd managed to hide the truth from our mothers until this point, but her luck couldn't hold out forever.

"All we have to do is keep it together until the wedding, which is in a few days," Thistle noted. "I know moving the wedding by a week and a half to coincide with the solstice was a blow, but I think it'll be better for us in the long run."

"How do you figure?" Clove's eyes filled with worry, something I didn't want to see because this was supposed to be the happiest time of her life. "I should already be married at this point. That was the original plan."

"Yes, well, you know our mothers." I flipped another page in the book and made a gagging sound. "Ugh. Why are there so many pictures?"

"These books are a cautionary tale of what happens when you let dudes have sex with you," Thistle replied, her lips twisting into a sneer. "Apparently all the bad stuff happens to women. I mean ... that is horrifying. Who knew the human body could stretch like that?"

"Giving birth is a natural process," Clove countered. "Women have been doing this for generations. I'll be fine."

She was much calmer than I expected. If I were in her position I'd be freaking out. That was usually Clove's default reaction. Now, though, she was focused on other things ... like keeping the pregnancy secret until after she'd successfully married her fiancé Sam Cornell. That happy event was right around the corner. It had snuck up on us much faster than I'd anticipated.

"You'll be fine," I agreed.

"I'm just worried that Mom and the others will find out before I'm ready to tell them." Clove chewed her bottom lip. "Do you think they'll be angry?"

I'd been considering that very question since Clove admitted to being pregnant. Her fear was palpable ... and that wasn't only because the pregnancy was wreaking havoc with her hormones and causing her to project emotions in a manner that had Thistle and me acting out of sorts.

The truth is, we were witches. We were born witches. Our mothers were witches. Our entire family was one long line of witches. Clove's emotions, which had always been on the surface, were now so out of control that Thistle and I were occasionally displaying uncommon personality defects because Clove was exerting magic without realizing it.

The situation wasn't good ... and yet we were so close to the finish line we could practically taste victory.

"It'll be fine," Thistle offered, forcing her attention away from the book and focusing on Main Street. We were seated in the living room section of Hypnotic, the store Clove and Thistle owned. "All we have to do is make it a few more days. Once you're married, it won't matter that you're pregnant."

"I can't believe we're even having this conversation," I said as Clove turned another page. "Mother of the Goddess," I hissed when I saw the photograph. "Is that what I think it is?"

"Stop looking!" Thistle barked. "Do you want to have nightmares? This will kill us all if we're not careful."

"Not me." Clove was firm as she smiled at the photo. "I'm looking forward to giving birth. No, seriously. I mean ... I'm scared of the pain and everything, but I'm looking forward to having a baby. How much fun will a baby be?"

That felt like a trick question. "Loads?"

Instead of being offended, Clove laughed. "You're hilarious. I forgot how much you hated babies."

"I don't hate them," I countered. "I simply don't like them."

"She's afraid of them," Thistle corrected. "They freak her out. If you want to know the truth, they freak me out, too. I'm not holding that thing until it's more durable and its head doesn't flop around. You've been warned."

Clove rolled her eyes. "You'll get over it and be great aunts. I'm not worried about that. I'm just worried about our mothers finding out."

To me, giving birth was the real fear. I would much rather put up with a little disappointment from my mother and aunts than have a baby ripped from my loins. Yeah, I said it. Ever since Clove had announced she was pregnant I'd been having a series of depressingly dark dreams that involved giving birth to various creatures ... including cats, dogs, rats and Kardashians. The last was the most horrifying prospect of all.

"I think you're worrying about nothing where they're concerned," I offered. "It's not like when we were teenagers. I mean ... if one of us ended up pregnant back then it would've felt like the end of the world. The thing is, we would've figured it out then, too.

"You're an adult now," I continued. "I know they warned us that we would be disowned if we turned up pregnant before marriage, but I think that was just a deterrent for when we were too young to take care of ourselves. You're getting married. In a few days, you're going to get everything you ever wanted. Why would they possibly be upset about that?"

"Because we're supposed to be married before having babies," Clove replied without hesitation. "They were adamant about that."

"Yes, and they were adamant that it was important not to have sex on the first date, but Aunt Winnie threw that out the window when she started having sex with Chief Terry," Thistle noted.

I frowned. I was still getting over the horror of finding out my mother was having sex with my favorite father figure. I was traumatized. "Do we have to talk about that?" I fought the urge to wrestle Thistle to the floor and start shoveling dirt from the nearby potted plant into her mouth. "I don't want to even think about that."

"Oh, poor Bay." Thistle's expression was mischievous as she poked my side. "We all have our hang-ups, don't we?"

That was an understatement. "Yeah. Some of us are convinced that Aunt Tillie is spying on us even though she's been distracted by other things ... like her new pig."

Thistle scowled. "Aunt Tillie *has* been spying on us. I know she has. I caught her peeking through the window of the store the other day."

I had to bite back a laugh. "Your storefront consists of two big windows," I reminded her. "Whenever someone walks past they have to look through the windows. That doesn't mean they're spying."

"Oh, grow up." Thistle's tone was withering. "She's spying. That's what she does."

"I think Thistle might be right," Clove acknowledged. "Aunt Tillie has been acting weird ... and that's saying something, because she bought a pig and named it Peg."

"I like Peg," I countered. "She's good for Aunt Tillie. She keeps her distracted."

"That is always a plus," Thistle agreed. "She's still spying. I haven't figured out what she's up to, but I will. I won't let her out-maneuver me. I'm done letting her win."

That was a conversation for another time. Thistle's paranoia was starting to rocket off the charts. It was a concern, but not one we could focus on now. We had other things to worry about, mainly Clove.

"The other witches start arriving tomorrow," I offered. "Once that happens, our mothers won't be able to focus on anything but them. This is a big deal."

"I actually think one or two are showing up tonight," Thistle countered, thoughtful. "Do you remember the last solstice celebration?"

"We celebrate the solstice every year," Clove countered.

"I know, but ... I'm talking about the last big gathering."

"We were teenagers," I answered, my mind drifting back to the day in question. "I remember it pretty well. There was a lot of naked dancing and wine drinking."

"There was a lot of fighting, too," Clove added. "That's why they canceled the big gathering the year after ... and things sort of snowballed from there."

"That's exactly what I'm talking about. This is the first big gathering in twelve years at least. These witches haven't been together in a long time. I can't be the only one worried that some of them might've forgotten their manners."

"Oh, don't kid yourself," Thistle supplied. "You're worried Aunt Tillie will forget her manners."

I'd definitely been worrying about that. "Landon asked me about the gathering last night," I said, referring to my live-in boyfriend. We'd taken over the guesthouse I used to share with Clove and Thistle and were happily cohabiting. "He's really excited to meet these other witches. I don't know what to tell him."

"Why not tell him the truth?" Thistle prodded. "Tell him that Aunt Tillie is often considered the sensible witch when it comes to the other coven members."

I made a face. "I don't want to scare him away."

"If Aunt Tillie's leggings haven't scared him away yet, it won't happen. Still, I get what you're saying. This is a big deal for all of us. I think that's the only reason our mothers haven't figured out Clove is pregnant. I mean ... they would have to be blind not to notice."

Clove, always concerned about her appearance, turned huffy. "You take that back." Her agitation was on full display. "I look the same as I always have. I've put on only two pounds."

Thistle snorted. "Oh, please. You've easily put on twenty pounds. We're just lucky that they think you're stress eating because you're nervous about the wedding."

"Twenty pounds?" Clove's eyebrows hopped halfway up her forehead. "Bay, tell her that's not true. I haven't gained twenty pounds."

I felt caught. On one hand, Thistle was right. Clove had definitely put on more than a few pounds. It was noticeable ... unless you were our mothers, apparently. On the other hand, I enjoyed messing with Thistle to the point I found true joy in torturing her.

"You look exactly the same, Clove," I lied. "Pregnant women the world over would be thrilled to look like you."

Clove preened as Thistle scowled. "Thank you."

"Liar, liar, witch on fire," Thistle hissed under her breath.

I pinched her flank, causing her to squirm as Clove went back to looking at her freaky book. "If she wants to believe she's still thin, who are you to ruin it for her? She just needs to get through a few more days. Is that too much to ask?"

Thistle glowered at me but ultimately lowered her eyes. "Fine. I'll keep playing this ridiculous game for a few days. After that, I'm going nuts."

I was right there with her. "I think we should be thankful that the coven elders decided to reinstate the group solstice celebration," I said, smoothly changing the subject back to a topic not quite so dangerous. "We're hosting it, so our mothers have something to obsess about other than us. That's a good thing."

"That *is* a good thing," Thistle agreed. "It's just ... I don't remember these solstice celebrations being relaxing events. I remember our mothers freaking out, barking a lot of orders and insisting that we be on our best behavior."

"I was always on my best behavior regardless," Clove offered.

"Thank you," Thistle drawled. "The Goddess of Sucking Up is apparently reporting for duty early."

I couldn't hide my smile despite Clove's pronounced pout. "We don't live under the same roof with them," I pointed out. "It was different when we had to help with the cooking and cleaning. They'll be taking all that on themselves this time. We can hide ... which is exactly what we need to do to keep Clove's pregnancy a secret until the wedding."

"And then you're telling them before you go on your honeymoon?" Thistle pressed. "You're not going to drag it out, are you?"

"No." Clove's lips curved down. "I thought about trying to pretend I got pregnant on the honeymoon, but odds are probably slim they would believe that."

"Especially with the baby coming in a few months," I shot back dryly. "You need to tell them before you go. That way they can fume for two weeks and be over it by the time you get back."

"Which means they'll take out their aggression on Bay and me while you're gone," Thistle added. "Not that we're not happy to take one for the team or anything."

Clove's expression turned rueful. "I appreciate you guys doing this for me. It means a lot." Her voice cracked and, oddly enough, I felt tears clogging my throat.

"Stop that," Thistle hissed, swiping at the tears appearing on her cheeks. "You can't keep projecting emotions on us. This will blow up in our faces if they figure out what's happening before the wedding. You need to hold it together."

"I will," Clove promised. "I promise I will. It's just the hormones get me occasionally."

"Well ... make them stop." Thistle lowered her face to Clove's stomach. "Stop being a whiner, baby. We're trying to protect you here. Get with the program."

I laughed, my eyes flicking to the window when I caught a hint of movement. At first glance I thought I was seeing things. Aunt Tillie wasn't just walking past the window, she looked to be flying at a high rate of speed. Then I realized she had her hands on a set of handlebars and wasn't flying as much as gliding.

"What is that?" I was already on my feet and heading to the window before Thistle and Clove could say a word.

"Was that a scooter?" Clove asked, joining me so we could stare at the sidewalk. Aunt Tillie had already disappeared around the corner.

"I think it was," I confirmed, lost in thought. "That must be the thing Mom and the aunts were complaining about her buying the other day. She ordered it from Amazon. Mom was furious because she said Aunt Tillie was going to break a hip or something."

"It's a kick scooter," Thistle pointed out. "Why did she get that instead of one she could sit down on?"

I shrugged. That was a good question. "I don't know. All I know is it's motorized and she's going really fast."

"You can say that again," Clove supplied. "Here she comes again. Wait ... what is she doing?"

I narrowed my eyes and watched as Aunt Tillie circled onto the sidewalk again, her eyes fixed on the store down the way.

"She's taunting Mrs. Little," Thistle surmised, shaking her head. "She's riding that thing around the block over and over because she knows it will drive Mrs. Little crazy."

Margaret Little was Aunt Tillie's nemesis, so that was a fair bet. "Well ... at least a new toy will keep her busy for a few days." I smirked as Aunt Tillie flew by the store window again, heading for the end of the block. "That's always a bonus."

"That's true." Thistle brightened considerably. "In fact ... ." She trailed off when a distinct sound filled the air, the sound of what had to be at least fifty crows cawing in unison as they took to the air and fled the downtown area. They dotted the sky, a mass of moving black targets, and the noise was deafening.

"What is that?" Clove asked, her hand flying to her mouth. "Is that what I think it is?"

I was familiar enough with signs to confirm it without a second thought. "Harbingers," I muttered, my witch training taking over. "They're harbingers. Something bad is about to happen."

I was already moving Thistle and Clove away from the window when a rumbling started shaking the building. The sound of something exploding echoed from farther down the street. It was close enough to be worrisome, and the force of the blow was enough to rock Hypnotic to its very foundation. On instinct, we all dived behind the couch and took cover.

Yes, something very bad was happening ... and it wasn't over.

TWO

Thistle and I instinctively shielded Clove with our bodies. The store shook with the power of the explosion, several items falling off shelves, but the roof held steady and the rumbling quickly ceased.

"What was that?" Clove lifted her head, her eyes wide. "Was that an earthquake? Oh, geez. What do you think Aunt Tillie did this time?"

My heart skipped a beat as Thistle jerked up her chin to meet my gaze.

"Aunt Tillie," we said in unison, hopping to our feet and racing toward the door. It wasn't that we thought she was responsible — for once, the odds seemed unlikely — but she'd been zipping around outside. She was in the open when whatever it was happened. We had to find her.

"Stay here!" I ordered Clove as I rushed through the door.

"Stay here?" Clove turned shrill. "What are you talking about?"

"Stay here," Thistle echoed as she moved in behind me. "We don't know what this is. You're safer here." She smacked into my back, but only because I'd pulled up short when I reached the sidewalk. "Oh, why don't you stand in the middle of the sidewalk and do nothing or something, Bay?" she complained. "That will help."

I didn't answer. I couldn't. My mind had gone temporarily blank.

"Why are you standing here?" Thistle gave me a vicious shove and I stumbled forward. It was her turn to be gobsmacked when she realized what had caught my attention. "Is that ... ?"

"That blacksmith shop," I replied grimly, pushing against Thistle's car to make sure I stayed on my feet. "I'm pretty sure it exploded."

We exchanged a heavy look.

"We need to get down there," she said. "We have to find Aunt Tillie."

She wasn't wrong. Our great-aunt might've been a royal pain in the keister — and that was putting it nicely — but she was still family.

"Stay here, Clove," I instructed again when she appeared in the open doorway. "If you see Aunt Tillie, grab her and make her stay inside."

Clove shook her head. "I should go with you," she countered. "I ... you shouldn't go without me."

"I don't see that we have much choice in the matter. You can't go with us. The smoke isn't good for ... anyone." I didn't mention the baby. No one on the street was paying attention to us — there was a fire to watch, after all — but now wasn't the time to be reckless. "We'll be in touch when we know what's going on. For now ... just stay here."

Clove opened her mouth to argue again, but she was too late. Thistle and I were on the move, our attention trained on the inferno raging at the end of the street.

"How did this happen?" Thistle asked blankly.

"I don't know. Maybe it was a gas leak or something."

She slowed her pace. "If there's a gas leak we shouldn't leave Clove in the store. We should put her in a car and get her out of here."

That was actually a good idea. "You do that. I'll go down and see what I can find out."

"No way." Her hand snaked out and grabbed me by the wrist. "You need to come with me."

"I can't." I felt helpless in the wake of her glare. "I need to know what that is ... and I have to find Aunt Tillie. Clove should be your responsibility. I'll make Aunt Tillie mine."

On a normal day Thistle would've jumped at the chance to foist

Aunt Tillie off on somebody else. Actually, it wouldn't even have to be a family member. Any random stranger would do. Today, though, she was clearly torn. She glanced back at the store and then at me. The serious set of her jaw told me she'd made up her mind.

"We're going together." She was firm.

This time when we started running, a sense of urgency had somehow kicked into gear in the back of my brain, forcing me to increase my pace until I was gasping for breath. When we arrived in front of the blacksmith shop, all hell was breaking loose ... and not in a fun way like we were used to in Hemlock Cove.

"Adam! Adam!"

A woman was wailing. It took me a moment to find her in the smoke, which was so black that I feared I wouldn't be able to find my way back out if it should become necessary to escape. Lorna Harris, her ashy blond hair jutting haphazardly from what had once been a severe bun, stood in the middle of the road screaming as she stared at the building.

Well, what was left of the building really. The burning structure wasn't original. When Hemlock Cove rebranded as a magical vacation destination years before, the town had to erect a few buildings. The blacksmith shop was one of them. There simply wasn't a need for a fancy barn with outdated equipment before the town took the plunge into the kooky.

"Adam!" Lorna was seemingly blind to Mrs. Gunderson, who had managed to beat us to the fire. The bakery owner was trying to calm the hysterical woman ... and not having much luck.

"What's going on?" I asked as I shielded my watering eyes from the smoke. "What happened?"

"The building blew up," Mrs. Gunderson replied simply.

"We figured that out ourselves," Thistle snapped. "How did it blow up?"

"I have no idea. I was in the front of the bakery when I heard it. I came right down because ... well ... just because."

I understood "just because." I had a reason for racing to the scene, but it was unlikely that I would've remained at the store even if not for Aunt Tillie. This was a big story, after all. I had to cover it for The Whistler.

"Adam!" Lorna screeched so loudly that I thought her vocal cords might snap. She continued to struggle against Mrs. Gunderson's iron grip. The baker was stronger than she looked.

I swallowed hard as reality set in. "Was Mr. Harris in there when it exploded?"

"I don't know." Mrs. Gunderson looked as bewildered as I felt. "You know what I do."

"Adam!"

I sucked in a breath, which was filled with smoke and made me cough. When I recovered, I strode in Lorna's direction. I wasn't sure what I was going to do until I was directly in front of her. "Is he in there?"

Lorna seemed surprised to be addressed so directly. She clamped her mouth shut and nodded, tears streaming down her soot-stained cheeks. "I was outside," she hiccupped. "I was getting the mail from the box. I felt the ground shake and then ... it happened so fast. I just remember thinking, 'The roof is gone.' Then I realized Adam never came out."

I turned my eyes to Thistle, wondering if she had the same thought. She was already shaking her head, so it seemed not.

"Don't even think about it," she hissed, moving closer to me. "We can't go in there." Even as she said it, her eyes traveled back toward the building. The flames stretched high into the sky, the roof completely obliterated. The first floor looked relatively unscathed, which seemed to be something of a minor miracle.

"We won't go far," I reassured her, my voice more solid than I expected given the fear coursing through me. "We'll just look through the door."

Mrs. Gunderson, perhaps reading our minds — or even lips – extended a warning finger in our direction. "You can't go in there."

"Adam!" Lorna was back to screaming. "Adam!" She would lose her voice soon, or maybe even pass out from the overwhelming smoke.

"We have to at least check," I insisted. "We'll be okay. We know what we're doing."

The look Thistle shot me was incredulous. "You get more and more like Aunt Tillie with each passing day. That's something she would say."

Well ... that was hurtful. "That's the meanest thing you've ever said to me."

"And I stand by it." Thistle refused to back down, her blue hair picking up flecks of gray from the small bits of ash and debris raining down on us. "You don't run into a burning building. That was one of the first lessons that crazy old bat taught us when we were kids."

"Since when do you listen to Aunt Tillie?"

"Since she occasionally makes sense. We're not going in there."

She was right. It wasn't smart or safe. Slowly, I nodded, causing her shoulders to relax. Then, because I couldn't get the notion of Adam suffering and dying on the ground only feet from us out of my mind, I tore in that direction before she could stop me. "I have to look."

"Son of a witch!" Thistle screeched behind me. I heard her feet pounding on the gravel as she followed. "You'd better hope that fire kills you, because if it doesn't I'm going to rip your hair out and choke you with it."

As far as threats go, it wasn't even close to her usual level of snarky sass. I couldn't dwell on that, though. I had a mission, and I couldn't turn away from it.

I pushed through the swinging doors. It was an enhancement added two years ago. It gave the building an "Old West" vibe that most tourists found charming. It was helpful now because there was no way we could get trapped without an exit.

"This had better be worth it," Thistle griped from behind me. "I'm not kidding. If he's already dead, you're going to join him."

It was an empty threat and we both knew it. Sometimes when fear overtakes a person it comes out as belligerence. That's how Thistle always rolled, ever since we were kids. She couldn't show the fear, so she had to control it. If that meant threats, so be it.

I paused for a moment to get my bearings. I'd visited the building a number of times for photographs and to collect ad information from Adam. I was familiar with the layout. The thick smoke momentarily threw me for a loop. Once I regained my senses, I pointed to the right.

"That's the workshop," I rasped. The smoke, in addition to causing my eyes to water, was overtaking my lungs. This would have to be a quick search. "If he's anywhere, he's there."

"Then let's go." Thistle wrapped her hand around my wrist. At first I was taken aback because I thought she might be feeling vulnerable. Then I realized it was simply because she didn't want to lose me should darkness overtake us. "Stop dilly-dallying. We have to find him and get out. This building won't stay erect forever."

She had a point.

I put one foot in front of the other as I cut through the building. It was hard to see because of the smoke, and the occasional sound of something falling from above was nerve-wracking. Thistle kept up a nonstop litany of curses and threats as she followed. Her fingernails dug into the soft flesh of my wrist and I tried to push the pain out of my mind. Now was not the time to complain.

There was a change in the amount of available light when we reached the workshop. Thanks to a window on the west side of the building, we could see at least part of the room. It was there, on the floor behind a bench, that a pair of legs were clearly visible.

"Is that ... ?" Thistle drew up beside me, releasing my wrist.

"Adam." I dropped to my knees. He was covered in debris, but I didn't have to clean him off to know that he was dead. His eyes were open, sightless, and his lungs had stopped drawing oxygen before we made the decision to enter the building.

"Oh, well, this is just great," Thistle drawled, glaring at me. "He's dead. We came in here for nothing."

I shot her a dirty look. "Are you honestly telling me you would've been okay with not checking?"

"I would've been fine with it."

I didn't believe her, but it hardly mattered. "He's gone. I'd suggest we drag him out, but I think it will take longer than we have." The sound of something falling on the floor above us caused me to cringe. "We have to get out of here."

"Oh, do you think?" Thistle's eyes flashed as she stomped back in the direction from which we'd come. "I could've told you this was a bad idea. Does anyone listen to me, though? Of course not. I'm just the youngest cousin. Nobody listens to the youngest cousin." She was silent for a beat. "Are you even listening to me?"

"Of course not. You're the youngest cousin. Why would I listen to you?" The words were meant as a joke, but there was no mirth in my tone because at that moment Thistle moved to slide through the opening, and a cavalcade of whispers assailed my senses.

I reacted on impulse. I still don't know why. It wasn't as if I could make out a single voice in the din. That didn't stop me from grabbing the back of Thistle's shirt and pulling hard. Murder etched across her face as she swiveled, and I knew I was in trouble. Before she could say a word, the ceiling in the room we were about to enter gave way with enough force that we both fell backward, landing on Adam's body.

"We can't go out that way," Thistle said dumbly, her face blank.

For some reason, her reaction struck me as funny and I laughed.

"It's not funny," she argued, adopting a dour expression. "Why are you laughing?"

"I don't know." That was the truth. I had no idea why I was laughing. "It just struck me as funny."

"That's because you're a moron." She flicked me between my eyebrows and glared. "How are we going to get out?"

I sobered. The lack of oxygen was causing us to act stupidly. It most certainly wasn't a good thing. I didn't want to suffocate. I didn't want to burn. We had to get out. I thought it was a great idea to enter in the first place. It was on me to get us out.

"I think we should go through there." I pointed to the window, which was now only offering the faintest bit of light.

"That's great." Thistle grunted as she stood. "How do you think we should do it?"

That was a ridiculous question. "We break the glass."

"Great, Einstein. With what?"

"Well ... ." I was starting to feel fuzzy around the edges. What I really wanted was to curl up in a ball and sleep, but I knew better than to give in to that urge. "Just a second."

Aimlessly — because having direction was more difficult than it should've been — I wandered toward the work bench and picked up the first thing that I found. It happened to be a hammer, which was good because I was certain a hammer could break glass.

"I've got it." I reared back with the tool and aimed at the window. I felt weak and struggled to stay upright. The voices in the back of my head were back ... and they were warning me.

"You can't throw that without help now," a woman whispered.

"You need help," another voice added. This one sounded decidedly male.

"Let us help you," the first voice persisted. "You'll die here if you don't."

I was confused. I'd never heard voices before. Okay, that wasn't exactly true. I talked to ghosts, ethereal beings others couldn't see. But they were real. These voices sounded otherworldly, as if they were talking to me from a great distance.

"Did you hear that?" I asked.

Thistle shook her head. "Bay, we need to get out of here. I can't last much longer."

The somber admission was enough to jolt me out of the floating reverie. She was right. If we didn't get out of this building now, we never would. Because it seemed like a good idea — I really did need help — I opened myself to the voices. They reacted in an instant, helping me lift the hammer. When I let it go, it soared faster and harder than it should've under only my power, and when it hit the window the glass exploded.

I was too slow to cover my face, and a few stray pieces landed on my cheeks. The rush of fresh oxygen was welcome. The second I inhaled, my brain started firing on all cylinders.

"We have to get out of here right now." I hopped on the bench by the window and poked my head out, sucking in gaping mouthfuls of air. When I turned to make sure Thistle was with me, I almost fell out of the window because her face was so close to mine. "Make a noise next time," I complained.

"Oh, I'm going to make a noise." Thistle's voice was low and full of warning. "I'm going to make so much noise you'll hear me in your dreams the rest of your life."

That was an ominous threat. "Hey ... we're both alive. In fact, ..." I yelped when I felt a set of hands on my hips. I was flying through the air before I could register what was happening. As I turned, I found Chief Terry Davenport's eyes on me as he gripped me tightly against him.

"I'm going to lock you up for the rest of your life for stupidity!" he barked. "And then I'm going to tell your mother what you did and laugh when she withholds dessert from you."

Ah, well, at least I was alive.

THREE

Chief Terry didn't stop until we were safely away from the building.

"Thistle?" I struggled against him, but he didn't release me.

"She's fine."

"Where is she?"

"She's fine!" He snapped out the words with enough force that I jolted. He must've immediately regretted being so harsh, because he held up his hands. "I'm sorry. I just ... are you stupid?"

That didn't sound like a rhetorical question. "Not last time I checked," I said dryly, rubbing at my irritated eyes. "Adam Harris is inside. He's dead."

Chief Terry's eyebrows rose. "You saw him?"

"He's in the workshop."

"Do you know how he died?"

I shook my head. "He had debris on him and his eyes were open. Maybe something hit him in the head. I would think if he was overcome by smoke his eyes would've been closed, but what do I know?"

He held my gaze for an extended moment and then snapped his

fingers to get a uniformed officer's attention. "Tell the firefighters to try to protect the workshop area," he ordered.

The officer didn't offer up a word of argument, leaving Thistle with a paramedic as he disappeared toward the front of the building.

"She needs oxygen over here, too," Chief Terry demanded of the first responder, a pretty blonde with big eyes.

"I'm okay," I protested, taking a moment to catch Thistle's gaze. She looked blissed out as she reclined on a gurney, an oxygen mask covering her mouth and nose. "Don't worry about me."

"What makes you think I'm worried?" There was a darkness to his voice that I'd heard only a time or two over the years I'd known him. I sensed trouble ... and it wasn't the sort I wanted to grapple with right now.

"I'm just saying ... ."

He barreled forward as if he hadn't heard me. "Only an idiot rushes into a burning building. I knew you were rash, but I never thought of you as an idiot. Well, that's not entirely true. There have been a few instances when I've wondered after you let your cousins talk you into the most moronic things imaginable. This, this is too much."

I opened my mouth to argue, but I didn't get a chance. The paramedic directly in front of me slapped an oxygen mask over my mouth.

"We had to look," I protested, my voice muffled.

"Take it easy," the woman instructed. "You've been through an ordeal."

"She's only been through half of an ordeal," Chief Terry countered, his expression serious as he held my gaze. "It's going to get worse when her mother and aunts find out. Oh, and her boyfriend. I can't wait to see his reaction."

My heart stuttered at the thought. "You're not going to tell them?"

"Of course, I'm going to tell them. I can't keep this to myself. You were reckless ... and I can't abide recklessness."

I didn't know if I wanted to laugh, yell or cry. In all honesty, it was a mixture of all three. "You can't tattle. That's not allowed."

"I can do whatever I want."

"But ... ."

"No!" His eyes flashed with fury. "You're in big trouble. Do you have any idea how terrified I was when I found out you were in that building? You're in deep, Missy, and I'm looking forward to you getting punished."

I wasn't used to being on his naughty list. "Will you change your mind if I cry?" I had to try something. This would spiral out of control quickly if I didn't manage to contain it.

"Nope. I'm holding strong."

CHIEF TERRY WAS IN THE MIDDLE OF a serious conversation with the fire chief when Aunt Tillie finally showed up. Her scooter, which had running lights that glowed in the smoky curtain billowing through the street, came to a screeching halt when she saw Thistle and me resting beneath oxygen masks.

"What happened to you two?" she asked, abandoning the scooter and moving toward us. She didn't look concerned as much as curious.

"They ran into a burning building," Chief Terry barked. I wasn't even sure he was monitoring us until he yelled.

"Why?" Aunt Tillie wasn't nearly as worked up as everybody else.

"Because Lorna was screaming that Adam was in there and we thought we should check," I replied, my voice hard to make out behind the mask.

"Was he in there?"

I nodded, briefly pressing my eyes shut. "He was already dead."

"That's too bad. I always liked Adam. He complimented my scooter yesterday. He had good taste."

Thistle propped herself up on her elbows and slanted her eyes in Aunt Tillie's direction. "Speaking of that, what's the deal with the scooter? Where did you get it? Oh, and why did you get a kick scooter? That seems like a lot of unnecessary work."

"I found it on Amazon. You can find anything there, including these gummy bears that supposedly give you explosive diarrhea. No joke. It's in the reviews. I bought some."

I was confused. "You want explosive diarrhea?"

"No, but I have enemies."

Of course. I heaved out a sigh. "How do you even know that Mrs. Little likes gummy bears?"

"What makes you think they're for Margaret?"

That was a sobering thought and I made a mental note to stay away from anything gummy on the rare occasions we served ice cream with a multitude of toppings at the inn. "You haven't explained about the scooter," I prodded. It seemed a safe topic. "Does Mom know you bought it?"

Aunt Tillie's gaze darkened. "First, I don't have to register my purchases with your mother. I'm an adult and can buy what I want. I wanted this, so I bought it. Secondly … I guess I don't have a second. That's a first."

"Really, I don't care either way. We saw you zipping around the block right before the building exploded and we were afraid."

"Oh, well ... that's kind of sweet." She patted my hand. "I was stalking Margaret at the time. I was nowhere close to the blacksmith's. You don't have to worry."

"We stopped worrying once we saw the fire," Thistle offered. "At least about you. Adam was another story."

"At least you looked," Aunt Tillie noted. "You would've questioned yourselves after the fact if you hadn't."

"See." I pinned Thistle with a pointed look. "Aunt Tillie gets it."

"Yes, the one person who agrees with what you did is our great-aunt, a woman who wears leggings with penises on them and rides around on a scooter so she can terrorize the woman who owns the porcelain unicorn store. That seems like a strong argument."

I wanted to smack her, but that would involve getting up, and I was too tired. Besides, she had a point ... which was beyond frustrating.

"You're on my list, mouth," Aunt Tillie warned, extending a finger in Thistle's direction. "I hope you're happy."

Thistle offered up a haphazard wave. "I'm too tired to deal with your crap. We'll argue about the list later."

"Fair enough." Aunt Tillie shuffled closer to Thistle and stared into her eyes. "Why do you look worse than Bay?"

"She always looks worse than me," I replied.

"In your dreams," Thistle growled. "Everyone knows I'm the hot one. You're the ... intellectual. Wait ... no ... I want to be the intellectual one, too. Clove is the whiny one, so that makes you the boring one."

I rolled my eyes. "Whatever you need to tell yourself to get through the day."

"I'm serious." Aunt Tillie's gaze darkened. "You don't look good." She turned her eyes to the paramedic. "Why is she so pale?"

"She inhaled smoke," the paramedic replied blankly.

"I know that, Dr. Obvious," Aunt Tillie snapped. "Why does she look worse than Bay?"

"She always looks worse than me," I repeated.

Aunt Tillie ignored me. "They went in together and left together. Shouldn't they be in the same condition?"

The blonde shrugged. "I don't know what to tell you. Some people are more susceptible to smoke. Your niece should be okay. We'll give her oxygen for another thirty minutes."

Aunt Tillie's expression was hard to read.

"She'll be fine," I reassured her. "We'll both be fine."

"It sounds to me like you were lucky," Aunt Tillie noted after a beat.

"Yeah."

"That luck is about to run out."

I groaned as I followed her gaze, my heart pinching when I caught sight of Landon Michaels. He was striding across the street, his long black hair fluttering in the breeze he created because he walked so fast. His blue eyes were full of fire as they searched the area. When he caught sight of me, a flash of relief appeared ... but it was followed quickly by anger.

"Oh, man," I complained, squeezing my eyes shut. "He's going to start yelling."

"Good." Aunt Tillie was blasé. "You've got it coming after running into a burning building. Have I taught you nothing?"

I protested. "You said you understood why we went into the building and that it made sense because we had to know if Adam was alive."

"I say a lot of things that are utter nonsense. I've changed my tune on this one. I'm looking forward to 'The Man' putting his foot down. That's always entertaining."

She was the only one who did.

Landon was on me within seconds. "Are you okay?" Concern swamped his eyes as he brushed my hair from my face.

I nodded. "I'm fine. Don't worry."

Landon didn't look convinced. "I was at a meeting with my boss in Gaylord when the news crossed my phone. I thought it was weird and planned to head out here eventually until an update said that a blonde and a woman with blue hair rushed into a burning building."

Uh-oh. "How did you know it was us?"

He didn't immediately respond, and I could tell he was reining in his temper.

"Lorna was screaming for her husband," I offered by way of explanation. "We felt we didn't have a choice because the fire looked to be contained to the second-floor roof."

Landon folded his arms across his chest and simply waited.

"Fine." I threw up my hands in defeat. "We shouldn't have gone in. Is that what you want to hear?"

"Yes." He leaned over and pressed a kiss to my forehead. "You frightened me, Bay." He lowered his voice. "I don't want to hear that you and your wacky cousin ran into a burning building ever again. You've done a lot of stupid things, but this takes the cake."

"We just had to be sure."

He blew out a sigh. "You're in trouble," he said finally. "I'm going to punish you severely later."

Aunt Tillie snorted. "I don't think she finds your kisses nearly as gross as I do. It won't be punishment to her."

Landon rolled his eyes. "And where were you when these idiots were running into a burning building? Why didn't you stop them?"

"I had no idea it was happening. I can't watch them twenty-four hours a day. They're adults now. They should no longer be idiots."

"Well, apparently your wise teachings failed." Landon's brow furrowed when he caught sight of the scooter. It had streamers and one of those cages for a water bottle. It only lacked a bell. "What is that?"

"That's my new ride." Aunt Tillie was calm. "I was giving it a test run when this happened."

"And what was 'this'?" Landon asked as he turned his eyes to an approaching Chief Terry. "Was it a gas leak?"

"That was my initial assumption," Chief Terry replied, grim. "The medical examiner managed to get the body out, and he has another opinion. By the way, the building is going to go any second. Don't be alarmed when it happens."

I moved my hand to the oxygen mask to remove it — I was feeling much better — but Landon slapped it back into place.

"You're not taking that off until the nice paramedic says it's okay," he ordered.

The blonde smiled coquettishly at Landon. He had a way about him that most women found impossible to resist. I should know. I was one of those women. Inexplicably, he'd fallen for me and we'd settled into a life together. I couldn't even work up a good head of jealousy because I knew he was interested only in me. It was a strange phenomenon.

"She should be good in another ten minutes or so," the paramedic noted. "She's better off than her friend here."

I thought about the whispers, the way the voices had tried to bolster me, and wondered if they had something to do with the outcome. Rather than dwell on it, I filed the notion away to ponder later. We had other things to worry about now.

"What did the medical examiner say?" I asked Chief Terry. "Was it an accident?"

He shook his head. "Adam was most likely dead before the fire started, although they'll have to confirm that in the lab. Right now, it appears he was stabbed twice in the back."

I was flabbergasted. "What?" I moved to sit up, but Landon applied pressure to my shoulder and forced me to remain prone.

"Not until I'm sure you're okay," he countered. "Stay there."

Ugh. He was going to baby me, I just knew it. "I'm fine."

"You're not fine. Only an idiot would run into a burning building. I'm thinking about forcing you to get a psychological exam."

Aunt Tillie brightened considerably. "That's a great idea. Most families have an eccentric uncle or grandparent. It would be fun to have an eccentric niece. We need confirmation from a professional before I can get a T-shirt made and start using her as a threat against my enemies. Everyone is afraid of those who are genuinely crazy."

Landon took a moment to look over her outfit — which included a pair of psychedelic leggings and an oversized shirt — and shook his head. "Some families have more than one eccentric relative."

"How awesome for them," she drawled.

I was already bored with this conversation. "What's going to happen with Adam?" I asked. "I mean ... do you have any suspects?"

"You know what I know," Chief Terry replied, his hand automatically going up to stroke my hair. "You need to rest and not worry about this."

That wasn't likely. "What about Lorna?"

"She said it was a normal day and she was going out to check the mail when it happened," Chief Terry replied. "I have no reason not to believe her ... at least right now. We need to wait for the full autopsy."

"When will that be?" Landon asked.

"We'll have the final results tomorrow," Chief Terry answered. "Don't worry. I have no intention of dragging you away from Bay today. I expect you to take care of her."

"Oh, I'm going to take care of her."

"I don't need anyone to take care of me," I groused, feeling a full wave of poutiness coming on. "I'm perfectly fine."

"I'm going to lock her in the guesthouse for the rest of her life ... or at least until she capitulates that she'll never again run into a burning building."

"I already said it was a mistake," I complained. "What more do you want from me?"

"A little common sense might be nice," Chief Terry replied without hesitation. "You scared ten years off my life, Bay. It's not funny."

"I never pretended it was funny." I shifted my eyes to the street, where a teenaged boy and girl were rushing in the direction of the commotion. I recognized them right away. "Dani and Nick," I murmured, my heart giving a heave when they caught sight of their mother.

Chief Terry followed my gaze, a muscle working in his jaw. "This is going to be hard for them."

"Are they Adam Harris's kids?" Landon asked.

I nodded. "They're teenagers. I think they're only about eleven months apart. They're really close."

He linked his fingers with mine and gave them a squeeze. "It's sad that they've lost a father," he noted. "You could've compounded things by sacrificing yourself. You need to be more careful, Bay. We just bought a piece of property to settle on down the line. That's our future. I don't want to lose it before I get a chance to enjoy it."

I wanted to crawl into bed and cover my head. "I said I was sorry."

"You're going to be sorry later," he muttered.

"You get her," Aunt Tillie encouraged, her eyes never leaving Dani and Nick as their mother explained what had happened.

I could tell the moment Lorna delivered the crushing blow, because Nick's face went slack and Dani started sobbing, her shoulders shaking uncontrollably.

"Aw, hell," Chief Terry muttered. "I suppose I should get over there and see if I can help." He paused long enough to give Landon a serious look. "These three are your responsibility. I expect you to handle them."

"Why not just task me with the impossible?" Landon asked dryly. "How am I supposed to handle them?"

"You're an FBI agent," Chief Terry reminded him. "Figure it out." With those words, he left us to our potential domestic squabble so he could handle a true tragedy.

Slowly, Landon's gaze bounced between us. "The first one who gives me any trouble is being locked in a cage overnight."

"That's something a dirty pervert would say," Aunt Tillie complained. "I always knew you were a dirty pervert."

He sighed. It was obviously going to be a long afternoon.

FOUR

Once Landon was satisfied that my oxygen levels were fine, we dropped Thistle at home with her boyfriend Marcus. He'd been so busy with work that he hadn't heard about the fire, and he was furious Thistle hadn't called him. We left them to their dispute and headed home.

We were barely through the door when Landon began barking orders. "Strip."

I stilled, surprised. "That's really romantic, Landon. I don't know that I'm in the mood, though."

He smiled, although he fought to maintain a stoic countenance. "You need to get in the bath," he said. "As much as I love you, I can't kiss you until you wash your face and get that smell off you."

"That doesn't sound like unconditional love."

He shook his head. "Strip. I'll put your clothes in the washing machine and then join you."

"Oh, so this is a bath for both of us."

"Absolutely."

That was an activity I could get behind. I left him with my filthy clothes and filled the tub with steaming water, dropping in some bubble bath. I groaned in relief when I slipped into the water. I was floating by the time he joined me and barely noticed when he slid me forward so he could climb in behind. His hands immediately went to my neck and started rubbing.

"I don't want to belabor the point, but ... ."

"You will," I muttered.

He ignored my grouchiness. "Running into a burning building ranks right up there as one of the dumbest things you've ever done."

That was hard to argue. "You wouldn't say that if we'd found Adam alive."

"You didn't."

"I know."

"And I still would've been angry," he added. "I know you're a hero and want to save lives, but forfeiting your own during the process is unacceptable. I don't want to keep harping on this, but ... ."

"You will."

He lightly pinched my flank, causing me to yelp. "We're building a life together. That won't be possible if you're not here. I need you to promise me you won't do that again."

I let loose a sigh. "Fine. I promise."

"Then I'll let it go." He pressed a kiss to my cheek and tugged me back against him. "I don't suppose you saw anything out of the ordinary before the fire today?"

Oddly enough, I was happy to focus on the logistics of the case rather than my inherent stupidity, so I eagerly embraced the conversational shift and shook my head. "I wasn't really paying attention. We were in the shop looking at a pregnancy book — talk about traumatizing by the way — when we noticed Aunt Tillie on her scooter. We were watching her when it happened."

"Did you know what it was?"

"Kind of. I mean ... I knew something exploded, if that makes any sense. We took cover, and when we were sure it was over Thistle and I ran out. We were looking for Aunt Tillie, not trouble, if that makes you feel any better."

"Aunt Tillie *is* trouble."

"Fair enough. She's still my aunt. I had to find her."

"And I can't argue with your instincts on that, but she wasn't in a burning building."

"No." I thought about the moments before I managed to break the window. "Something else happened." I related the tale to him as best I could, keeping my voice low and even because I didn't want him to melt down. When I finished, he was perplexed.

"What do you think it was?"

I'd been giving that a lot of thought. "I think it was the dead."

He shifted. "Like ... ghosts?"

"Maybe. Or maybe it was voices from the other side. I shouldn't have been able to throw that hammer the way I did. I was feeling weak."

"Maybe your body responded out of desperation and you simply didn't realize how much force you were putting into the effort."

"That doesn't explain the voices."

"I guess not." He tightened his arms around me. "I'm just glad you're okay."

"You're being fairly reasonable about this," I noted. "I expected you to scream, stomp and yell."

"That rarely goes over well."

"That doesn't stop you from doing it."

"I figure your mother will go after you — and Chief Terry once he's had a bit of breathing room and gets over his terror — so there's no need for me to be the bad guy when they're willing to take up the mantle."

"Smart."

"I thought so."

We lapsed into silence for a moment. I was the first to break it.

"Whoever killed Adam set the fire to cover it up, right?"

"That would be my guess. It seems like too much of a coincidence to be anything else."

"So, we have a murderer in town who just happens to be a firebug on the side. That can't be good."

"Nope. I'm worried, too."

At least we could agree about that.

. . .

I OPTED FOR COMFORTABLE JEANS and a T-shirt for dinner. Now that I was several hours removed from the situation, I felt like a bit of a dolt. Running into the building was definitely stupid. I had no doubt I would get an earful from the rest of my relatives ... and I wasn't looking forward to it.

"We could skip dinner tonight," I offered helpfully once we reached the back door. "I'll buy and everything."

Landon's expression reflected amusement. "I believe your mother said it was Mexican night. I can't miss out on tacos."

He was messing with me and we both knew it. "You just want to watch her yell."

"Maybe a little." He put his hand to the small of my back and prodded me toward the door. "The faster you get it over with, the faster they'll go back to obsessing about this witch gathering and Clove's wedding. I don't think I've ever seen them this manic about a group of guests before."

I had, in years past. "This is a big deal." I stepped into the family living quarters when he opened the door for me, pulling up short when I heard snorting. It didn't take long for Peg, Aunt Tillie's new pig, to come running for attention. The spotted swine was ridiculously cute, if impractical. Today she was wearing a pink tutu that made her look like a farm animal fairy.

"Look at you!" Landon was delighted as he forgot all about me and raced toward Peg. "Who dressed you up?"

"It wasn't me," Aunt Tillie said darkly from the couch. She was in her usual spot watching *Jeopardy*. "There's no way I would've purchased that monstrosity."

Given how Aunt Tillie dressed, the fact that she could cast aspersions on anybody's clothing choices was mildly amusing. Still, she looked relatively morose, so I asked the obvious question. "Did Twila buy this for her?"

"Actually, it was your mother."

I was beyond surprised. "My mother bought Peg a tutu?" That was hard to wrap my head around. "Why?"

"You'll have to ask her. I've been warned if I remove the tutu that my still will go up in flames. She sounded serious."

I smirked. "You can't be surprised."

"I didn't say I was surprised," Aunt Tillie growled. "I just can't stand it. They're witches, not celebrities. They mount brooms the same way we do: one leg at a time."

"Who's a pretty girl?" Landon enthused. He'd moved to the floor and was rolling around with Peg, who greeted him with excited kisses and snorts. I was starting to realize that Landon desperately needed a pet. He'd mentioned a dog recently, and I was considering asking my mother if she would allow us to adopt one and keep it in the guesthouse. It probably wasn't a good day to broach the subject.

Aunt Tillie rolled her eyes at Landon's antics. "For the record, I don't think this gathering is a good idea. You know how I feel about those women."

Landon reluctantly dragged his attention from Peg and focused on Aunt Tillie. "What's wrong with the women who are coming? I thought you were familiar with all of them."

"That doesn't mean I like them," Aunt Tillie sneered.

"Aunt Tillie is proud of being a witch — and she wants all of us to be badass witches — but she's not particularly fond of other witches," I explained. "She's jealous when others have magic at their disposal."

Aunt Tillie's glare was withering. "I'm not jealous. Why would you even say that? It's absolutely ridiculous."

Amusement flitted across Landon's handsome features. "Tell me more."

"Don't tell him anything." Aunt Tillie jabbed a finger in my direction. "It has nothing to do with you. You don't need to stick your long law enforcement nose into this. Just ... stay out of it."

Landon's eyes lit with exaggerated merriment. "Oh, something tells me I'm missing part of the story. What's going on? I want to know what to expect."

I opened my mouth to answer, but Aunt Tillie quashed the urge before I could utter a single word.

"Why do you even care?" she challenged. "No, I seriously want to know. This gathering has nothing to do with you."

Landon wasn't about to be dissuaded. "That's not true." He used his "practical" tone, which often drove me crazy. I had a feeling that was his aim with Aunt Tillie. "Bay is my girlfriend. She's a witch. These other witches are coming to town for some ritual. I'm obviously curious about what this entails."

"It's a solstice celebration," I explained. "It basically involves a blessing, a lot of alcohol and a bit of naked dancing."

"Oh, good," Landon said dryly. "I don't see nearly enough naked dancing."

Aunt Tillie rolled her eyes. "Such a pervert."

While stroking Peg's head, Landon looked back at me. "Give me the rundown on these witches. I don't need the nitty-gritty, but I want to know why Aunt Tillie has her nose out of joint. If there's going to be a problem, I want to be prepared."

"There won't be a problem," Aunt Tillie insisted. "I have everything under control."

Those were empty words, but Aunt Tillie would never admit it. "Most of the witches are fine," I volunteered. "They're earth witches who spend all their time cooking and gardening."

"Like your mother and aunts."

I nodded. "When it comes to coven work, very few witches are as powerful as us," I continued. "We're something of anomalies in the paranormal world. That means we're often revered ... and sometimes feared. The only witch who does neither is Hazel Weller."

"Ah, now we're getting somewhere." Landon rubbed his hands together before grabbing Peg around the waist and transporting her to his lap. The pig was in absolute ecstasy as he petted her. "Who is Hazel Weller?"

"She's a nobody," Aunt Tillie automatically responded. "If there was a witch hierarchy — which there's not — she would be on the last rung. She's a bottom feeder."

"Tell me how you really feel."

"I just did."

Landon stared at Aunt Tillie for a long beat before switching his gaze to me. "What's the deal with Hazel Weller?"

"She's stronger than the other witches," I explained. "She's not an earth witch. In fact, she's a fire witch, which makes her stronger than us."

Landon didn't look convinced. "I don't believe that's possible. You guys are the strongest."

"See." Aunt Tillie preened. "He's smarter than he looks, and we've trained him well."

"Perhaps 'stronger' wasn't the correct word," I hedged, shrinking under the weight of Aunt Tillie's glare. "Fire witches are rare, especially in this area. We get more earth witches and air witches in these parts."

"Which are you?" Landon looked genuinely curious. "I thought you were a necromancer."

"I am. That's an entirely different thing. It doesn't play into my elemental magic."

Landon dragged a hand through his dark hair, confusion evident. "I'm not sure I understand."

I couldn't blame him. When it came to magic, I'd fallen down on the job explaining things to him.

"Necromancy isn't an elemental power," I started. "I'm mostly an air witch with a touch of water and fire."

"You just said fire witches were rare."

"True fire witches are very rare. Hazel is a fire witch and nothing else. It's ... odd."

"It's evil," Aunt Tillie corrected, stirring. "Every witch who has ever gone evil has been a fire witch. It's like being a Slytherin."

Landon's lips quirked. "I see."

"That's not true," I protested, pinning Aunt Tillie with a quelling look. "Don't tell him that. I don't want him to fear fire witches. We have some fire in our lineage."

"I will never be frightened of you," Landon promised. "Frightened for you is a different story, but we've decided to table that discussion for the remainder of the evening. I want to know more about this specific fire witch."

"There's nothing wrong with her," I offered hurriedly. The last thing I wanted was Aunt Tillie riling up Landon. He rarely fell for her shtick, but there were times he lost his head and embraced whatever conspiracy theory she was floating for the week. Now was not a good time for that to happen. "She's a perfectly nice woman ... who has a tendency to mouth off, talk down to Aunt Tillie and try to compete with her on every front."

"Oh, wow." Landon's eyes lit with genuine mirth. "You're saying she's another version of Aunt Tillie."

"You take that back!" Aunt Tillie poked a threatening finger into his chest. "I am nothing like that woman."

"They're fairly similar," I acknowledged, taking an inadvertent step back when Aunt Tillie trained her furious gaze on me. "Aunt Tillie is way better, though."

Landon snickered. "I have no doubt. I don't understand why you stopped having these gatherings if they were such a big deal. I mean ... if they're so important, why cease having them?"

I risked a glance at Aunt Tillie and found her watching me with an expectant gaze.

"Well, tell him," she prodded after a beat. "Blame it on me, like your mother does."

"I have no intention of running into a burning building twice in one day," I countered. "I don't blame you for what happened. In truth, I was happy when the gatherings stopped. Mom, Marnie and Twila used to go crazy when it came to planning. It was a relief when things came to an end."

"I need more information than that," Landon pressed. "What happened?"

"There was an incident," I offered, choosing my words carefully.

"Oh, let me tell it." Aunt Tillie made a face. "You'll do it wrong."

Landon remained where he was on the floor, Peg curled into a ball on his lap and snoring lightly. She was all tuckered out after the initial excitement.

"Hazel wanted to institute a coven council," Aunt Tillie started.

"She thought it was best to have a panel of witches who could dole out punishment for certain individuals if they stepped out of line."

"And she didn't want you on the council."

"I didn't want to be on the council," Aunt Tillie shot back. "There's nothing worse than telling others how they should act. I mean ... nothing."

"I would argue that it's worse to be on the receiving end of other people's orders, but this is probably a bad time to argue about the merits of that," I offered.

Landon met my gaze. "I definitely wouldn't go that route this evening. You'll tick me off if you even try."

"See, he would be good on a coven council," Aunt Tillie drawled. "He loves bossing people around."

"No, I love keeping people safe," Landon countered. "That's neither here nor there, though. I want to hear more about the witch council."

"You really don't," I said. "The story isn't as entertaining as you envision. Hazel wanted to institute a council. She had a lot of people who agreed with her and was well on her way to setting up elections — where she would be the head witch, mind you, by design — when Aunt Tillie instigated something of an uprising."

Landon's shoulders straightened. "Oh, now we're getting to the meat of the story. What did you do to Hazel?"

"I didn't do anything to her," Aunt Tillie sniffed, averting her gaze. "I simply made the others aware that she would be an absolute tyrant if we gave her any real power. It's not just the big things Hazel wanted to control. It was the small things, too."

"Like what?"

"Like what spells could be cast and when," I volunteered. "She wanted to make everyone in the coven request permission before using their magic. That information was hidden deep in the bylaws she'd been working on, almost as if she was trying to hide her true intentions."

"Oh." Realization dawned on Landon's face. "She wanted to take away your autonomy."

"Exactly." Fury sparked in Aunt Tillie's eyes. "She wanted to be the one to say who we helped ... and when we helped ... and how we helped. I'm not living in a world ruled by anyone other than me."

"Why didn't you run against her?" Landon asked. "I mean ... it seems to me the best way to ensure that she couldn't institute her plans was to make sure she had no real power."

"I don't want to be in charge," Aunt Tillie replied sharply. "I know you believe the opposite, but I'm a big fan of free will."

"The coven sort of fell apart when all the sides started fighting," I said. "This will be the first time everybody has been together in more than a decade. I wouldn't be surprised if the council is brought up again."

"And I'll be right there to squash it again," Aunt Tillie promised.

Landon's smirk couldn't be contained. "Is it wrong that I'm looking forward to the drama? It's nice when the fighting doesn't revolve around us for a change, isn't it, Bay?"

I wasn't exactly on the same page, but he wasn't altogether wrong. "It will be interesting," I agreed. "I'm a little curious to see how things go myself."

FIVE

Dinner went exactly as I'd expected. It was two hours of recrimination and threats from my mother and aunts. Thistle wisely opted to stay home, so I took the brunt of the admonishment, to the point I felt wrung out by the time we left.

Landon, full of tacos, nachos and flan, was in a great mood when we tumbled into bed. He'd managed to avoid being the bad guy and yet I was still verbally flogged to within an inch of my life. He was still smiling when we returned to the inn for breakfast the next morning.

"We need to buy groceries so we can eat at home occasionally," I complained as we walked into the inn. We'd parked at the front so we could head to town once the meal was finished, so at least I didn't have to risk running into Aunt Tillie before I had a dose of coffee in me.

"Why would we want to do that?" Landon asked. "We have the best breakfast in town within walking distance."

"You're just saying that because you can smell the bacon from here."

"Like I said, it's the best breakfast in town." He kissed my cheek before picking up his pace. He could detect bacon from a hundred feet away. Despite his love for Peg, there was no way he was giving up the crispy goodness that was his favorite food.

Chief Terry was already seated at the table drinking coffee when we arrived. He slid his gaze to us and I was disappointed to see annoyance lurking in the depths of his normally kind eyes.

"How long are you going to punish me?" I lamented as I slipped into my regular spot, which happened to be located on his left. "I said I was sorry."

"You're only sorry because you got yelled at," he replied as Landon grabbed the coffee carafe from the center of the table and started pouring. "You don't believe you did anything wrong."

That wasn't entirely true. "What I did was moronic," I countered. "But I had to check. I couldn't stop myself."

"And that's why I'm still angry." Chief Terry turned his attention to Landon. "There's a state fire inspector on the scene. He's expecting us in an hour. I figured you would want to be part of this even though we have no reason to believe this was anything other than a lone targeted attack … at least right now."

"I don't have anything pressing otherwise, so you figured right," Landon said. "Besides, we don't know that it won't happen again. If this was about the fire instead of a specific victim, things could go badly. We need to make sure that we don't have an arsonist on the loose."

I'd done enough research on firebugs to know that it was the blaze itself that excited them. Once they got the urge, the only thing that usually stopped them was death or incarceration. "Could it be a teenager?" I asked. "Don't fire fanatic tendencies usually start during the teen years?"

Chief Terry didn't immediately respond, so Landon took pity on me.

"In a hunch, yes," he answered. "But that's not always a given."

"Oh." I frowned at Chief Terry. I hated it when he was angry with me. "I really am sorry." My voice was low as I leaned my head against his shoulder. "You can't stay mad forever. It's not fair."

Landon smirked as he slid his arm around the back of my chair.

"We both know you're going to forgive her. You're not going to be able to hold out. Why not get it over with now and stop torturing her?"

Chief Terry's eyebrows migrated higher on his forehead. "I would think you'd be as angry as me," he argued. "She could've been killed. I know you would miss her if something happened."

"I would most definitely miss her," Landon acknowledged. "But she did what she thought was right. She knows it was a stupid move. I don't see how dragging this out helps anyone. She's sorry."

"I am." I jutted out my lower lip and stared soulfully into his eyes. "Please don't be angry."

He held my gaze for an extended beat, much longer than I thought he would be able to manage. Finally, he heaved a sigh. "I'm not being mean just to be mean. You need to be careful, Bay. You could've died."

"I know. I'm really sad. I hate it when you're angry with me. It makes almost dying even worse."

"Oh, that was beautiful," Landon teased, grinning as Chief Terry huffed. "How can you be mad at this face?" He grabbed my chin and gave it a squeeze. "I mean ... look how sad she is. Do you want her to cry?"

"Knock that off." Chief Terry pushed Landon's hand away from my face. "I can't just switch off my emotions. I'm angry. You have no idea how afraid I was when I heard you were in that building, Bay. We could hear the ceiling give way. I imagined it was falling on you."

"That was probably hard for you," I said solemnly. "The last thing I want to do is upset you. I love you so much."

"Oh, geez." Chief Terry slapped his hand to his forehead. "You make it impossible to stay angry with you."

That was my goal. "So ... you forgive me?"

"I forgive you but reserve the right to call you an idiot for the next week."

I cocked my head, considering. "I can live with that. Just don't be angry. I hate it when you're angry."

"I'm not angry." He sipped his coffee and shook his head, glaring as Landon snickered. "You just double-teamed me and I don't like it. I preferred it when you were the one yelling because she did stupid things."

"Yes, but that never ends well for me," Landon noted. "This is really the best of both worlds. I get to annoy you and keep my Bay happy. In turn, she keeps me happy. What's not to love about that?"

"I'm going to lick all the bacon before you get a chance to eat it," Chief Terry warned. "I'm going to laugh like a loon while I'm doing it."

"That won't stop me from eating it."

"You're a sick man."

"Yes, but I'm a sick man who can eat his weight in bacon. That should be an Olympic category if you ask me."

"Only you would think that."

CHIEF TERRY AND LANDON WERE ALREADY standing in front of the burned-out husk of the blacksmith shop when I pulled myself away from a few curious looky-loos on Main Street. They had their heads bent together, talking in hushed tones, which I found interesting. Before I could ask them what they were conversing about, a hint of movement caught my eye inside the building.

"Is someone in there?" I asked.

Landon slid his eyes to me, confused. "No. We're waiting on the state arson investigator. He was here already and went to the diner for breakfast. He's ten minutes out."

That made what I saw doubly confusing. "Someone is in there."

"What do you mean?"

"I saw someone inside." I was firm. "I swear it. I'm not making it up."

"You rarely make things up, sweetie. It's just ... I don't see anyone. Are you sure the wind isn't moving something?"

"I'm pretty sure I know the difference between a person and the wind."

Chief Terry and Landon exchanged weighted gazes before Landon put his hand to the small of my back and prodded me forward.

"Then we'll check it out," he said. "Be careful and watch your step. There are a lot of fallen boards with nails in them."

I wasn't worried about a nail going through my foot — although that would suck — as much as I was interested in figuring out who would have the gall to enter a burned-out building that was marked off with police tape.

Chief Terry took the lead, making sure to position me between Landon and himself. If they thought they were playing it coy with their protective stances, they were wrong. I had other things to worry about, though. The whispers were back inside my head and they were loud enough to send a chill down my spine.

"I don't think it's a human," I whispered, my blood running cold as one of the voices began talking.

"She's back," it said.

"What is she doing here?" another voice answered. "She shouldn't have returned. It isn't safe."

"She needs to go. I told you she wasn't all that smart."

"Hey!" My temper got the better of me and I brushed past Chief Terry to enter what used to be the workshop ahead of him.

He growled and grabbed me by the back of the neck before I could put too much distance between us. "What do you think you're doing?"

I couldn't answer. My mind had gone blank upon entering the room and finding three ghosts standing guard in the middle of the fallen building.

"Bay?" Landon snapped his fingers in my face to draw my attention to him. He looked concerned. "What is it?"

How could I explain without looking like a freak, especially in front of Chief Terry? "There are ghosts here." I blurted it out even though I knew the state arson inspector was due to arrive at any moment. "They're talking ... and they say I'm an idiot."

"I don't believe that's the word we used," the male ghost replied. He didn't look familiar. In fact, I was fairly certain I'd never seen him before. He certainly didn't resemble Adam.

"It's not the wrong word," a female ghost offered. She wore a pair of simple jeans and a hoodie … and she looked amused. "Only an idiot runs into a burning building."

"You wouldn't believe how many times I've heard that the last two days," I grumbled.

"What are they saying?" Landon asked. He looked genuinely curious. "Is one of them our dead guy? It would be helpful if he could tell us what happened to him."

"Yes, that would be lovely," Chief Terry drawled, sarcasm dripping from his tongue. "There's nothing better than explaining to a judge that our evidence came from a ghost."

"I'm not saying we can use it as evidence," Landon argued. "It's a place to start, because we have nothing."

"We have an arson investigator who is going to give us information," Chief Terry pointed out. "Once he shares what he's discovered, we'll have a place to look."

"If Adam tells us who attacked him we'll have two places to look."

I bit back my annoyance and rubbed my cheek. "It's not Adam," I explained. "It's … people I don't recognize." I was flustered, and confused. This felt somehow off, and I couldn't explain why. "Who are you guys?"

"Don't you know?" a pretty brunette asked. She had a sharp nose and her voice was rough, almost as if her vocal cords had been rubbed with sandpaper a few times before her death. "You called to us."

"I … called to you?" My confusion was complete. I didn't understand any of this. "How did I do that?"

"How should we know?" The woman's annoyance was obvious. "We were in the middle of our own deaths when your voice invaded our minds and demanded we join you here. We don't even know where here is."

"Hemlock Cove," I replied numbly, racking my brain for an acceptable explanation for what they were saying. "Wait … you're saying you died and I somehow called to you."

"You needed help," the man offered. "We came to this place to make sure you didn't perish … and then you left us here. We're trapped until you release us."

Well, that wasn't what I wanted to hear. Not even a little. This necromancer thing was getting stranger and stranger. "I'm sorry." I felt like an idiot. "I didn't know I called to you."

"That's probably because you were in the middle of dying," the brunette supplied. "You called out without understanding what you were doing. We helped you escape and then you trapped us here."

"I didn't mean to trap you."

Perhaps sensing my unease, Landon moved his hand to the back of my neck. "What's wrong? What's happening?"

"I was right about having help with the hammer," I replied dumbly. "I called them here as they were dying and then I didn't help them pass on. This is on me."

"You didn't know," Chief Terry argued. "Can't you release them now?"

I nodded as I chewed my bottom lip. "I really am sorry," I offered. "I didn't realize what was happening."

"You should be a little more careful with your magic," the man noted. "It's not the end of the world. Go ahead and cut us loose now. I don't know about my friends here, but I'm anxious to see the other side. I've seen enough of this place."

"I don't blame you." I raised my hands and exhaled heavily, screwing my eyes shut as I let the magic flow through me. When I opened them again, the spirits were gone and I was left with nothing but self-recrimination and two confused men. "I need to get a better handle on what I'm doing. That was ... stupid."

"You're doing the best you can," Landon countered, pressing a kiss to my forehead. "I don't like that you're blaming yourself for this. It's not fair. Running into a burning building was something stupid that you could control. This ... this is a work in progress and you're trying really hard. That's the most important thing."

That was true. "I still need to do better. I should've realized what was happening yesterday. I was confused."

"I'm pretty sure that was the lack of oxygen," Chief Terry noted. "It's done now."

"Yeah. I ... ."

"Shh." Chief Terry gave me a small shake of his head before inclining his chin toward the parking lot. A man in khaki pants and a gray coat was exiting a vehicle with a briefcase in hand. "It's the arson investigator."

Which meant I had to put on a brave face. "Gotcha."

Landon left his hand on my back for another ten seconds before moving to intercept the man. He introduced all three of us, explaining that I worked for the newspaper and was part of the rescue attempt the previous day. He didn't touch on our relationship, which was probably wise.

"I'm Todd Bennett," the man announced. "I've been over your scene once and plan to make my rounds again, but I figured you would want to hear my initial report."

"Absolutely." Chief Terry enthusiastically bobbed his head. "What do you have?"

"The place was doused with accelerants," Bennett replied, matter-of-factly. "We're not talking about anything fancy. It was simple gasoline, which you can probably smell."

"I only smell smoke," Landon admitted.

"I can smell the gasoline a bit," Chief Terry offered. "I'm not sure I would've noticed if you hadn't pointed it out."

"Well, when you've been in this business as long as I have you learn to notice things like that right away."

He didn't look all that old. He had one of those faces that could be considered ageless. If he'd told me he was forty, I would've believed him. The same if he claimed his age was thirty.

"What else can you tell us?" Landon asked.

"Whoever did this had no idea what they were doing," Bennett replied. "This was not a professional. My guess is we're dealing with a novice. He probably killed the owner and assumed that the fire would burn so hot there would be no way to ascertain what happened to the body. Unfortunately for him, he made a mess of the gasoline distribution."

"How so?" Chief Terry prodded.

"All of the gasoline was poured at the base of the walls. That means the fire climbed up instead of over. I mean ... I guess it's possible the roof could've caved in over the workshop at some point, but that part of the building looks as if it was added on after the rest of the building was erected. It was more insulated."

"Do you think we could be dealing with a teenager?" Landon asked.

"It's entirely possible," Bennett confirmed. "Whoever did this doesn't have much experience with arson. He's either just getting into his infatuation or the fire was just a way to cover his tracks."

"You keep saying 'He,'" I noted. "How do you know it's a male?"

Bennett shrugged. "Statistics. The ratio of people who turn to arson, whether as a countermeasure or murder weapon, skews overwhelmingly toward men. It's not impossible that we're dealing with a woman, but statistically that would be an anomaly."

"Still, we can't rule it out," Chief Terry noted. "You're saying we have to find a motive to track down a killer because there's nothing in the evidence."

"At least so far," Bennett agreed. "I'm not done yet, but I have nothing concrete to offer at this point."

"That's a disappointment."

I couldn't help but agree. Fire made me nervous. I wanted to put this one to bed as soon as possible. That wouldn't be an option if we didn't luck into a motive, and fast. The problem was, I had no idea where to start gathering information. Adam wasn't the sort of man who inspired hate. He was, in fact, rather boring.

So, the question was, who wanted him dead? What didn't we know about him? Did he have secrets, and how grave were they? If we could answer those questions, we would better understand who we were seeking.

SIX

I was still bothered by the ghosts when I hit Main Street. I assumed Landon would stay behind with Chief Terry. Instead, he was right on my tail.

"Hey." He caught my chin and planted a long kiss on my lips, taking me by surprise.

"What was that for?"

His smile was enigmatic. "Can't I just want to kiss you?"

"Not usually."

His eyes flashed. "I can be romantic."

"I'm sure you can."

"No, really. I can be romantic. I'm awesome at it."

There was something so amusing about his reaction I couldn't stop myself from smiling. "You're a romance machine." I patted his shoulder. "Is that all? I have things to do."

This time the frown he offered wasn't even remotely playful. "Bay, this isn't your fault. Whatever happened ... whatever you did ... ." He couldn't even finish the statement because he didn't understand any of it.

"I ripped them out of their afterlives and drew them here, where I forced them to save Thistle and me before leaving them in a burned-out husk to do nothing but hang around while I went home with you."

"Going home with me is always a good idea," he insisted. "As for the rest ... I'm not sure what to say. If you expect me to be upset because they saved you, I won't."

"It's not about them saving me." I chose my words carefully. "I don't have a death wish. You don't have to worry about that."

"I know." He slid his arms around me. "You have me. That's worth celebrating ... with bacon-flavored pie. I can't imagine there ever being a time when you're not excited about spending time with me ... which means your life is a constant party."

His response was enough to cause me to laugh. "I don't think there's bacon pie."

"There should be."

"Maybe." I rested my forehead against the side of his face. "If I hadn't gone with you this morning I never would've known what I did to them. Those ghosts would've been trapped there indefinitely ... because of me."

He sighed and stroked his hand down the back of my head. "I know you don't want to hear this, but motive is important when assigning blame," he started. "You didn't know what you were doing. You can't be blamed for that."

"Is ignorance a defense in other crimes I don't know about?"

"Oh, don't go there." He wagged a finger and pinned me with a serious look. "You didn't commit a crime. You were confused and called for help. Sure, the help that came was in the form of ghosts, but I'll never be sorry that you're okay."

"I'm not sorry I'm all right. I'm just ... angry that I didn't realize what was going on with the voices. I need to get this power under control, Landon. I could ruin a lot of lives if I'm not careful."

"You're dealing with ghosts. They have no lives."

"No?" I folded my arms over my chest and narrowed my eyes. "Say I died before you ... ."

He immediately started shaking his head. "I don't like this game."

"I know you don't, but suck it up. I have a point. Say I die before you and another necromancer pulls me out of my intended trajectory and locks me in a different location. When you die three days later of a broken heart, too upset to even eat bacon, you'll move on to whatever is out there and I'll be stuck here forever. There will be no afterlife for us to share."

Landon looked taken aback. "Why won't I be able to eat bacon?"

I elbowed his stomach, annoyed. "As cute as you think you are, there are times I want to shake you. No, truly. I have to figure out what I'm doing with this power. I can't keep winging it."

"You do a great job of winging it," he countered. "You're doing the best you can. No one else in the family has this power. What are you supposed to do? Last time I heard there's not a necromancy school ... and that would be one creepy school with all the ghosts running around. Speaking of losing your appetite for bacon."

Even when I wanted to yell at him he was adorable. He had a charm streak wider than a galaxy. He also was loyal and determined to keep me from feeling sorry for myself. What wasn't to love about that?

"A bunch of witches are descending on the town today," I reminded him. "Hazel knows a lot. She might be able to help me with this."

Intrigue lit his features. "Do you really think she can help?"

"It can't hurt to feel her out. Heck, even if she can't help there's a chance some of the other witches can. They're due to arrive on a bus within the hour. I mean ... I won't hop on them the second they arrive, but I'll definitely poke around to see if enlisting them is an option."

"I don't have a problem with that." He leaned forward and pressed a kiss to my lips. "In fact, of all the ideas you've had the last two days, that's my favorite. It's so much better than that, 'Let's run into a burning building.'"

My lips curved down. "You're not going to let that go, are you?"

"Not until every hint of a bad dream that involves you dying in a fire disappears."

"Did you have one last night?"

He nodded. "I can't stop myself from being afraid for you, Bay. I know better than pushing you on certain things, though. We'll deal with this — and I'm talking all of this, from both our ends — together. That's what we do."

"That's what we do." I gave him a hug, putting as much effort as I could muster into it. "I love you."

"I love you, too." He rested his cheek on top of my forehead. "See, this isn't so bad."

The simple statement was enough to jinx us as a low whir caused me to jerk my head just in time to see Aunt Tillie cruising down the sidewalk on her scooter. Today she was dressed in a pair of plain black leggings, something so staid I couldn't imagine her picking them out. She also wore her combat helmet and had a whistle around her neck, but those items were part of her regular ensemble.

"Stop fornicating in the middle of the street," she barked as she zipped by.

"Where are you going?" Landon called out.

She didn't answer because she was already gone. And, to make matters worse, from the rear I saw her leggings weren't bare of a pattern after all.

"Is that a pair of ... lips?" Landon, horrified, asked after a moment.

I nodded grimly. "Yup. Right on the keister. I believe the message is obvious."

"She's going to be difficult because of this Hazel woman, isn't she?"

"Oh, you have no idea."

CONVINCED THAT I was no longer drowning in melancholy, Landon returned to Chief Terry, leaving me to my work. I let myself into The Whistler and headed straight to my office. There, I wasn't surprised to find Viola, the resident ghost, waiting expectantly. She peppered me with questions as I handled a bevy of busywork tasks and then lost interest. She'd wandered back into the lobby by the time I remembered she was still in the building, and that only happened because she let out a few excited yips.

"What now?" I asked as I plodded out of my office. Viola was the excitable sort and there were times she made noises simply because she saw a dog. She couldn't help herself.

"Look." She excitedly gestured out the front window.

"What is it?"

"Look." When I didn't immediately rush to join her, she gave me an impatient stare. "*Look.*"

I heaved out a sigh and moved to her side, my eyes going wide. "Oh, my ... ."

The witches had arrived. There were too many to stay at The Overlook, so some had registered at other inns. They'd all joined together to ride the bus into town, and it was something to behold.

"The Samhain Train," I read aloud from the side advertisement panel. "Well ... that's new."

"It's inspired is what it is." Viola's eyes danced with excitement. "I mean ... seriously. Look at that thing. It's amazing."

I could think of a few other words to describe it. "It's purple."

"But an awesome purple."

I couldn't argue with that. Out of sheer curiosity I tried to keep track of the number of witches exiting the bus. I lost count after a bit, but it was clear we were dealing with more than one-hundred women. Apparently the coven was bigger than I remembered ... or it had somehow grown over the years.

"Who is that?" Viola looked in awe as she extended a finger and pointed toward a specific woman. She wore a purple pantsuit, a fancy hat that would've been more at home at the Kentucky Derby, and she clutched what looked to be an expensive bag with feathers in her right hand.

It had been years since I saw her, but I recognized Hazel right away. She hadn't aged a day. "That's the woman who is going to turn Aunt Tillie into a nut the next few days."

"That's not Margaret."

I chuckled. "That's the *other* woman who is going to turn Aunt Tillie into a nut," I corrected. "Her name is Hazel."

"And Tillie doesn't like her?" Before her death, Viola and my great-aunt had something of a tempestuous relationship. Viola aligned herself with Mrs. Little, thus proving herself an enemy of the witch state in Aunt Tillie's mind. After her death, Viola decided to mess with both women ... something I often found amusing. That wasn't the case today.

"Aunt Tillie and Hazel have differences of opinion when it comes to policy," I corrected. "It's not as if they hate each other." Even as the words escaped I knew they weren't quite true. "It's not as if they hate each other a lot," I clarified.

Viola snickered. "I get it. Tillie is difficult."

"She's not altogether wrong on this one," I supplied. "I don't know if I think a witch council is a good idea. I do know that I don't like the idea of anyone telling us what we can and can't do. Hazel is just as much of a control freak as Aunt Tillie, maybe worse in some ways."

"That's a frightening thought."

"You have no idea."

I TRIED TO RETURN TO MY WORK, but it didn't go well. Once I knew the other witches were in town they were all I could think about. That meant it was time to shunt my work to the side and head outside for a little fun.

I was already downtown, a cup of gourmet coffee in hand, before I realized what I was doing. I sat on the bench in front of the police station to watch the shenanigans. That's where Landon found me a few minutes later.

"May I ask what you're doing out here?" he asked, tipping his head to his side. "Besides getting loaded up on caffeine, that is."

"Just watching the show." I smirked when two women squealed in delight at the sight of Hypnotic and immediately headed for the shop. "I find the witches fascinating."

"Oh, yeah?" Landon was clearly dubious. "They don't look like witches to me. They look like wannabes."

"And what do real witches look like? If you think they all look like me, you're sadly mistaken."

"Oh, I know they don't all look like you. My head would implode if there were a hundred Bays in town. No, seriously. I would explode from all the beauty."

I cast him a sidelong look. "Was that your attempt at romance?"

He turned sheepish. "Maybe a little."

"You should probably work on it."

"Yeah. I knew the second it came out that it was too much."

I patted his knee, sympathetic. "All you need is a little practice." I turned my eyes back to the witches. "The one in the hat is Hazel."

He chuckled when he caught sight of her. "That's somehow fitting, isn't it? Look who's riding her scooter around behind the other queen witch."

I didn't have to look to know he was referring to Aunt Tillie. Still, it wasn't as if I could ignore the potential disaster. Sure enough, Aunt Tillie was deftly navigating her scooter between the throngs of witches, circling Hazel as she glared. If Hazel was aware of Aunt Tillie's actions, she didn't show it. Instead, she kept up a running commentary with several younger witches surrounding her.

"I have to give her credit," Landon said after a beat. "She knows exactly how to drive Aunt Tillie nuts. Pretending she doesn't see the commotion is a surefire way to have Aunt Tillie popping her top by the end of the day."

"Oh, she won't make it that long. If she makes it an hour without trying to run someone over with that scooter I'll be stunned."

"Won't that be fun?" He rubbed his hand over my neck. "You okay?"

"I'm fine." I meant it. "You don't have to worry about me. I'm okay."

"Worry comes with the territory. I'm actually glad you showed up. Lorna is on her way to answer some questions. She's bringing her daughter. Lorna insists we don't question the children, which seems weird to me, and says she will call an attorney if we try."

I understood what he was getting at without him laying it out. "You want to see if I can talk to Dani."

"I'm not specifically asking you to do that because it would be unethical."

"You're not exactly dissuading me either."

"You're so smart." He gave me a kiss and a wink and then stood, his attention immediately going back to Aunt Tillie, who was making rude honking noises to get people to move. "We should get her a bell."

"I can't believe you're encouraging this. She could kill someone."

He snorted. "It's a kick scooter. The only one she's in danger of hurting is herself. She'll be fine."

I hoped that was true. For now, though, I had bigger things to worry about.

Lorna and Dani arrived several minutes later. Lorna strode directly into the police station, not so much as giving me a sidelong glance. She appeared to be in her own world, her eyes red and puffy, her face devoid of makeup.

Dani looked equally distressed. She remained outside the building, staring at the witches as they took over Main Street.

"Interesting sight, huh?" I prodded, forcing a smile for the girl's benefit. She was sixteen if I remembered correctly, but looked a little younger.

"Oh, hey, Ms. Winchester." Dani offered me a small wave. "I didn't see you there."

I was offended at being called "Ms. Winchester." Old people are referred to in that manner. I was far from old. "You can call me Bay."

"My mother says that's not polite when talking to adults."

I bit back a sigh ... but just barely. "Sit down and watch the witches with me," I instructed, patting the bench. "You've obviously had a rough night and should rest."

Dani didn't put up any complaint. Instead she readily slid into the spot next to me and turned her eyes back to the show on the street. "What is Miss Tillie doing on that scooter?"

"Messing with the other witches. That's what she does."

"She looks like she's having fun."

That was the truth. Aunt Tillie might've been a righteous pain in the behind for most of her life but she was almost always fun.

"I'm sorry about your dad," I offered, briefly wondering if I should refrain from bringing it up. Landon wanted me to get information, but I felt skeezy being underhanded in the attempt. Everything I knew about Dani suggested she was shy and well-behaved. I didn't want to manipulate her.

"Thank you." Dani's voice momentarily cracked. "I heard you tried to save him and almost died. I wanted to thank you for trying."

I felt bad for her. She was painfully polite even in grieving. "I liked your father," I offered. "He was always really nice and he had a wicked sense of humor. He made people laugh all the time at the festivals."

"Yeah. He was a good dad."

"He was a good man," I corrected. "He helped a lot of people in town, volunteering his time at various events. We're really going to miss him."

"I don't know that I would call him a good man." Dani's expression darkened, but she didn't expound on the statement. That put me in the awkward position of having to prod her, and I wasn't necessarily comfortable doing that.

"What do you mean by that?" I asked finally.

"He was cheating on my mom," she replied simply, her gaze never leaving the witches. "Everyone knew about it. He pretended to be a good guy, but he wasn't. He broke her heart ... and I can't help wondering if this is karma."

Well, I wasn't expecting that. I'd never known Adam to have a wandering eye. Still, Dani would know better. "I've never heard that rumor."

"It's not a rumor. I heard my parents screaming at each other in the bedroom about it the other night. Mom says Dad betrayed her. He told her to stop whining, but he admitted to it." Slowly, she tracked her eyes to me. "When you do bad things and other bad things happen to you in return, that's karma, right?"

She asked the question with such blank-eyed earnestness I felt put on the spot. "Some people consider that karma," I replied finally.

"Basically he got what he deserved." She turned back to the cavorting witches. "That scooter looks fun. Maybe I should see if my mom will buy me one."

And just like that, Dani was done talking about her father ... and I had more questions than answers.

SEVEN

I sat with Dani until her mother exited the police station. I had a million questions, but no matter how I tried to direct the conversation back to the bomb she'd dropped about her father's affair, Dani wasn't volunteering more information. She wanted to talk about the witches and nothing else.

Once Dani and her mother left, I headed for Hypnotic. It buzzed with activity — excited witches "oohing" and "aahing" over the assorted items for sale — so I wedged myself behind the counter to talk to Clove and Thistle without drawing too much attention.

"So ... I just had an interesting conversation with Dani Harris," I announced.

"Oh, yeah?" Thistle slid her eyes to me. She was busy wrapping a stone mortar in tissue paper. "How is she handling her father's death?"

"Not in the way you might think. She says her parents were arguing earlier in the week because her father was having an affair."

Clove furrowed her brow. "Adam? That doesn't sound like him. Are you sure she wasn't confused? Grief can make people act out of sorts."

"It can," I agreed. "She didn't seem confused. She refused to give me more information after dropping the bomb. I don't suppose you guys have any ideas on who he might've been having an affair with?"

"I don't think Adam was the type to have an affair," Thistle replied, studying her handiwork. She was an artist at heart and even her wrapping job showed a bit of flair. "I've never seen him with anyone, if that's what you're asking."

"That's what I'm asking." I'd searched my memory for instances of seeing Adam with a woman who wasn't his wife and come up empty. "I don't know what to make of it. She was really flat when she delivered the news, as if it wasn't a big deal."

"Maybe it wasn't a big deal for her."

"She asked a few questions about karma."

"Really?" Thistle arched an eyebrow, intrigue washing over her features. "Well, that's weird."

That's exactly what I was thinking. "I know, right? I find the whole thing weird."

"You could ask Lorna," Clove suggested. "She might own up to having marital issues."

I thought about Lorna's demeanor when she passed me in front of the police station. "I don't think Lorna is in the mood to answer questions right now. She has her hands full."

"If she was angry about Adam having an affair she did a masterful job of covering for it yesterday," Thistle noted. "I mean ... she was screaming and carrying on. If Mrs. Gunderson didn't have a firm hold on her she would've raced into the flames to try to save him."

"She was beside herself," I agreed.

"That could've been an act," Clove pointed out. "That could've been for your benefit ... and it obviously worked, because you guys ran into that building to try to save him, which was an absolutely moronic thing to do."

I murdered her with a dark glare. "Thank you so much for your opinion. It's valued and appreciated."

Thistle snorted. "You took the words right out of my mouth. She's been whining about being left behind all morning."

"You should be glad you were left behind." I kept my voice low.

"The paramedics were on us the second we left the building. You would've had to admit you were pregnant if you'd been there ... and you would've been in more danger than Thistle and me. Is that what you want?"

"What I want is not to be cut out of things now that we're living apart," Clove replied primly. "Our lives are different. That doesn't mean I want to be ignored. I'm having a baby, not dying. I want to be included in the adventures."

That seemed unlikely. "And how are you going to do that? Are you going to bring the baby with you when we're breaking into stores ... or traipsing around the cemetery ... or throwing magic at whatever evil pops up at any given moment?"

"If need be."

"What about when we're looking for Bigfoot?" Thistle challenged. "Are you going to bring the baby on those excursions?"

"Bigfoot isn't real." Clove said it with conviction but doubt clouded her eyes. "We won't be looking for Bigfoot because he's not real ... probably."

I smiled. Still, I understood what she was saying. We were creatures of habit. We didn't embrace change all that well. "We have no intention of cutting you out. It's just that your reality is a little different from ours right now. You can't be involved with everything because it's not safe for the baby."

"But ... you know I hate being left out," she whined.

"Yes, Clove suffers from a debilitating case of FOMO," Thistle drawled. "She'll succumb and die if we're not careful."

Clove's glare was pronounced when it landed on Thistle. "I know you think you're being funny, but you're not. I don't want to be left out. I'm becoming a mother, and that's a good thing. But I was your cousin first. I don't want to be forgotten."

My heart went out to her. "We're not going to forget you. We're going to include you in as many things as possible. But it will never be exactly the same again. That's not a bad thing. It just ... is."

Tears flooded Clove's dark eyes. "But that's not what I want."

I found my eyes burning with tears. Clove's magical emotion cloud was back in action. "Oh, man." I swiped at the tears beginning to trickle down my cheeks. "Why do you keep doing this?"

"Knock it off!" Thistle jabbed a finger at Clove as she grabbed a tissue from the box on the counter. "Do you have any idea how much I hate crying? I'm not even crying over things I care about. I'm crying because you're a kvetch."

"I can't help it," Clove offered with a half sob. "Sometimes it just happens. I'm not always in control of my emotions."

"It's the hormones," I complained. "She can't control them. We'll have to make do until she pops out that kid ... or miraculously manages to turn this particular power off. Speaking of powers, something weird happened to me this morning."

I told them about my run-in with the three ghosts. When I was finished, Clove's tears had miraculously dried and Thistle looked legitimately intrigued.

"Well, that's interesting," Thistle muttered, shaking her head. "I was so confused at the time I didn't realize that we had help escaping. This is turning into a handy little power."

"Except for the part where I'm turning ghosts into slaves. I don't like that part."

"I don't blame you, but you'll get over it." Thistle refused to back down. "Odds are we would've become overwhelmed with smoke yesterday if they didn't help. I'm glad your subconscious took over and protected us."

"Me, too," Clove agreed. "Thistle told me what happened. It sounds terrifying."

"I was too slow because of the lack of oxygen to be terrified," I admitted. "I was more numb than anything else."

"Me, too," Thistle admitted. "As soon as we got fresh oxygen to our brains, things cleared. We were lucky ... and I've had to hear nothing but complaints from Marcus about how stupid we were since it happened."

"Join the club."

"Yes, but I didn't want to be stupid," she reminded me. "I wanted to stay outside. I only went inside because you insisted on going and I couldn't very well leave you. That essentially means you're the reason I'm being called stupid."

"You can't blame that on me."

"I just did."

"Let's not get in an argument about this," Clove said firmly, shooting us both warning looks before gesturing toward the busy store. "I don't want to lose customers. I think this is going to be a good week for us and I'm saving for a crib."

Thistle made a face. "You don't pay for that stuff yourself. You wait and have a baby shower and make everybody else pay for it."

"Yeah, but ... nobody knows."

"Yet," I corrected. "They don't know yet. In another week, they will know and then we can start planning. Don't buy anything until after you get back from your honeymoon."

Clove looked happy at the prospect. "I hope you're right. Circling back to your other problem, I think you should talk to Mrs. Little."

I'd almost forgotten I'd had a purpose when I entered the store. "You want me to talk to Mrs. Little about Adam? Why? I very much doubt he was having an affair with her."

Clove's expression was withering. "I wasn't suggesting that. Mrs. Little knows all the gossip. She can't keep her nose out of other people's business. If you want to know if Adam was really having an affair, talk to her."

The idea of talking to Mrs. Little about anything often gave me indigestion. Still, it was a place to start. "That's not a bad idea. Does anyone want to go with me?"

Thistle's snort of disdain echoed throughout the store. "Nice try. We're busy, and no one wants to talk to Mrs. Little. If you really want to dig on this, you're on your own."

THERE WERE TIMES I THOUGHT Mrs. Little was the worst person imaginable. No, seriously. I grew up with Aunt Tillie and she taught me a thing or two about vengeance and enjoying the misery of others, but Mrs. Little was far worse.

I knew about evil, understood about sociopaths. I recognized some people couldn't change because of their nature. Mrs. Little was different. It wasn't that she *couldn't* change. It was that she *wouldn't* change. She didn't want to make herself better. She was fine being horrible.

That didn't mean she wasn't occasionally a fount of good information.

"Hello, Bay." She stood behind the counter, feather duster in hand. The look on her face was unreadable.

"Hello, Mrs. Little." I refused to show weakness. She had frightened me when I was a child. There was just something about her. As I grew older and watched Aunt Tillie make her life miserable, I found amusement in her antics. It wasn't until I was an adult, though, that I realized what she truly was.

Aunt Tillie found joy in smiting her enemies. She never went after a person who didn't deserve it ... or at least earn a reckoning in her head. Mrs. Little went after the weak and shy. She went after the young and old. She went after anyone who got in her way. She was a conqueror ... although in recent years she'd been conquered herself more than once.

That included recently when Landon purchased the piece of property she'd had her eye on right out from under her. I'd made sure to avoid her since that news became public. I'd heard from the bank owner that she was on a rampage.

"I'm surprised you're cavorting with your fellow witches outside," she offered calmly. There was no hint of mayhem in her eyes, which I found suspicious.

"I'll visit with them later. They'll be here for days."

"Yes, they will." She returned to her dusting. "Is there something specific you need?"

She sounded on edge, which made me wonder if she expected me to be the one to strike first blood. She would enjoy that, of course. She liked to retaliate so she could play victim. I wasn't keen on facilitating that.

"Actually, there is. I'm sure you heard about Adam Harris's death yesterday."

Surprise crawled across her face. Clearly she was expecting me to bring up the campground that she wanted so she could lease the property to the township for a financial killing. Landon wanted the property because that's where we'd met years ago — even though we didn't know it until recently — and he was incensed at the idea of her taking what he believed should be ours. With Aunt Tillie's help, he secured a mortgage and closed on the property in almost record time — although I had a feeling Aunt Tillie worked a little magic to make that happen. It was a done deal before Mrs. Little found out about it. Her rage was legendary and I was still waiting for her to react. She would blow eventually.

"You're here to talk about Adam?" Mrs. Little's expression was quizzical. "I don't understand. It was a fire. I keep trying to get the fire department to tell me if we should all be worried about gas leaks, but the chief won't respond to my calls."

"He probably has other things on his mind," I replied dryly. "You know … what with the building that's falling down and the dead body inside."

Mrs. Little's demeanor turned icy. "If there's nothing else … ."

"It wasn't an accident," I volunteered, taking her by surprise. "He was murdered before the fire was started. That wasn't a gas leak either. Accelerants were used."

I didn't feel all that guilty about sharing the information. It would be public knowledge within a few hours anyway. Hemlock Cove never met a secret that could be kept. Even the ones that were buried under a mountain of time and a name change couldn't remain hidden forever.

"You're kidding." For the first time since I'd entered the store, she showed real animation. "I hadn't heard that. Why are they keeping it secret?"

"I don't know that they're keeping it secret," I said. "They had to call in an arson investigator from the state and he only confirmed it this morning. I was there when he talked with Landon and Chief Terry."

"You were there?" Mrs. Little's disdain was evident. "I'm on the town council and I wasn't invited to the party. Why were you?"

"Oh, well ... ."

"Never mind." She waved her hand imperiously. "You don't have to answer that. I already know why you were invited. You have a special ... power ... over those two men."

I didn't like what she insinuated. However, if I picked a fight with her now I would never get the information I needed. "I'm actually here for a specific reason," I stressed. "I've heard through the grapevine that Adam might've been having an affair." There was no way I would mention Dani's name. Mrs. Little would spread that information through the town in five minutes flat. The family was dealing with enough. "I was wondering if you'd heard anything."

"Me?" Suddenly Mrs. Little looked like the poster child for the Innocence Project. "Why would you ask me that question?"

"You're a wise woman." I decided to blow smoke even though I wanted to choke on it ... again. "You know a lot of things. People confide in you. You've got your finger on the pulse of Hemlock Cove."

"I do indeed," she agreed, her gaze speculative. "I know almost everything ... except when certain individuals plan to buy property I've had my eye on for a great deal of time."

Oh, well. It was bound to happen eventually. She couldn't keep her mouth shut forever, no matter how she plotted to punish me otherwise. "I'm not here to talk about the camp. I know you're upset, but ... Adam's murder is more important. We have a dangerous individual on the loose."

For a brief moment I thought she was going to laugh. Instead, she pulled herself together and offered me a watery smile. "I'm not upset about the property. I mean ... I might've been at first. I've had some time to think about it, and I believe it's good that you and Landon own the property."

I was instantly suspicious. "You do?"

She bobbed her head. "That property is important to the history — and future, for that matter — of Hemlock Cove. You will take care of it, keep it in the family so to speak. That's important to me."

She was lying. I had no doubt about that. But if she wanted to save face I wouldn't begrudge her the opportunity. "Well, thank you for that. I appreciate the sentiment. Back to Adam ... ."

"Yes, Adam." She made a tsking sound with her tongue and shook her head. "Adam has been a bad boy. I heard the whispers, too. He wasn't very discreet when cheating on his wife. It's a travesty really."

"Do you know who he was cheating on Lorna with?"

"I never saw them together," she cautioned. "But I know others who did."

Finally, we were getting somewhere. "And?"

"Sheila Carpenter."

"Sheila? Are you kidding me? She's married ... and a deacon at the church."

Mrs. Little held her palms out and shrugged. "I don't make the moral decisions for the denizens of this town. I only report what I've heard ... like you."

I was insulted by the comparison, but held it together. "Are you sure?"

"Like I said, that's what I heard."

"Okay, well ... thank you for your time."

"Don't mention it. Oh, by the way, I hope you and Landon have endless happiness in your new home."

Something was definitely off here. That was for pondering at another time, though. For now, it was best left ignored. "Thank you. We will."

EIGHT

I wasn't what you'd call a regular church-goer. That was surprising to absolutely no one who knew me. We were witches, after all. Our version of worship came on different altars and under the full moon. Still, I was familiar with the local church. It was non-denominational and Christian. That's all I knew about it.

As far as I could tell, everyone who attended the church was a good person … other than Mrs. Little, I mean. They donated their time at festivals and didn't go out of their way to make problems for people. Sure, there was the occasional jerkwad who couldn't stop himself from being an asshat, but in general I'd never had a problem with the congregation.

I still felt like an outsider walking through the front door.

"Hello, Bay." Denise Pritchard greeted me with a happy wave when I slipped into the coolness of the shade. The weather in Michigan hadn't yet turned hot and humid, which was a bonus, but the air conditioning felt nice ... especially because my cheeks were burning.

"Hey, Denise." I felt out of place and hated what I was about to do. "How's it going?"

"Good." The woman, a mother of two who spent all her time

volunteering for various functions, fixed me with a puzzled smile. "Do you need something specific?"

That was a loaded question. I swallowed hard. "Actually I'm looking for Sheila Carpenter. Is she here today?"

"Sheila?" Denise's eyebrows drew together. "She's here. She's in the main office working on the books. Can I perhaps help you instead?"

"No, I really need to talk to Sheila."

"Can I tell her what it pertains to?"

Absolutely not. "It's private." I shifted from one foot to the other, uncomfortable. "I don't want to take up much of her time but it's important that I talk to her."

"Is this for the newspaper?"

"Yes." That wasn't technically a lie. I was most certainly digging into Adam's personal life because of the way he died and I was writing an article for the newspaper. How much of this would be included was up for debate. "It's for a story I'm working on."

"Fair enough." Denise's smile never wavered as she motioned for me to follow her. She led me through the rectory, not stopping until we were at the back of the building. "Hold on." She knocked on the closed door and poked her head inside when a voice beckoned. "Hey. Bay Winchester is here and she wants to talk to you."

I couldn't see Sheila, but I could picture her face. It wasn't a pretty scene. She invited me in without hesitation.

"Go ahead." Denise encouraged me to slide around her and into the office. "I'll be out front if you need anything."

I had no idea if she was talking to Sheila or me. It didn't matter. I planned to get in and out as fast as possible.

"Hello, Bay. Close the door."

I was happy to accede to her wishes and found my palms sweaty when I sat in the chair across from her desk.

"What can I do for you?"

Ah, well, so much for pleasantries. I was certain I would have to engage in some ridiculous idle chatter before getting to the meat of the conversation. Apparently, I was wrong.

"So ... um ... I'm here about Adam Harris." Playing games seemed a waste of time so I cut straight to the heart. "I understand you were close."

"Adam and me?" She looked legitimately puzzled, which caused me more discomfort than I'd envisioned. "I heard what happened to him, of course. What a tragic accident."

"Yeah, it wasn't an accident." Obviously she wasn't yet up on the newest gossip. That didn't surprise me. It wasn't as if she ran in the whispering circles that Mrs. Little ruled with an iron fist. "He was murdered."

"I'm sorry?" Genuine shock reverberated through the room. "I heard it was a fire. A gas leak, in fact."

"There was a fire, but it was set to cover up what happened to Adam. He was stabbed ... in the back." Saying it out loud made me realize there was quite possibly some symbolism attached to that act. That was something to ponder at a different time. "It wasn't discovered until after his body was removed from the building."

"Well, that is absolutely terrible." Sheila shook her head. "I had no idea. I assumed it was an accident. I feel horrible for Lorna and the kids."

For some reason, that struck me as funny. "I bet."

Her forehead wrinkled. "I don't understand why you're here."I licked my lips and pushed forward despite my unease. "I know about your relationship with Adam."

"My ... relationship ... with ... Adam." She repeated the words, as if trying to absorb them rather than delay responding to them. "I guess I'm not getting your meaning."

Oh, geez. She was going to make me spell it out. I kind of wanted to pull her hair for that, or at least make her eat dirt. I didn't like it one little bit. "The affair you were having."

I expected denials, maybe a few choice words. Instead, Sheila barked out a laugh that was so raucous it caused me to jolt. "Affair? You think I was having an affair with Adam?" She snorted through her nose, the sound unladylike ... and yet I was the one who felt uncomfortable. "May I ask where you heard that?"

This was starting to feel wrong. Way wrong. "Margaret Little." I felt no compulsion to protect the woman. "I was just at her store and she told me that she heard you and Adam were, um, an item."

"I see." She made a clicking sound as she moved her jaw back and forth. "I don't know how to tell you this, Bay, but I believe Margaret might've been having a little fun at your expense ... and mine. This probably stems from the fact that she wants to give the sermon next week — the pastor will be out of town and there's a competition of sorts brewing to see who will be in charge of the service. Margaret was ruled out by the deacons because ... well ... you've met her."

Things slid into place. "That horrifying witch," I hissed. I should've seen this coming. She was far too easy to get along with. I should've known it was a trap. "I'm sorry," I said hurriedly. "You probably frown on the name-calling."

"It's not something we embrace, but in this particular instance I don't believe it's out of line."

"It's definitely not out of line. I'm going to ... ." I mimed ripping an invisible head off someone I violently disliked, earning a genuine chuckle from Sheila. "I'm sorry. I just can't believe I fell for it. I knew she was being far too helpful."

"It doesn't surprise me that Margaret tried to damage my reputation. That's who she is. I am a little disappointed that you believed it, but ... well ... I guess that's on me."

"No, it's not on you." I felt like a complete ninny. "I voiced disbelief when she told me. It was my initial reaction. But she was very convincing."

"Yes, well ... she's a piece of work," Sheila said. "Was Adam really murdered?"

"Unfortunately, yes. It's also come to my attention that there's a possibility he was stepping out on Lorna. I was trying to ascertain who with and keep it under the radar to cause as little strife as possible, but apparently I went about it in the wrong manner."

"I would definitely say so. The thing is ... I know who Adam was with."

I wasn't expecting that. "Are you serious?"

She nodded. "I don't like idle gossip, you understand, but a lot of people have been talking about it. Adam was a regular parishioner here ... as is Lorna."

"I know. Can you tell me who it was?"

"I would rather not."

I decided to change tactics. "I need to know. It would be better if you told me. If Chief Terry and Landon have to come calling, things will get worse. If there's a chance I can talk to this woman before them ... well ... it might be easier coming from me."

She cocked her head to the side, considering. Finally, she offered me a slow nod. "That actually makes sense. I would prefer the information not be tracked back to me if you can help it."

"Sure. You're not Mrs. Little. I never divulge a source ... unless that source happens to be evil. You don't fit that bill."

She chuckled. "That's good to know. It's Lisa Newman."

I was taken aback. Lisa was a local seamstress. A lovely person, she made costumes for all our festivals. Two years ago, her husband had fallen ill and died a few days later. I couldn't even remember what he died from. It was sudden, though, and Lisa was an absolute wreck for months.

"Are you sure?" I felt mildly sick to my stomach.

She nodded. "I know what you're thinking. Her husband Barry was best friends with Adam. My understanding is the relationship grew out of their mutual grief."

In my mind, that didn't make it better. "Do you know how long it's been going on?"

"No, but I'm pretty sure it's been more than six months."

Well, great. "Okay. Thanks for letting me know." I slowly got to my feet. "As for Mrs. Little, don't worry about her. I'll handle it."

"And how will you do that?"

"Send Aunt Tillie after her. She's always looking for a reason to torture her."

Sheila laughed so hard I thought she might cry. When she finished, she simply nodded. "If there was ever an apt punishment, it would be that."

I couldn't agree more.

. . .

IT DIDN'T TAKE LONG TO find Aunt Tillie. She was zipping around the downtown area on her scooter, casting scathing looks in Hazel's direction. For her part, the top witch of the gathering was doing a remarkable job of ignoring Tillie's antics. It was a master class on how to derange Aunt Tillie. I would've applauded her under different circumstances.

"Aunt Tillie ... ." I tried to get her attention as she zoomed past me, but she didn't as much as glance over her shoulder.

When she did it twice more, I outright glared ... and then grabbed her by the back of the shirt when she tried to fly past me a fourth time. She lost contact with the scooter during the process and it smacked into a garbage receptacle, causing her to howl in fury.

"What are you thinking? Are you trying to kill me? I swear, Bay, it's as if you want me out of your life."

I didn't bother hiding my eye roll. "Cut the drama." I released her shirt so I could retrieve the scooter. "I need to talk to you."

"Oh, like I'm going to talk to the person trying to murder me. By the way, you're on my list. Be thankful that someone else has the top spot reserved because otherwise, whoa baby, you would be crying."

I was thankful for that. I knew I wouldn't last long on her list, though, because I was about to give her a big prize. "I have a mission for you."

Her glare was withering. "Oh, now you want me to be your errand girl. Won't happen. Besides, I have other things going on."

"It's about Mrs. Little."

No matter how focused Aunt Tillie was on Hazel, Mrs. Little was her true nemesis. Nothing would stop her from torturing her if the opportunity arose. "I'm listening."

I told her about what happened with Sheila, leaving nothing out and embellishing just a little so Sheila looked particularly pathetic in the scenario. Aunt Tillie hated it when good people were trampled upon.

"I think you should split your focus," I offered. "Mrs. Little needs a good lesson."

"She does." Aunt Tillie looked thoughtful as she switched her attention to the Unicorn Emporium. "Why do you think she went after Sheila that way?"

"Sheila said it's because there's some sort of competition to see who gets to deliver the sermon next Sunday. Pastor Mark is going to be out of town and it's apparently a big deal."

"I never understood things like that." Aunt Tillie worked her jaw. "Still, maybe I can somehow snag that spot."

"How do you think you're going to manage that?"

"I'm gifted, Bay."

She was ... something. "I don't care how you get her back. I just want her to think twice before messing with me again. This is all because of the campground. She acted fine, said she was glad we got it because that meant it would remain important to the town, and then lied to my face and tried to hurt an innocent woman in the process."

"She's so full of crap even the most dedicated sanitation workers won't touch her," Aunt Tillie groused. "I knew that campground steal would cause her grief. We hurt her first, which I always appreciate."

"You always told me it didn't matter who hit first. It was the last hit that counted."

"And I stand by that. We're definitely going to strike her again. I just need to decide how."

"I don't care how you get her. I just want her crying. Oh, and if you could get photos of her crying, that would be great."

The look she shot me was appraising. "You get more and more like me with each passing year."

"That's the meanest thing you've ever said to me."

"No, it's a thing of beauty. I'm serious. If you're like me, you'll be happy for another ninety years."

It seemed unlikely I would live that long, but I was fine agreeing if it meant she would give Mrs. Little her full attention. "Just get her ... and get her good."

"Oh, you don't have to worry about that. I have a few ideas I've been gnawing on. I'll figure out which operation to launch before the end of the day."

"Great." I moved to leave and then stilled, something occurring to me. "What's your deal with Hazel? I know you promised Mom that you would at least try to get along with her. This doesn't look like getting along."

"What your mother doesn't know can't hurt her."

"I have no intention of tattling on you. Quite frankly, I've never been Hazel's biggest fan either. It's been more than a decade, though. Don't you think you should give her a chance to see if she's changed? I mean ... that's been known to happen. Not to you or anything, but to others."

"I know exactly who Hazel is." Aunt Tillie's expression darkened. "I'll handle Hazel and Margaret, don't worry about that. I'm good at what I do."

I was familiar with that firsthand. "Okay. Well ... I need to run and do a few more interviews. You haven't heard anything about Adam having an affair, have you?"

"No, but I paid very little attention to him. Do you think he was really having an affair?"

"Yeah. It just wasn't with Sheila. She knew who he was having an affair with ... but I'm not supposed to tell anyone that she supplied me with the information."

"My lips are sealed. I have bigger whales to harpoon."

"Okay, well ... try not to get arrested. It won't go over well if Chief Terry has to take you into custody and then explain to Mom what you were doing. She'll be furious."

"You let me handle your mother. I'm not afraid of her."

If Aunt Tillie was afraid of anyone, it was Mom. Still, it was none of my business. Their relationship was between them. "Okay. I'm heading to Lisa Newman's shop. I'm not sure where I'll be after that, but if you're interested in lunch we'll probably be ordering in to Hypnotic later."

Shrewd as always, Aunt Tillie narrowed her eyes. "Why are you going to the seamstress shop?"

"Why do you think?"

Her mouth dropped open. "No way. She was schtupping Adam? That is so wrong. Her husband and Adam were best friends."

"Yes, it seems like a huge betrayal on just about every front. I think it might be true. Either way, I have to talk to her."

"That sounds like a terrible conversation."

"I'm not looking forward to it."

"I'll go with you." She volunteered without hesitation, which made me uneasy.

"I don't think that's a good idea," I hedged. "This is a delicate conversation."

"Which is why you need me. Nobody does delicate better than me."

I knew a hundred frustrated women — and even more men — who could argue with that statement. "Why do you really want to go?"

"I've been thinking that the one thing this scooter needs is a cape for me. Lisa could make one ... and I bet she could do it fast."

Huh. Never what you expect. "Fine, but don't say anything embarrassing."

"Do I ever?"

She was doing me a favor, I reminded myself. There was no sense buying trouble. "Of course not."

NINE

I thought Aunt Tillie's cape plan was a joke until she strolled through the door of Lisa's store and planted her hands on her hips. "Where's your Wonder Woman section?"

I practically choked on my own tongue.

"My Wonder Woman section?" Lisa looked up from the sewing machine she was working at and frowned. "I don't technically have a Wonder Woman section."

"How can you not have a Wonder Woman section?"

"I haven't gotten around to it yet," Lisa replied. "Perhaps if you tell me what you're looking for I can help you with something from a different section."

Instead of immediately answering, Aunt Tillie sighed. "I don't know. I had my heart set on being Wonder Woman … at least I think."

She was being purposely difficult, which wasn't unusual. "She needs a cape," I volunteered. "Something satin ... maybe blue. She wants to wear it around her neck while she's riding around on her scooter so it streams behind her. I think that's a good way to get snagged on something and accidentally hang herself ... but I don't get a vote in the matter."

Instead of reacting to the news with an appropriate sneer, Lisa nodded and stood. "I think I have what you're looking for." She gestured for Aunt Tillie to follow her to the far corner of the store. "These are durable synthetic fabrics that mimic satin but come with a much smaller price tag."

"Oh, cool." Aunt Tillie brightened considerably when she saw the fabrics. "Do you only have solid colors?"

Lisa looked rueful. "I'm afraid so."

"Ah, well." Aunt Tillie tapped her chin as she regarded her options. "Can I have one that's double-sided?"

"You should probably ask how much it's going to cost first," I pointed out. "You might decide you don't want to spend that much."

"Don't be ridiculous." Aunt Tillie's lip curled into a sneer. "I'm going to wear a cape on a scooter. In what world won't I want to do that?"

She had a point. "It's up to her," I said, waving my hand as Lisa started pulling out bolts of fabric.

"What colors do you want?" Lisa asked Aunt Tillie. "We can do double-sided. Maybe you can have two sides of your superhero personality."

"Actually I prefer being a super villain on my off time." Aunt Tillie ran her fingers over the fabric. "Go green for one side and purple for the other."

I furrowed my brow. "Why not red and blue for Batman and Superman? Or red and yellow for Wonder Woman? You just said you wanted to be Wonder Woman."

"I don't want to be either of those goons."

"Wonder Woman is red, too."

"Yes, but the Hulk is purple and green. I've decided if I was ever to turn into a superhero, it would be the Hulk. He most closely matches my personality."

I could see that. "Do what you want."

"Thanks for your permission," she shot back dryly. "Do you need to measure me?"

Lisa shook her head. "It should be fairly easy. I'll make sure it's not too long because I don't want you tripping. I saw the scooter. If it gets tangled under your foot or in the spokes, that could be a recipe for disaster."

"Good point." Aunt Tillie flopped in a chair and watched as Lisa started measuring fabric. "So, word on the street is that you were having an affair with Adam Harris. Is that true?"

I wanted to kick her ... or at least slap myself in the face for telling her in the first place. I had no one to blame but myself. Aunt Tillie never met a secret she didn't want to blab.

"I can't believe you just said that," I gritted out.

"Sure you can. You knew I would broach the subject from the start. That's why you invited me."

"I didn't invite you."

"That's not the way I remember it." Aunt Tillie's gaze remained clear and keen as it rested on Lisa. "You don't have to talk to us if you don't want to, but it's better to spill your guts to Bay than 'The Man' ... and I guarantee 'The Man' will find a way to stick his nose in your business. He's threatened to take my still and wine so many times I've lost count. And don't get me started on my pot field."

She was referring to Landon. They had a tempestuous relationship at best. Landon had threatened her pot field on more than one occasion. Unfortunately for him, Aunt Tillie cursed the field so anyone trying to find it would get diarrhea.

Yeah, she's a horrible woman when she wants to be.

Now that recreational pot was legal in the state of Michigan, we were at a crossroads. You could legally own eight plants. Aunt Tillie had way more than that. But the field was cloaked, so there was no way to prove she was breaking the law. Chief Terry had long since given up trying to get her to follow the rules. Landon wasn't quite done smashing his head against the wall yet.

"I don't know what you're talking about," Lisa said. Her full attention was on the fabric she was cutting, but it was impossible to miss the stiff set of her shoulders. The question had clearly hit the mark.

I felt bad for her ... and a little annoyed at the same time. "I don't think you were as stealthy as you thought when it came to hiding the relationship," I offered. "More than a few people know the particulars."

"I see." She held up the fabric, comparing the panels to ensure they were the same size, and then moving back to her machine. "I guess it's a mistake to deny it given what happened?"

"I would definitely say so," I confirmed, resting my hands on my lap as I regarded her. She was steadfastly avoiding eye contact. I couldn't blame her. This could hardly be the way she envisioned things ending when she embarked on the affair. "Why didn't you come down to the blacksmith shop after the fire yesterday?"

"I was out of town," Lisa replied, grabbing a container of pins from the counter and carefully inserting them in the fabric. "I had to run to Traverse City for supplies. That's a normal run for me. I do it at least once a month. Actually, Adam was supposed to go with me this time, but he had to back out at the last minute."

"Why?"

"Lorna couldn't handle the shop herself and everyone kept saying these witches coming into town were a big deal. Tourism is the name of the game in Hemlock Cove. We have to keep the tourists happy ... and these particular tourists are bringing a lot of money to the town."

"They are," I agreed. I felt woefully out of my depth. "How long were you and Adam involved?"

"About a year."

"So ... a year after Barry's death."

"I know what you're thinking." Lisa finally lifted her head and I saw the strain lining her pretty features. She was in her late forties, but looked younger. "You think I'm a horrible person for carrying on with a married man."

"I didn't say that."

Aunt Tillie lifted her hand. "I didn't say it, but I think it. I don't like cheats."

I slapped at her hand. "Knock that off." I was firm. "You've already caused enough trouble."

"What trouble?" Aunt Tillie's face was blank. "If I hadn't come with you the question never would've gotten asked."

"That's not true. It just would've taken longer."

"Okay." She turned back to Lisa. "Didn't it bother you that Adam was married?"

"Of course it did." Lisa sat down at the machine with her basted project. "We didn't plan for it to happen. You should know that. It was an accident. It just sort of popped up out of nowhere."

"Did he fall on top of you or something?" I asked blankly. It was an old joke, but I didn't buy "accidental" affairs.

"Of course not." She let loose a sigh. "It started when he volunteered to help me around the house. After Barry's death, I had a rough time of it. He died so suddenly. We weren't expecting it. People say that it's better to go fast than linger. I believe that, deep down, but not being able to say goodbye wrecked me. There has to be a happy medium between the long goodbye and the nonexistent one."

"Barry was a good guy," I offered. "He used to help Aunt Tillie pull her plow truck out of the snowbanks by Mrs. Little's house."

Lisa chuckled at the memory. "He didn't even need to drive in that area. He just liked going down there and finding you. He thought it was funny the way you used to torture Margaret by plowing the end of her driveway in so she couldn't escape. But he never understood how you turned the snow yellow."

"She's gifted when it comes to torture," I drawled. "That still doesn't explain how you ended up with Adam."

"I'm getting to it." She flashed me a tense smile. "Like I said, he came around to help me after the fact. Barry left a lot of unfinished projects ... like replacing the electrical socket in the bathroom and updating the trim in the dining room. Adam volunteered his time to help.

"I thought he just wanted to keep an eye on me at first," she continued. "He was a good man but out of his element. He was worried I would harm myself because I was so upset over Barry."

I remembered that time well. A lot of people were worried about that exact scenario. "So he came over a lot."

"There was no definitive moment," she supplied quietly. "It wasn't as if it was a conscious choice. We spent a lot of time talking about different things, including history — we both loved learning about the World War II era — and art. It got to where we'd read the same books and talk about them, like our own personal book club. It spread to watching the same shows and sending emails when we weren't together. Then it grew to phone calls. Before we realized what was happening, we were looking forward to seeing each other ... and it only snowballed.

"You have to understand that we didn't plan this. We didn't want to hurt or embarrass anyone." Her tone turned pleading. "All we wanted was to be together. We couldn't stay apart."

On one hand, I felt sorry for her. The man she'd loved died and left her alone. I couldn't imagine that happening to Landon. The mere thought gutted me. On the other hand, Lorna was supposed to be her friend. Adam broke his vows and cheated, but Lisa was complicit.

"You think I'm rationalizing what I did," she said quietly. "Go ahead and say it."

"It's not my place." I meant it. "It's not for me to judge. It's not my business. It's just ... Adam was stabbed in the back and then a fire was started in his shop to cover his slaying. I can't help but think an affair makes for an interesting motive."

Lisa was taken aback. "What?"

It was only then that I realized she wasn't aware of the truth. "Oh, geez." I felt like an idiot. "You didn't know."

"Adam was murdered?" Her voice was shrill as she stood and then sat again. It was as if she didn't know what to do with herself. "I don't understand."

"I'm sorry." I held my hands up, helplessness washing over me. "I assumed you knew."

"I thought it was an accident. A tragic accident, but an accident nonetheless."

"Not quite." I pressed the heel of my hand to my forehead. I was starting to get a whopper of a headache. "Did Lorna know about your relationship with Adam?"

She nodded without hesitation, catching me off guard.

"She did?" I was surprised. "But ... how did that work?"

Lisa chuckled, the sound low and utterly humorless. "It's not as convoluted as you might think. Adam was a good man. At a certain point, he told Lorna that he didn't think their marriage was healthy, that it wouldn't survive the long haul. She actually agreed. She didn't put up an ounce of fight.

"They had a very long discussion, something I wasn't a part of because it wasn't my place, and agreed to keep the marriage together for Nick and Dani," she continued. "The kids were sixteen and fifteen at the time. Now they're seventeen and sixteen. The plan was for Lorna and Adam to remain together until the kids graduated from high school. After that, they would get a quiet divorce."

"Just like that?" I had my doubts. No divorce I'd ever heard of was that simple. "No tears? No names? No threats?"

"I wouldn't say there were no tears. They were married a long time. They cared about each other. There were no names or threats, though."

I looked to Aunt Tillie to see what she was thinking. "If Landon ever does that to me there's going to be more than names flying about."

My great-aunt snorted. "He'll never do that. He's not the type. Even if he did, he would live to regret it."

Lisa shook her head. "Not all relationships are based on the sort of love Landon and Bay share. I've seen them together. They have a fiery love. It will never be truly easy because they'll often argue and fight, but it will never be boring.

"I'm not trying to be derogatory to Lorna," she continued. "I like her very much, although the friendship has basically disappeared at this point. As much as she was okay with letting Adam go, she didn't feel all that comfortable with me."

"Do you blame her?" I asked. "I mean ... even if she realized the marriage wasn't going to last, the way things went down had to hurt."

"I'm sure it did and I'm genuinely sorry for it. The thing is, after a few weeks, Lorna was not only happier, she was more relaxed. She didn't even realize how tense she was in the marriage. She didn't initially want the marriage to end because it made her feel like a failure, but when the decision was taken from her, she felt lighter."

"She told you that?"

"She told Adam."

"So … there were no hard feelings between them?" I found that hard to believe. "Nothing at all?"

"Not to my knowledge."

I thought about what Dani had said to me. "What if I told you they'd been fighting and Lorna threw the affair in his face? Would you find that out of the ordinary?"

"Yes."

She seemed certain of herself, which left me scrambling for the right words. "Adam was stabbed in the back. Someone wanted him dead."

"And you suspect Lorna?"

I thought back to the way she'd carried on in front of the blacksmith shop. If Lisa was right and she was fine with the divorce, it didn't make much sense.

"I don't know what I believe," I replied. "Lorna seemed distraught about what was happening when we saw her yesterday."

"Of course she was distraught. Adam was still one of her closest friends. He was the father of her children. The love they shared didn't go away. It simply changed into something new. Why wouldn't she be distraught?"

Perhaps I was looking at the situation the wrong way. It all felt off. I didn't know how to balance my questions, empathy and suspicions. "Lorna might've been putting on an act," I said finally. "She might've pretended to be fine even though she was actually angry."

"I sincerely doubt that."

"Why?"

"Because she was involved in another relationship."

Oh, well, the hits just kept on coming … and coming and coming. "With who?"

Lisa chewed her bottom lip, uncertain. "I'm not sure I should say."

"Either you tell me or Landon and Chief Terry will confront her.

That'll probably make things worse." Actually, there was no "probably" about it. Things were definitely going to get worse. "The news will come out either way."

She heaved a sigh and I saw the resignation dragging down her shoulders. "Fine. But I would prefer the information not being tracked back to me."

That was turning into the main game of the day. "No problem. Who is it?"

"Paul Masterson."

I nearly fell out of my chair. "Paul Masterson? The guy who owns the real estate office?"

"That's him."

"The old guy who is also on the township board?"

"One and the same."

"Oh, geez." I pinched the bridge of my nose and looked to Aunt Tillie. "This just keeps getting uglier and uglier."

"Yeah, but I'm getting a cape out of the deal," she said. "That's the most important thing."

TEN

Lisa finished Aunt Tillie's cape, making sure to test it by tying it around her neck and tugging from five different directions before sending us on our way. She looked exhausted, to the point I was certain she was back to where she was right after her husband died.

I made a mental note to say something to Chief Terry. He had connections with the county mental health facility and might be able to send a counselor her way.

"What do you think?" Aunt Tillie twirled in her cape, studying her reflection in the front window.

"You look like a grown woman dressed like a superhero," I replied automatically.

She scowled. "Not about that, you ninny. I'm talking about the story she told. Do you believe her?"

"I don't have any reason not to. Still ... it seems a little weird, right? I can't imagine being okay with my husband having an affair, and certainly not to where I take off and have an affair of my own."

"That's because you've already bonded for life with your Fed. Not everyone bonds as strongly as the two of you."

"I think I prefer being bonded."

"That's not always the easiest way to go," she noted as she gripped her cape tighter and twirled again. I didn't need to see inside her mind to know what she was thinking. She had bonded for life, too. Only her husband, my great-uncle Calvin, died when they were still in their prime. She'd spent the decades since without him.

Sure, she'd dated a bit. Her last boyfriend, Kenneth, had seemingly disappeared into the ether when she lost interest. I'd considered asking why she'd dumped him, but I recognized it wasn't my place. If she didn't want to talk about it, she didn't have to.

"Yeah, well ... that doesn't explain the fact that Lorna is dating Masterson." I made a face as I moved to the edge of the sidewalk and focused my attention on the town square. It was set up for a festival — which was always the case in Hemlock Cove — and the witches raced around the open area, having a good time. In the middle of it all were several local politicians, chatting up the guests, putting themselves on display and feeding off the attention. Masterson seemed deep in conversation with a pretty, dark-haired witch.

I didn't know him well. He was in his late sixties and boasted snowy hair. There were lines around his eyes, but otherwise he carried himself with the strength of a younger man. He was always impeccably dressed, never a hair out of place. I honestly didn't know if I liked or hated him.

"What do you think of Masterson?" I asked after a beat. Aunt Tillie knew him better. While she tended to take the theatrical route with enemies, she was a good judge of character when it came to others.

"He's kind of an enigma," Aunt Tillie said, turning her full attention to the town square. "I mean ... I've talked to him here or there. He's never really pinged my radar. Why? Do you think he killed Adam?"

"I think this entire relationship game is a big problem," I admitted. "We have a quadrangle that was messy, no matter what Lisa said. We also have at least one kid in the mix who knew about the affair. What are the odds Nick was in the dark if his sister knew?"

"You think the kids did it?" Aunt Tillie wrinkled her nose. "That's quite a stretch."

"I didn't say that. The thing is, if the adults thought they were hiding it from the kids — and that seems to be the sole reason Adam and Lorna were staying together — maybe they weren't as under the radar as they thought. It's possible a lot of people knew about the affair.

"I don't know what that means in the grand scheme of things," I continued. "It could mean absolutely nothing. It could also mean there's a clue in there we simply have to sort out."

"Who is this 'we' you're referring to?" Aunt Tillie queried. "I'm not involved in this. I have my own mischief to manage."

She wasn't wrong. "You're going to the festival tonight?"

"Of course. Margaret will be there ... and Hazel." Aunt Tillie's eyes turned dark. "There has to be a way for me to punish them both with the same plan. That will make me look like a genius and force them to turn into whiny babies who curl into balls and cry for days."

"I doubt they'll do that."

"You don't know. I'm good at what I do."

That was true. "Just be careful when you're doling out punishment. If Mom finds out ... ." I left it hanging. My mother had been in a remarkably good mood of late — finally embarking on a real relationship with Chief Terry had seemingly made her a happier person than I ever remembered — but that didn't mean she would simply sit back and watch Aunt Tillie run roughshod over the gathering's premier guest.

"How many times do I have to tell you I'm not afraid of your mother?"

We both knew that was a lie, but I decided to let it go. I needed Aunt Tillie on top of her game. "Just be careful." I patted her shoulder. "Try not to get your cape tangled in any tree branches while you're riding. You might get hurt."

She turned haughty as she retrieved her scooter and moved it toward the street. "Don't you worry about that. I've got everything under control."

"How can you control an accident?"

"With magic. You keep forgetting, Bay, we're witches. We can do whatever we want. That includes casting a spell that makes capes something more."

I didn't want to know what that "something more" was. "Just be careful. We have enough on our plates."

LANDON PICKED ME UP AT THE Whistler shortly after his shift ended. He greeted me with a friendly kiss and then linked his fingers with mine before dragging me toward the festival.

"You must be hungry," I noted as I struggled to keep up. His legs were longer than mine and he appeared to be a man on a mission.

"How do you know I'm not in a hurry to get you in the kissing booth?" he asked, slowing his pace a bit. "This could all be about you rather than my stomach."

I shot him a dubious look.

"Or it could be about the new bacon food truck that I saw earlier," he added sheepishly.

"There's a bacon food truck?" Seriously, how did I miss that? "Who's running it?"

"Who cares? It's bacon. I saw the menu when I was walking past and it's glorious."

He looked like a kid who had just gotten the new bike he really, really wanted for Christmas. "What if I don't want bacon?"

"Don't tease me, Bay." His response was dry. "Everybody wants bacon."

"Not all of us love it as much as you. Besides ... how many different things can they make with bacon?"

"I'm glad you asked." He tightened his grip on my hand and his expression turned distinctively dreamy. "They have maple bacon doughnuts, bacon-stuffed fried Twinkies, bacon-wrapped chicken drumsticks, bacon sliders and something called bacon-wrapped cheese bombs. I have no idea what those are, but I'm eating ten of them."

"Well, at least you have a plan."

"I do," he agreed, his eyes sliding to me. It was only after a moment of searching my face that he appeared to slow down. "Tell me about your day."

He was perceptive. That was one of the best things about him. He might've initially missed the hints about my mood because of his bacon mania, but it didn't take him long to catch up.

"I learned a few interesting tidbits," I admitted. "I think you need to hear them ... but I come off looking like an idiot at the beginning of the story."

"Did you put yourself in danger?"

"No. I simply believed something Mrs. Little told me that turned out not to be true."

He scowled. He hated Mrs. Little as much as the rest of us. Sometimes I thought more. We were used to her, had grown accustomed to her nonsense over the years. He didn't have the luxury of finding any of her antics funny. "Did she say something to you about the campground?"

"Not exactly." I told him about my afternoon. I did a run-through of my discussion with Mrs. Little, included my embarrassment at interrogating Sheila and finished with my distaste following my conversation with Lisa. It took almost twenty minutes.

"You've been busy," he said as he gently slid a strand of hair behind my ear and considered what I'd told him. "That's quite the romantic quadrangle there. What do you know about this board member?"

"Not much. I even asked Aunt Tillie about him. She said he's never pinged for her, but the truth is that she's never paid that much attention to him. With Mrs. Little constantly acting up, there was no reason to focus on Masterson."

"You must've had some run-ins with him."

"I guess." I searched my memory. "I don't remember talking to him more than a few occasions. I interviewed him a few times. He's simply a non-entity."

"We'll still have to talk to him."

"I figured." I leaned close and rested my head on his shoulder as he pressed a kiss to my forehead. "I should probably tell you now that I enlisted Aunt Tillie to go after Mrs. Little. I was frustrated at the time because she sent me after Sheila. Now I'm starting to wonder if it was a terrible idea."

Instead of commiserating with me, Landon snorted. "Please. That woman has it coming. I can't wait to see what Aunt Tillie dreams up. Now that she has a cape there will probably be a superhero theme to her punishments. That sounds entertaining."

I hadn't told him about the cape. "Did you see her in it?"

He nodded. "She's zipping around on the scooter and having a grand time."

"She could hurt someone."

"She won't." He sounded sure of himself. "She's more responsible than we give her credit for ... at least most of the time. Don't get me wrong, she does the occasional idiotic thing. Okay ... she does a lot of idiotic things. But at her core she's a good person with a wicked sense of justice. Whatever she doles out to Margaret Little, that horrible woman has it coming."

I arched an eyebrow, unable to hide my surprise. "Tell me how you really feel."

"That is how I really feel. I want Aunt Tillie to make her cry. I've had it with her."

"You know, earlier today Aunt Tillie said I was getting more and more like her with each passing year. I didn't want to hear it. Now I'm starting to wonder if you're getting more like her."

Instead of being offended, Landon laughed. "You know what? I'm fine with it, especially where Mrs. Little is concerned. I don't want to talk about her, though. I want to talk about the bacon truck. Can we please go there before my stomach implodes?"

He was too earnest to deny. "Okay, but I might be getting my dinner from a different truck. I don't think I want huge chunks of cheese wrapped in bacon as my primary source of nutrition this evening."

"Do what you want, but you'll be missing out."

"I can live with that."

. . .

LANDON HAD SEVERE BACON BREATH when he dragged me into the kissing booth. It was one of his favorite festival attractions, which always made me laugh. He'd overdosed on bacon to the point I was convinced he would be sweating grease later, but he was in a ridiculously good mood so I was willing to put up with it.

Masterson was one of the first people I saw upon leaving the kissing booth. He was holding court in the middle of the festival, a bevy of witches surrounding him, and telling jokes that didn't sound even remotely funny. The brunette I saw earlier guffawed and I figured it had to be an act ... or she was an airhead who didn't get the idea of true humor.

"Not tonight," Landon admonished, lightly grabbing me by the back of the neck to keep me from crossing over to Masterson. "There are too many people here."

I was surprised he cared. "We need to talk to him."

"Technically *I* need to talk to him ... and Terry. You don't need to be involved in this at all."

I narrowed my eyes. "You can't cut me out of this. Not after everything."

He sighed. "I have no intention of cutting you out of this. Believe it or not, I consider you a valuable part of the team." He kissed the tip of my nose by way of proof. "But you have to wait. We can't draw attention to a murder in the middle of a festival. That's not the way to keep the tourists happy."

I was dumbfounded. "I had no idea you cared so much."

"Yeah, well ... I love this town. I fell in love with you first and your love of this town caused me to take a long, hard look at what we were dealing with. We're going to live here forever. I don't want to do anything to hurt Hemlock Cove's future prospects."

That was an adult viewpoint ... which I didn't necessarily like. "So ... we're going to talk to him tomorrow?"

"We're going to discuss a game plan tomorrow," he countered. "I don't know how we're going to approach this. Technically it's Terry's case. That means you and I are the subordinates."

"I don't like being a subordinate."

He lightly patted my behind and prodded me forward. "It can be fun if you play it the right way. Later tonight we can play that game. I'll be Mr. Montague and you can be my long-suffering secretary."

I shot him a dirty look. "That is not funny."

"Oh, it's funny if you think about it."

"I don't want to think about it. In fact ... ." I trailed off when I heard crows cawing. It was much louder than we'd normally hear at this time of night. "Where is that coming from?"

"What?" Landon's gaze was on the ice cream truck. "We should get sugared up and go back in the kissing booth."

I ignored the suggestion and lifted my eyes to the sky. There, a swarm of black birds circled at the far edge of the town square ... almost as if they were stalking prey. "Harbingers."

Finally, as if sensing that I was distracted, Landon followed my gaze. His frown was pronounced. "What kind of birds are those?"

"Crows."

"Why are they doing that? This isn't going to turn into a horror movie, is it?"

I wasn't sure. Until this exact moment, I'd forgotten about the birds I saw right before the explosion. "We should head over there."

"Why? Crows aren't scavengers, are they? I doubt they're circling a body."

"No, but a big murder of them appeared right before the black-smith shop exploded."

He stilled. "Murder?"

"That's the term for a flock of crows."

"You didn't mention the crows at the blacksmith's shop."

"I forgot. Between Adam dying and the lack of oxygen to my brain, it had slipped right out of my head."

Landon didn't look happy at the news. "Maybe we should stay away from that area if it's dangerous."

"We have to look." I was firm. "If another fire breaks out ... ."

"People could be in trouble," he finished, shaking his head. "I don't know that I like this, Bay."

"Do you have a better suggestion?"

He didn't, so we wordlessly headed in that direction. His earlier bacon euphoria had diminished, and that made me sad. That didn't mean we could shirk our duties.

When we arrived at the spot the birds were circling, we found a lone figure sitting on a bench. It was a woman; I could make that out right away despite the dwindling light. I had to stare a bit longer, peer through the shadows, to make out the features.

"Is that Lorna?" Landon asked after a beat.

I nodded, confused. There was nothing in this area to set on fire. Also, Lorna didn't appear to be communicating with the birds. Instead, she sat beneath them, staring into nothing.

"What is she doing?" Landon whispered. "Is she gathering those birds to attack?"

That was a good question. "I don't know."

"So ... why are they gathering?"

"I have no idea." I was flummoxed. "I think we should watch her a bit longer."

"Maybe we should try to talk to her."

I flicked my eyes to the birds again and shook my head. It wasn't that I feared them — well, not exactly — but they made me leery. "Let's just watch for now. We don't have a reason to question her yet."

Landon didn't look convinced, but he acquiesced. "Okay, but if those birds attack I'm going to be really ticked off."

"Better birds than sharks."

ELEVEN

I was lost in a dream. I realized that right away, but my heart still pounded. The landscape I found myself in was stark. It was Hemlock Cove ... only altered.

The downtown was dark, red clouds filling the sky. The street lamps were operating, but they cast an eerie pink glow, bordering on magenta.

"Landon?"

I knew it was futile to call his name. It was my dream. The odds of him being there were slim. I was doomed to disappointment ... and yet I wanted him anyway.

"What are you doing here?" The voice that ruthlessly questioned me didn't belong to the man who I knew was actually sleeping in bed beside me in the real world. When I swiveled, I found Lorna watching me.

She sat on the same bench I'd seen her on earlier, her expression grave. Behind her, black birds perched on a fence that didn't exist in real life. All of them watched me with predatory eyes, looking as if they wanted to peck me to death and then tear off strips of my flesh. Of course, that could've just been more horror-movie knowledge influencing me.

"What are you doing here?" I shot back, doing my best to appear bold. This Lorna was a figment of my imagination, but I didn't want to appear meek.

"I asked you first."

"Yeah, well ... I asked you second."

There was no amusement in her gaze. "You shouldn't be here, Bay. You're separate from what's going to happen. This doesn't concern you."

"What doesn't concern me?" I was frustrated. "Did you kill Adam?" It was a ridiculous question given the fact that I was caught in a dream, but still I wanted to know.

"No. Did you?"

"Of course not. I tried to save him."

"I wanted to save him, too. I tried. I ... really tried." For the first time since she appeared she showed a hint of real emotion. If I had to give a name to what I saw, it was forlornness. She was legitimately sad. "Still, it's too late to save him now. If you persist in this, you'll only put yourself at risk. Is that what you want?"

"I never want it. That doesn't mean it doesn't occasionally happen."

"You should stay out of this."

Another voice joined the fray. "You really should."

I jolted at the new player and frowned when I saw the three ghosts I'd released earlier in the day standing in the middle of the road. I could see through them. The weird lights made them look evil, but I knew that wasn't the case.

"I'm sorry for what I did to you." I meant it. "I didn't realize I'd summoned you."

"That hardly matters now," the brunette said. "What's in the past is beyond changing. All you can do now is keep your future safe."

"Do you have any advice on how to do that?"

"Watch the birds."

"Watch the birds?" That seemed like a silly statement and yet I understood, deep to my bones, what she said. "The birds are the key, aren't they?"

She nodded. "Yes, but you can't control them. You can only wait for them to tell you where to look."

I pursed my lips as I shifted my gaze back to the crows. Suddenly, they and the fence they perched on were closer. "I really wish they wouldn't look at me that way."

"They're not malevolent," the brunette warned. "They're animals. They don't hate. It's the person who controls them who gives them their purpose."

I turned back to Lorna. "That's you, right?"

"Why are you focused on the birds?" she complained. "The birds aren't important. What's important is you minding your own business." There was an edge to her tone, and it was sharp enough that it caused several of the birds to rustle their feathers and caw.

"I'm not trying to hurt you," I explained to Lorna. "I only want to know the truth. Did you kill Adam?"

"How many times must I answer that question?" Her eyes filled with fire at the moment the crows started moving. They were moving in my direction. "Don't stick your nose in something you don't understand. This is none of your concern. You need to stay out of it."

As the last sentence escaped her mouth, the birds attacked. Instinctively, I covered my head and began to run. Dream logic is a funny thing. Even as I zigged and zagged to escape them, the crows were ahead of me at each turn.

I shrieked — something I was convinced I would never do in real life — and dropped to my knees as I tried to protect my face from the beaks. "Leave me alone!"

THE WORDS LEPT FROM my lips as I bolted to a sitting position on my bed. I couldn't stop from shaking my head and smacking at my hair to make sure no birds had followed me from the dream.

"Bay, look at me." Landon was firm as he grabbed my shoulders and forced me to stop freaking out. "You're okay. It was just a dream."

His voice was enough to soothe me. When I saw his features,

though, I was so relieved I threw my arms around his neck. "I was looking for you."

"Yeah?" He stroked the back of my hair. "Well, you found me. I'm never very far away."

That was true. He was always close when I really needed him.

"What did you dream about?" he asked quietly, his voice laced with concern. "Tell me."

"I ... it was weird."

"I want to know anyway. Unless it was a sex dream about someone other than me. If that's the case, keep it to yourself."

I laughed. "I only have sex dreams about you ... and the dude who plays Thor. Sometimes you're even in the dream together."

"That is disturbing." He readjusted to keep me close and lay back against the pillows. "I still want to hear about the dream."

I told him, feeling a bit foolish. When I finished, he seemed more confused than I was. "What does that mean?"

"I have no idea."

"Is Lorna a killer?"

"Don't know. It's not as if she was really in my head."

"No, but you're intuitive. If you had that dream, there must be a reason."

I could think of a few. "The birds. It must've been the birds."

"That was not normal bird behavior," he agreed, his hands moving to the base of my neck so he could rub at the tension there. "I can't help but think you had this dream for a reason."

"Maybe it was simply all the ice cream I ate reacting with all the bacon you ate."

"Maybe. Or maybe it was something more."

"Like what?" I was genuinely interested in his answer.

"I don't know, Bay. What I do know, without a shadow of a doubt, is that I love you. I won't let the birds or anything else get you."

I smiled in the darkness as I rested my head on his shoulder. "I never had a doubt in my mind that you would."

. . .

WHEN BREAKFAST rolled around I was feeling much better. I showered, changed into capris and a T-shirt, and walked with Landon to the inn. We entered through the back door and found Aunt Tillie in the middle of a screaming match with my mother.

"You're not the boss of me!" Aunt Tillie's hands landed on her hips. "I'm the boss of you. I'm older. There's a pecking order in this family and I'm at the top."

"Uh-oh." Landon grimaced as he regarded my tempestuous great-aunt. She was dressed to impress today, a pair of Wonder Woman leggings offsetting a military coat. She was the queen of clash ... and the purple and green cape only made things worse.

"There *is* a pecking order in this family," Mom agreed, her tone brutally pleasant. "I'm on top. You're somewhere below ... on the same level with Bay, Clove and Thistle. Do you want to know why?"

"Because you're getting way too big for your britches," Aunt Tillie replied without hesitation. "That's why."

"No, because you often act like a child ... just like them."

"Hey." I was offended by the remark. "I'm rubber and you're glue," I started.

Mom extended a finger in my direction but kept her eyes on Aunt Tillie. "Don't add to this madness, Bay. I'm not kidding. I'm not in the mood."

That was obvious to pretty much everyone. "Why are you even fighting?" I asked after a beat, hoping to smooth things over. "It's too early for yelling."

"It's never too early for yelling," Aunt Tillie countered, her gaze withering. "Have I taught you nothing?"

"Speaking of people who are in trouble." Mom turned her eyes to me. "It's come to my attention that you were with Aunt Tillie when she selected this lovely ensemble. Would you like to explain yourself?"

Oh, well, now I was on the hot seat. I didn't like that one little bit. "When were we discussing people who were in trouble?"

"That's a regular conversation when Aunt Tillie is around," she replied blandly. "Explain about the outfit."

"How am I supposed to explain that outfit? Besides, I was only with her when she had the cape made. The rest is out of my control."

Mom didn't look convinced. "She said you helped her select all of it."

"And you believe her?" I gestured toward the leggings. "Like I would pair red and yellow with camouflage. Get real."

Landon, clearly bored with the conversation, craned his neck. "Where is Peg?"

"She's in the dining room entertaining all the witches," Mom replied. "She's a big hit."

"We're still getting bacon for breakfast, right?"

Mom rolled her eyes, but nodded. "We are. You know, if bacon ever makes it on the illegal substances list you'll have to go to rehab."

"It will be totally worth it." Landon started toward the kitchen, not letting go of my hand. "Come on, Bay. I want to meet these other witches. Is Hazel the Horrible out there?"

Mom glared. "I see you've been getting an earful. I wonder who from." Her eyes were glittery slits when they landed on me.

"Hey, I just told him why Aunt Tillie disliked her. I didn't say anything about my personal preferences."

"That's true," Landon noted. "Bay is a good girl." He squeezed my hand. "Now I want to meet the evil witch."

Mom made a disgusted sound deep in her throat. "You'll all be the death of me. Is that what you want?"

"Better you than me," Aunt Tillie replied, skating around Mom and hurrying to catch up with Landon and me. "I'll protect you from Hazel, Landon. Stick close to me."

He winked at her. "Always."

THE DINING ROOM THRUMMED WHEN we entered. Landon immediately followed the sound of snorting, leaving me to greet women I hadn't seen in more than a decade.

"Who's a good girl?" Landon crooned, dropping to the floor.

"You really need to get him a pet," Aunt Tillie muttered, shaking her head.

"I've been thinking about it. What sort of pet doesn't require a lot of attention and will let Landon pet it for five hours straight?"

"Other than the attention part, you just described yourself."

I scowled. "You're bugging me."

"That's what I do."

I pasted a bright smile on my face when I settled next to Chief Terry. He looked overwhelmed by the sheer number of women at the table. He sent me a welcoming smile and then frowned at Landon.

"Can't you make him stop doing that?"

Landon was making kissing noises for Peg's benefit.

"Not so far," I replied ruefully, pouring myself a cup of coffee. "I wish he would kiss me that way; alas, I don't rate as high as the pig."

"Don't be jealous, Bay," Landon chided. "I have room in my heart for both of you."

I shook my head and focused on the woman staring at me from the other side of the table. I recognized her, of course. I'd managed to avoid her for the better part of the day yesterday. Apparently my luck wasn't going to hold. "Hello, Hazel."

"Bay." The smile she shot me was full of sunshine. "It's good to see you. I was beginning to wonder if you were avoiding me."

"Avoiding you? No. I don't live in the inn."

"Oh, no?" Hazel's eyebrows drew together. "I was under the impression you lived here."

"I live in the guesthouse on the property, but it's a decent walk, and we were out late at the festival last night."

"Yes, I think I saw you." Her eyes drifted to Landon. "Your friend was dragging you into the kissing booth and you were complaining about bacon in his teeth."

"That's a regular occurrence for them," Aunt Tillie replied as she sat at the head of the table. "Why are you so interested in Bay anyway?"

"I'll have you know that I'm an interesting person," I countered.

"She totally is," Landon offered from his spot on the floor. "She's the most interesting person I know, isn't she?" He smiled indulgently at Peg as the pig wiggled her butt. "She's awesome."

"I've always been interested in Bay," Hazel replied. "She's an interesting girl. As for you, Mr. ... I'm sorry, I didn't get your name."

"Landon Michaels," I supplied. "We live together."

"I figured that out myself," Hazel noted. "How did the two of you meet?"

Oh, well, that was an interesting story. "Um ... ." I trailed off, uncertain, and found the brunette I'd seen with Masterson the night before eyeing me curiously from the other side of the table. She didn't look impressed with what she saw.

"I'm an FBI agent," Landon volunteered. "I met Bay when I was undercover and she was working on an article." He was purposely vague. "We hit it off and have been together ever since."

"Not the entire time," Aunt Tillie muttered, referring to a brief period after Landon learned I was a witch. He said he needed time to think. It was enough to break my heart, but in hindsight he wasn't gone all that long.

"Thank you for bringing that up," Landon muttered, his gaze dark. "I don't think we hear that story nearly enough."

"There's a story?" Hazel brightened considerably. "I love stories."

"It's not a story for you," Aunt Tillie chastised. "It's only a story for me."

"It shouldn't be a story for anyone," Landon groused. He'd apparently lost interest in Peg, because he was sliding into the chair next to me and pouring coffee. "I hate that story."

I patted his knee under the table. "She's just trying to irritate you. Let it go."

"Well, either way, you make a strikingly handsome couple," Hazel offered. "It's obvious you're happy, which is exactly what I always wanted for you. When you were a child, I saw a hint of darkness in you that I wasn't always comfortable with. You still have the darkness, but you seem to have mastered it."

Landon frowned as he cupped his hands around his mug of coffee. "Bay isn't dark."

"I didn't mean her hair or anything," Hazel said with a laugh.

"And darkness isn't always bad," the brunette added with an annoying chortle. "Oh, I'm Evie, by the way. Actually Evanora, but I go by Evie."

I frowned. "Like after the witch in *The Wizard of Oz*?"

She nodded. "Exactly!"

"Was your mother a fan?"

"Oh, no. I chose the name myself. My old name was boring. This one fits me better. As for darkness, like I said, it's not always bad."

"And I really didn't mean anything bad by it," Hazel stressed.

"I know what you meant and she isn't dark." Landon was firm. "Everything inside of her is goodness and light."

"Except for when she's crabby in the morning," Aunt Tillie added, causing Landon to nod.

"Except then," he agreed. "Once she's had her morning dose of coffee, she's fine."

Hazel was clearly taken aback by his vehemence. "I wasn't trying to upset you. You mustn't think that. I just ... Bay was always an interesting child. She had a lot of power, but didn't use it. She spent all her time running around with her cousins rather than studying."

"And now she spends all of her time running around with this one." Aunt Tillie jerked her thumb in Landon's direction. "Bay isn't interested in studying. Never has been."

I wanted to argue the point. The problem was, it was true. Aunt Tillie tried to give us magical lessons as kids. She insisted it was crucial. We always bowed out because we had more important things to do ... and Aunt Tillie was often tyrannical when it came to serving as a tutor. Now, given what I'd done to the ghosts, I couldn't help wondering if that was a mistake.

As if reading my mind, Landon leaned closer. "You're perfect the way you are. Don't listen to either of them."

He was so earnest I couldn't stop myself from smiling. "Thanks."

"You're welcome ... and it's true."

"Knock that off," Aunt Tillie warned, jabbing at us with a crooked finger. "You have sex in your eyes and I don't like seeing it when I'm about to have breakfast. Stop being gross."

I sighed and dragged my gaze from Landon. "I'm sorry. What is everyone planning to do today?"

"We're going to hang out at the festival, maybe do some circle work on the bluff later if you're interested," Hazel replied, exchanging a bright look with Evie. "We don't have a set plan."

"Oh, well ... I appreciate the offer, but I probably won't have time for circle work." Her steady gaze made me distinctly uncomfortable. "I have other work to do. A local man was killed recently and I'm helping Chief Terry and Landon solve the crime."

Chief Terry stirred, arching a dubious eyebrow. "You are?"

"I am." I bobbed my head and gave him my best "Don't even try arguing with me" expression. "I'm in this one for the long haul."

"Wonderful," he said dryly.

"That's too bad," Hazel volunteered. "You'll be missed on the bluff. Perhaps another day."

"Perhaps." When Aunt Tillie's pig started magically flying around, that is.

TWELVE

Landon dropped me at Hypnotic. He thought he was being sly by suggesting we ride together, but I recognized what he was doing.

"I'm not going to purposely find trouble," I promised as I hopped out of his Ford Explorer. "You don't have to worry about me." We hadn't talked about the dream since waking, but it was obviously bothering him.

"Did I say anything?" He was the picture of innocence.

"No, but you're thinking really hard."

"I am. Now ... come here and kiss me."

I was instantly suspicious. "Why? You're not going to handcuff me to you to make sure I don't stick my nose into things, are you?"

"I wasn't considering it, but I find the suggestion interesting." A sly smile spread across his face. "I just want a kiss."

I rolled my eyes, but it was mostly for form's sake. When I stopped in front of him, he took me by surprise by drawing me in for a tight hug. "Don't go running around and getting in trouble. If you find something you want to investigate, give me a call and we'll do it together. We're supposed to be working this case as a team."

I nodded as I leaned back and stared into his soulful eyes. "I need to research the birds."

He didn't argue. Instead he merely traced his thumb over my bottom lip. "I figured. I think that's a good idea. Just ... don't go after the birds without me."

"Why would I go after the birds?"

"I don't know why you do half the things you do." He grinned when I glowered ... and then he slowly sobered. "You'll go after them — or rather, the person controlling them. We both know it. I don't want you going alone. I'll help."

"Are you going to shoot the birds?"

"If need be."

That sounded overly simplistic, but we were nowhere near the point where it was a prominent concern. "I'll be fine." I squeezed his hand. "I promise not to find trouble today."

"We both know you can't promise that. Trouble often finds you."

"True, but ... ." I wasn't sure what to say.

"I'm not angry, Bay," he reassured me. "Worrying about you comes with the territory. I wouldn't trade you for anything - not a single thing - so I can live with pretty much anything. Just ... call me if you decide to start chasing birds. That's all I ask."

It seemed a reasonable request so I nodded. "I really will be fine," I promised him. "Trust me."

"With my heart." He gave me a kiss. "Try not to let Thistle and Clove get you riled up. That's my job."

I snorted as I headed toward the store. "You're in a good mood today. Bacon hangover?"

"The best of all hangovers."

"So you've told me."

CLOVE AND THISTLE WERE HARD at work when I entered Hypnotic. Well, Thistle was hard at work. Clove sat on the couch in the middle of the store, a catalog open on her lap and an order sheet perched on the cushion next to her as she elevated her feet on the table.

"Are you playing the pampered princess today?" I teased as I skirted the living room area and headed straight for the reference books.

"My feet are swollen," Clove complained, her expression dark. "I mean ... like big time. It's like walking around on two sausages."

"That sounds ... lovely."

"People always say pregnant women have a glow," Clove muttered. "I think that's a load of crap. I don't feel as if I'm glowing."

I spared her a sidelong glance. I couldn't help but agree. She looked pretty far from happy, and there was nothing shiny about her. "Well ... things could be worse," I said. "You could be pregnant with one of those monsters from *Alien* and about to give birth to a creature that punches through your chest."

Thistle snorted as Clove made a face.

"Oh, thank you for saying that to her," Thistle drawled once she'd recovered. "Now I'm going to have to listen to her complain for days because she has indigestion and believes it's an alien about to pop through her chest. You won't have to deal with it because you have an office you can hide in."

I hadn't really thought about it, but that was an added benefit. "I need a book." I decided to switch tactics because I didn't have time to dilly-dally. "I saw you had an interesting one here several months ago. It was on harbingers."

Thistle, her faux outrage over having to deal with Clove's meltdowns forgotten, furrowed her brow. "Harbingers? Why are you researching them?"

"I've seen them twice now."

"Oh, yeah?"

I reminded her of the birds we both saw right before the explosion rocked the downtown. Then I told her about what Landon and I witnessed the previous evening at the festival.

"That's weird," Thistle murmured. She looked lost in thought. "I don't even know what to make of that."

I was right there with her. "That's why I want to research harbingers."

"Go ahead. I'm kind of curious now that you've brought it up."

I found the book I was looking for and settled in a chair close to Clove as I read. Surprisingly — or perhaps unsurprisingly if you believed Hazel about me not wanting to be part of the witch learning crew — there was quite a bit I didn't know about the topic.

"Did you know there are harbingers of joy?" I asked when I was about thirty minutes into my research. "Hummingbirds. They're supposed to signify joy and victory over darkness."

"And here I thought they were just mesmerizing to watch," Thistle teased.

I ignored her and kept reading. "Owls are harbingers of doom and symbols of wisdom. They're considered wise and supposedly can communicate if you give them a chance."

"Oh, well, that sounds like a great idea," Thistle said. "I recommend the two of you not sit in the woods and talk to the owls."

I ignored the sarcasm. "For witches, owls are particularly important. They're drawn to us on an individual basis given the strength of our magic, and if we see one crossing our path we're supposed to pay it particular attention."

"I'll get right on that," Thistle muttered.

"I've always liked owls," Clove said. She'd given up the pretense of ordering things and was instead openly lounging. "I think they're cool."

"Owls are only harbingers of doom if we see them fighting," I continued, completely caught up in the material. "Otherwise they're carriers of wisdom."

"Something this family desperately needs," Thistle noted. "We should totally get a pet owl."

I moved on to the next section of text. "Crows and ravens have always been considered harbingers of death, but this says they get a bad rap. They can bring bad news, but not all the time, and are essentially the image of truth. What do you think that means?"

"Does it say what it means?" Thistle challenged.

"It says if you see a crow you're going to discover the truth."

"Did you see crows or ravens last night?" Clove asked. "I mean ... it might help to narrow down the sort of bird we're dealing with."

"I'm really not sure." I was hardly a bird expert. "I thought they were crows. Do we even have ravens in this area?"

"I have no idea," Thistle answered. "I could ask Marcus. He might know. He works a lot with animals."

"I'm not sure it matters." I turned back to my reading. "Hawks are symbols of good. If we're in a battle and can call upon a hawk, supposedly we're assured of a victory. If a falcon or hawk crosses your path you're supposed to be ready for battle ... but the hawk will more often than not join you in the battle."

"Oh, well, that's good to know." Thistle was clearly over bird talk. "Next time I decide to take on Aunt Tillie I'll take a hawk along. There's nothing scarier than a hawk when you're having a witch fight."

Clove pointed at her. "True story."

My lips quirked at their interaction, but I kept reading. "Bats aren't birds, but they're still harbingers. Almost everyone fears bats ... except witches. Bats don't signify death, they indicate a major transition.

"Oddly enough, storks aren't the bearer of babies as we've been taught," I continued. "Storks bring something new to your life, but not necessarily a baby. Hmm.

"Vultures aren't omens of death, despite what mass media would have us believe." I was really getting into it now. "I would've thought they were because of their scavenger nature. They're omens of fertility." I turned my eyes to Clove. "You didn't see a vulture before Sam knocked you up, did you?"

I was having a good time, something I previously would've thought impossible when talking about birds. I was so engrossed in what I was doing I didn't initially notice that the store had fallen into complete silence ... almost unnaturally so. After a few seconds, the hair on the back of my neck stood on end.

I slowly raised my eyes and found Aunt Tillie standing behind the counter. She must've come in through the back door without alerting us — perhaps to use the bathroom — and she looked utterly flabbergasted as she glanced between us.

"Uh-oh," I muttered, shoving the book to the side and focusing on our great-aunt. "How long has she been standing there?"

"Long enough to hear what you said," Thistle replied. She'd moved away from the shelves she was dusting and was completely focused on Aunt Tillie. "How did you get in through the back? We keep that door locked."

Aunt Tillie's eyes narrowed as her gaze bounced from face to face. Finally, she focused on Clove. "You're pregnant?"

Clove's lower lip trembled and I felt the panic washing over her. "I ... you ... ."

"You can't say anything," I barked, taking control of the situation. Aunt Tillie respected strength ... and I was about to show her mine.

Aunt Tillie ignored me and remained focused on Clove. "How far along are you?"

"Several months," Clove admitted, her voice tiny. "I ... um ... ."

"Give her a break," Thistle ordered, circling in from the other side. Much like me, she obviously sensed trouble. She wasn't about to let Aunt Tillie bully Clove when our cousin was at her most vulnerable. "She and Sam will be married before the end of the week. There's no reason to make a thing out of this."

"No reason?" Aunt Tillie's eyebrows hopped. "She's going to have a baby. I just ... how long have you been sitting on this information?"

She switched tactics quickly and it made me suspicious.

"Why does that matter?" I challenged. "We're not doing anything wrong. We're simply ... helping our cousin."

"Zip it." Aunt Tillie held her thumb and forefinger about an inch apart as she gestured toward me. "I'm not talking to you right now." Her gaze never left Clove's face. "When are you going to tell your mother?"

"After the wedding," Clove answered, breathless. "I swear I'm telling her after the wedding."

"Why not tell her now?"

"Because ... because ... ."

"You know why," Thistle argued. "This week is important to our mothers. Clove just wants some peace before her big day. We're almost there. We just need a few more days."

"I don't think I can keep this a secret," Aunt Tillie admitted. "It's not a little thing, like you guys risking your lives or breaking into a business to look for clues and potentially being sent to the big house, where you'll be molested by prison queens for cigarettes. This is a big deal."

"Why?" My temper was bubbling close to the surface, something I knew wasn't good but I couldn't stop myself from reacting with fury. "She's going to be married in a few days."

"Besides, this belief you guys have that we need to be married before procreating is antiquated," Thistle added. "I think those are probably ideal circumstances, but there's no such thing as ideal circumstances in life. Clove and Sam will be happy. More importantly, they'll be good parents. You need to leave them alone."

"I don't think I can." Aunt Tillie shifted slightly and I could tell she was about to bolt through the back door. I had no doubt what she would do if she escaped.

"You can't tell them." I was insistent. "You'll ruin everything."

"I don't see that I have much choice," Aunt Tillie shot back. "You can't expect me to keep this secret from them. It's not fair."

"You're keeping your mouth shut." Thistle took a menacing step in her direction. "If I have to curse your tongue myself, you'll keep this to yourself."

"Oh, well, that's a bold threat," Aunt Tillie said. "I think you'll have to catch me first." With those words, she nipped through the hallway and disappeared.

For a moment — one interminably long beat — Thistle and I just stood there. Then, as if propelled by the same force, we tore toward the door. Clove gave chase, too, but with her swollen feet she couldn't keep up. Thistle and I were already way ahead of her when we hit the street.

"Which way?" I asked, jerking my head left and right.

Thistle pointed. "There." Aunt Tillie was already on her scooter halfway down the alley. She glanced over her shoulder to see if we were giving chase and she grinned when she saw us.

"You can't stop me," she called out. "I have to do what I have to do."

"Like Hecate you do," I muttered.

The scooter was both a blessing and a curse for Aunt Tillie. She could ride faster than we could run, but the street was littered with people and she wasn't coordinated enough to smoothly navigate through the throngs without constantly having to stop and readjust.

Still, she managed to make it to the other side of the crowd. She was heading toward the part of town where the blacksmith shop was located when Thistle got fed up.

"Enough is enough." She narrowed her eyes and started muttering curses.

I didn't realize what she was doing until it was too late to stop her. "Wait ... ."

Thistle let loose a barrage of magic that caught up to Aunt Tillie with enough force to cause the scooter to careen sideways. Aunt Tillie couldn't control her velocity and pitched forward.

For one horrifying moment all I could picture was Aunt Tillie's head meeting the concrete. Would there be broken bones? Would the head injury actually be enough to kill her? Had we just traded Clove's secret for Aunt Tillie's quality of life?

And then Landon came out of nowhere and caught her before she hit the ground.

I wasn't sure where he'd been — although the blacksmith shop was right behind him and Chief Terry and Todd Bennett were watching the scene with something akin to awe — but he timed it exactly right to make sure Aunt Tillie incurred minimum damage.

"There now. You need to be careful," he admonished.

Aunt Tillie's eyes were wide when they landed on him, but they narrowed when she turned them to us. "Oh, you two are in so much trouble."

We were out of breath when we closed the distance.

"You're going to keep it to yourself," I argued, grabbing her wrist to make sure she didn't flee a second time. "It's important."

"I already told you I can't keep a secret like that," Aunt Tillie argued. "They're my nieces. They have a right to know."

"Oh, geez." Landon rubbed his forehead. "I take it you big mouths were talking about Clove's secret and she overheard. I told you this would blow up in your faces."

"Nobody wants to hear 'I told you so' at a time like this, Landon," I shot back. "She came in through the back. We didn't hear her. How were we supposed to know?"

"You should've been careful all the same."

Realization washed over Aunt Tillie's face and she became enraged. "Wait ... he knows before me?" Her cheeks flushed with color. "That is just the most insulting thing I've ever heard. Why would you tell him?"

"Because I can trust that he'll keep his mouth shut," I replied without hesitation.

"Do I even want to know what you guys are talking about?" Chief Terry asked.

I shook my head. "No. I can unequivocally say that you don't."

"I agree on that," Landon offered. "You're better being ignorant."

"I always think that." Chief Terry gestured for Todd to return to the hollowed-out shell that used to be the blacksmith shop. "Let's take another look around."

Todd nodded. "Sure. That sounds like a plan."

I waited until I was certain they were out of earshot to speak again. "You can't tattle on us. You'll ruin absolutely everything if you do."

"I don't know." Aunt Tillie chewed her bottom lip. "I'm not sure this is a secret I can keep."

"You have to hear us out." I refused to back down. "Once we tell you why it needs to be a secret, you'll agree with us. I know you will."

Aunt Tillie didn't look convinced, but she nodded. "I guess it can't hurt to let you make your case. I should warn you, though, my mind is already made up."

THIRTEEN

Clove finally caught up with us at the small park across the way. Most of the activity focused on the downtown area was at the far end of Main Street, so we were relatively assured of being able to talk without anyone eavesdropping.

"Listen," I lectured Aunt Tillie. "we're not trying to keep a secret just for the sake of keeping a secret. This is a stressful time for Clove. The last thing she needs is our mothers flying off the cauldron handle and adding to it."

Aunt Tillie folded her arms across her chest. "That's the lamest argument I've ever heard. You can do better."

"We don't have to do better," Thistle countered. "It's Clove's secret. She has a right to decide when it comes out."

"Better, but still lame."

I frowned. "What good will come from telling them before the wedding?" I challenged, appealing to her practical side. "It will only get them worked up."

"They'll get worked up anyway," Aunt Tillie pointed out. "I distinctly remember them warning you about getting pregnant before marriage. It was one of the few threats they issued."

"I'm pretty sure they have no right to issue those threats," Landon offered, speaking for the first time since we'd left the blacksmith shop. He'd opted to come with us, although I figured it was in more of a supervisory position than anything else. "What does marriage have to do with being a good mother?"

"I didn't say that marriage is important to being a good mother," Aunt Tillie clarified. "But she's an adult. She knows where babies come from. The whole point of stressing the importance of birth control to them was because we didn't ever want them to feel they had to get married."

Clove stirred. "Is that what you think? Sam and I were engaged before I found out I was pregnant. By a long shot."

"Fair enough. But that's what other people will say."

"Since when do we care what other people think?" Thistle challenged. "For the entirety of our lives you've insisted that we think for ourselves and not follow the crowd. I mean ... you're riding a scooter around and wearing a cape while terrorizing people, for crying out loud."

Annoyance flashed deep in her eyes as Aunt Tillie balked. "That's a smart look."

Thistle frowned. "No, it's not."

I held up my hand before this conversation could get away from us. "Aunt Tillie, only bad things can come of you opening your mouth now. Clove is going to tell them after the wedding but before she leaves for her honeymoon. That will give them time to cool down. Things will be fine by the time she gets back."

"Please don't tell them." Clove's eyes filled with tears and she looked pathetic as she beseeched Aunt Tillie. "I'm begging you. It's important to me that I be the one to tell them. I know you don't understand that, but ... it really is important to me."

"Ugh." Aunt Tillie growled. Given the way her shoulders slouched in resignation, though, I knew we'd won. "Fine. I won't say anything. I still think this is a bad idea. They won't be nearly as worked up as you think."

"That would be a nice surprise," I acknowledged. "I'm not sure I believe it, though. Still ... thank you. We need you on our side for this."

"Oh, I didn't say I was on your side," Aunt Tillie countered. "I said I wouldn't tell them. You're on your own when it comes to keeping this secret. I have bigger things to worry about ... like Margaret and Hazel. You're just lucky that I can't afford to have my attention split in a third direction."

"We feel extremely lucky," I reassured her. "You're the best aunt in the world."

"You're totally the best," Clove enthused.

Aunt Tillie's expectant eyes landed on Thistle.

"You're all right," Thistle replied after a beat. "You still tick me off."

"I feel the same way about you," Aunt Tillie shot back. "By the way, you're totally on my list for that little stunt you pulled with the curse and the scooter. I will find time to dole out some retribution for that."

Thistle made a face. "I can't wait."

ONCE THINGS WERE SETTLED WITH Aunt Tillie and she'd scootered off in the direction of the witches to continue her campaign of terror, Thistle and Clove returned to Hypnotic, which they'd left open and unlocked. That left Landon and me to ourselves.

"Why are you back here?" I asked. "Did the arson investigator come up with anything new?"

"This is just standard stuff. It's normal for him to come back because once the debris has settled he can find new evidence."

"Like what?"

He arched an amused eyebrow. "Do I look like an arson investigator to you?"

"I thought you knew everything."

"Cute." He poked my side. "You know that Aunt Tillie could've been injured by that move you guys pulled? I don't think you should do that again."

I didn't necessarily want to blame Thistle, but that's exactly what I did. "It wasn't my curse."

"I know, but be more careful next time. Believe it or not, you'll miss her when she's gone, and you would never forgive yourself if you were the reason she was hurt."

"I'll see what I can manage." I rolled my neck. He wasn't wrong. The horror I felt when I saw her fall was still fresh. "What are you guys up to next?"

"I don't know. I'm a little out of the loop right now. What are you going to do?"

"Visit Lorna."

Landon made a sound halfway between resignation and exasperation. "I thought we agreed you would wait for me before approaching her."

That's not how I remembered things. "I said I wouldn't go after the birds. I'm just going to question her ... and work at the same time. When someone dies, I like to do a story that's a tribute to his or her life. I need to talk to Lorna for Adam's story."

"Are you going to ask her about the affairs? What about Masterson?"

Both good questions. "I don't know yet. I'll have to play it by ear, gauge her mood."

"I would prefer you not get into too much trouble, Bay. I don't like this one ... and for a multitude of reasons. That bird thing is weird and I can't help but think you dreamt about the birds because they're somehow important."

"I agree they're important. That doesn't mean Lorna is controlling them."

"No? She was the only one on that bench."

"Yeah, but someone else could've sent the birds after her. I mean ... have you considered that maybe Lisa is the one putting on the act?"

"I haven't talked to Lisa yet. I'm sure that will be on the agenda for today. Since you've already talked to her she'll be expecting us, too. That means she'll have time to come up with a story."

"She already told me her story."

"And you seemed to believe her at the time."

That was true. Quite frankly, I couldn't decide how I felt about all the players. "I know but ... there are a variety of different things that could be happening here. I'm not saying I believe it, but what if Lisa decided that she was fed up with waiting for Adam to divorce Lorna and she snapped?"

"And ... what? Do you think she killed Adam in a fit of rage, covered it up with a fire, and is now after Lorna?"

"It's possible, right?"

He tilted his head, considering. "I guess it's possible," he conceded after a moment. "I'm not sure I believe it. I need to interview her myself before I form an opinion."

"I think that's a good idea. While you're doing that, I'll interview Lorna."

"What if she's the guilty party? What if she killed Adam and she's some sort of dark witch?"

The suggestion was enough to take me aback. "I've never sensed magic when I've been near her."

"Do you always?"

"No, but ... ." I heaved out a sigh. I had no idea how all of this was going to play out. "I think the only thing we can both be sure of is that we have to dig. That's all I'm going to do today. I'll be careful. I promise."

"I want you to text me when you leave, just so I'm not worrying. I know you don't like feeling as if I'm hovering but I can't help but worry. Something about this one feels off ... and that's saying something given the other stuff we've faced."

"I like facing things with you." I squeezed his hand. "I promise to call. I'll be fine. I know how to take care of myself."

"I have faith in you. I always have. That doesn't mean I can just shut off the worry. That's not who I am."

On that we would have to compromise. He couldn't shut off his worry and my curiosity couldn't be contained. It would forever be an issue. Thankfully it wasn't something we couldn't handle. We had that going for us.

"It'll be fine." I was sure of that. "I simply need some time alone with her. I think I'll be able to figure things out better after that."

"Fair enough. I still want a text."

"You'll get one."

A DISHEVELED LORNA answered the door.

I instantly felt like an intruder. "I'm sorry. Did I wake you?"

She looked as if she'd been on a bender. I really couldn't blame her given everything that had happened.

"Bay?" Her eyebrows drew together and it took her a moment to recognize me. "What are you doing here?"

"I came to see you." That wasn't a lie. Sure, I had ulterior motives, but at the heart of my visit was the desperate need to check on Lorna. "I was hoping to do a nice article on Adam. You know, talk about the things he did for Hemlock Cove, mention that he was a good family man."

If that wasn't an opening, I didn't know how else to pry open a door for her to walk through and start spilling her guts.

"Oh, that sounds nice." Vacantly, Lorna left the door open and disappeared inside the house.

I watched the empty spot where she'd been standing for a moment, confused, and then followed.

The house was dark, all the drapes drawn. The lights were on, but they seemed dim. I found Lorna in the kitchen. She was brewing a pot of tea. It was obvious she hadn't yet showered and was still muddled from sleep.

"How are you doing?" Even though there was a possibility she was evil, I felt sorry for her. "Did you sleep at all?"

"I tried." Lorna's smile was tight when she turned back to me. "I was exhausted, but I managed to conk out for only about an hour and then I was wide awake. I tried to take some sleep medication — probably too much if you want to know the truth — but it didn't really work for me. Now I feel listless and draggy, too exhausted to function, and yet I can't sleep. It's a vicious little cycle."

"Sit down," I instructed, moving to the stove. "I'll handle the tea."

"Are you sure? I don't mind."

"No, you should definitely sit down."

Lorna followed my instructions, plunking herself in one of the chairs. She didn't look comfortable when I joined her, the dark circles under her eyes proving to be so big I thought I might be able to hide inside them.

"Where are Nick and Dani?" I asked. The house was silent.

"They're both asleep. They were up late, couldn't fall asleep, but then they finally passed out. I'm going to let them sleep as long as they want. It's better for them than sitting here and wallowing. Besides, they keep asking questions and I'm not sure how to answer them."

"What sort of questions?"

"They want to know who killed their father," she replied simply. "I don't have an answer for them. I'm not even sure what I should tell them. It's all such a mess. Such a huge, huge mess."

If I expected a better opening than this one, I wasn't going to get it. I either had to be bold and tell her I knew about the affair or talk about absolutely nothing. I decided being bold was the best course of action.

"So ... I talked to Lisa Newman."

I expected Lorna to tell me I didn't understand the situation or at least swear violently under her breath at mention of the woman. Instead, she merely sighed.

"I guess I should've realized that information was going to come out. I haven't really thought much about it since Adam died. It's too much to think about."

The kettle had begun to whistle, so I removed it from the stove and shifted it to the pad she'd already laid out on the table. "I was surprised when I heard. I didn't realize you and Adam were having problems."

"I don't know that we were having problems," she countered. "It's more that we grew apart. We loved each other at the start. but somewhere along the way we became friends rather than lovers. I'm not even sure how it happened.

"I still loved him, don't get me wrong, but it was more of a friendship love," she continued. "I was hurt when I heard he had feelings for

Lisa, but the more I thought about it the more I realized that it made sense."

She was calm. I didn't understand the phenomenon, but I was grateful for it. "Lisa said that you guys decided to stay together until after the kids graduated from high school."

"Um ... I can't quite remember how that came up. I know that I was in favor of that because I didn't want the kids' grades to suffer or anything. Adam was all for it."

"Did you guys still share a room?"

"No. Adam slept in the guest room and I kept the master bedroom. He was leaving me the house so it made sense."

"Didn't the kids ask questions?"

"Honestly? I'm not even sure they noticed. Adam kept his clothes in the master bedroom and only slept in the guest room. We told the kids it was because he snored. They didn't say a word about it. I'm pretty sure they didn't realize we were planning on separating."

I knew that wasn't true because of what Dani had told me, but I decided to keep that to myself. The last thing the teenager needed was more pressure put on her. "I know it's difficult, but can you think of any reason Lisa might want to hurt Adam?"

Lorna shook her head. "Why would she want to hurt him?"

I shrugged. "I don't know. Maybe she thought she was going to get an inheritance or something."

Lorna waved off the suggestion as if I'd said that fat-free cheese tasted the same as the real deal. "No, that's not even remotely true. Adam and I had already gone through our finances. He switched his life insurance policy so it paid out to the kids. I did the same. As for the rest ... it's not as if we're rich."

Oh, well, that was interesting. "So you're not the beneficiary of his insurance policy?"

"Not for at least six months. I'll oversee the money until the kids are eighteen, but I can't touch it. We set up my life insurance policy the same way."

Huh. It seemed money wasn't an issue between them. I didn't

know whether to be relieved or suspicious. "Can you think of anyone else who would want to hurt Adam?"

"No. I just don't understand. I saw him twenty minutes before the fire. We'd been talking about the blacksmith business and what we were going to do after the divorce."

"What were you going to do?"

"He was going to keep the business and take out a small loan so I could set up my own dress shop. I saw these neat dresses and hats at a renaissance fair and I thought they would fit in well in Hemlock Cove. That was the plan once the kids were in community college and out of the house."

"It sounds like things were amicable between the two of you."

"They definitely were."

I wasn't getting nearly as much information as I'd hoped. "Well ... I really do want to write a nice story about Adam, something your children can cherish forever. I was hoping you had some photographs I could use."

"Absolutely." Lorna stood. "Let me find them and we'll go through them."

"Sure." I watched her leave the room, conflicted, and when I turned back toward the stove to finish gathering the ingredients for tea I found a ghost watching me with a pair of the grimmest eyes I'd ever seen. "Adam?" I gasped.

He stared at me for a long time, a sadness so profound emanating from him that it almost knocked me over. He tried to open his mouth but couldn't. No sound came out no matter how he struggled. It was then that I realized it was sewn shut.

"How did that happen?" I took a step in his direction, but he shook his head to stop me. There was warning in his eyes.

Then, as if on cue, birds began raising a ruckus outside. I moved to the window, pulled back the drapes, and found thirty of them – a variety of colors and sizes – circling the backyard. Some sat on an old grill, others on a fence. All of them stared directly at me.

FOURTEEN

I took copious notes during my time with Lorna. The interview lasted three hours, and by the time I left her house the birds were gone. Adam's ghost didn't linger. He disappeared before she returned with her stack of photos, which I promised to return as soon as possible.

I walked to The Whistler and wrote my article. It was a glowing piece, a profile of a man who donated his time to the town while also managing to be a good father. I avoided his marital issues. They weren't important, at least for this particular story.

When I finished, I met Landon and Chief Terry at the diner for lunch. They were deep in conversation when I joined them and I almost felt guilty for interrupting.

"Would you prefer I sit at the counter by myself?" I asked.

"Don't be stupid." Landon pulled out the chair next to him. "We were just talking about what Bennett told us."

I perked up. "Anything good?"

"It was … interesting," Landon replied, his hand lightly brushing over my back. "It seems that in addition to gasoline he found butane on the premises. That's what made the explosion so big."

I waited for him to continue. When he didn't, I held out my hands. "I don't know what that means."

"It's a strange choice," Chief Terry volunteered. "Butane comes in canisters and not usually in large amounts. It might be an important clue, or it might be nothing. Perhaps our murderer simply had some around."

"Could you track the sale?"

"No. You don't have to jump through any hoops to buy it. It's readily available."

"Did he say anything else?"

"Just that the gasoline was poured around the body, but none was dumped directly on Adam," Landon replied. "There are several reasons for that. Our killer might've assumed it didn't matter. This could be a first-time killer. Or our killer didn't want to get any gasoline on clothing or shoes that could be traced back."

I ran the information through my head. "Where was the butane?"

"On the other side of the workshop door."

I frowned. "That doesn't make sense. The fire was already raging when Thistle and I went in. We walked through that door. Nothing was on fire."

"And then you were quickly overwhelmed by smoke," Landon pointed out.

"I don't like talking about this," Chief Terry lamented. "It reminds me that she's an idiot. I prefer pretending she's still my little angel."

Landon smirked as I glowered.

"I'm not an idiot," I argued. "I was trying to save a man's life. I bet you wouldn't say things like that if I'd managed to pull Adam out alive."

"I'd still be saying them." Chief Terry didn't as much as crack a smile. "You could've been killed, Bay, and I don't like thinking about it."

"I don't like thinking about it either," Landon supplied, perhaps sensing trouble. He looked uneasy. "We agreed to give her a pass this time. I don't think this is a good time for an argument … because I just ordered a bacon cheeseburger and I want to eat it without getting heartburn."

Chief Terry grunted and shook his head. "You're whipped. I don't want to fight either, but you truly are whipped."

I cast Landon a sidelong look. "Do you think you're whipped?"

"Yup. I'm addicted to you, your mother's cooking and now Aunt Tillie's pig. You're never getting rid of me."

"I like a man who can admit the truth."

"Yeah." He swooped in and gave me a kiss. "Basically we're still figuring things out. We don't know if the new information means anything. It's entirely possible that it's not important."

"Well, you're handsome *and* wise. You'll figure it out."

"Oh, gross." Chief Terry rolled his eyes when Landon rested his forehead against mine and grinned. "You two are officially disgusting."

"Says the guy who slept with my mother on the first date," I shot back.

A flush stole across his cheeks. "I thought we weren't talking about that."

"I'll stop talking about it when you stop calling me an idiot."

"Believe it or not, Bay, I don't enjoy calling you an idiot. I love you. Always have. If something were to happen to you … ."

He left it hanging. I didn't need him to continue. The "I love you" was enough to melt my heart. "I promise not to run into a burning building again if I can help it. Is that enough?"

He sighed and nodded. "For now. Let's talk about something else. What did you do today?"

"I spent the morning with Lorna putting together an article about Adam. The freaking birds returned."

Landon sat straighter in his chair. "Excuse me?"

Uh-oh. I didn't think that out before dropping the bird bomb. "They didn't attack or anything. They were just outside the window … staring. They disappeared before I left. They're beyond creepy."

"I'll say. I knew letting you go there without supervision was a bad idea."

I cocked an eyebrow. "Supervision?"

"There's a danger alarm going off in the back of your brain right now," Chief Terry volunteered helpfully to Landon. "It's probably best you heed it and don't make matters worse."

"That came out wrong." Landon adjusted his tone. "I simply meant that it would've been wise for you to have backup. That's not an insult. I just love you so much that I constantly want to be with you."

"Nice save."

"I thought so."

Chief Terry shifted on his chair and tapped his fingers on the Formica tabletop to get our attention. "Does someone want to explain about the birds?"

I laid everything out for him. "And that's not the only weird thing. Adam's ghost was there and somebody had sewed his mouth shut," I said. "There's a whole dark magic thing going on, but I can't figure out who is doing it or why."

The waitress had arrived to take my order and deliver Chief Terry and Landon's food during my recitation so I helped myself to a fry from Landon's plate. "I'm starving. Give me a bite of your burger."

Landon's mouth was open in abject horror when I turned to him.

"What did I say?" I asked defensively.

"How does a ghost's mouth get sewn shut?" Landon kept his burger out of my reach as he asked the question. "And you ordered a salad because you're convinced the calories don't count if you pick off my lunch. You're stuck with your own lunch. You can't have my burger."

I lobbed a glare in his direction and sipped my water before answering. "I don't know how his lips were sewn shut. I could actually see the thread going through his skin … although he technically doesn't have skin. You know what I mean."

"I do," Landon confirmed. "That is freaking weird. I want you to stay as far away from Lorna as humanly possible."

"But … why?"

"Because I don't want your lips sewn shut. Believe it or not, I actually enjoy talking to you occasionally … when you're not trying to steal my burger, that is."

"I don't know that Lorna is responsible. I only know that it happened. She didn't act as if she could see him. Of course, he appeared after she left and then disappeared again before she returned."

"Shouldn't that be a sign that she's responsible?" Chief Terry challenged. "I mean … that sounds pretty damning to me. Too bad we can't arrest her because of birds and ghosts."

"I don't know that I believe she's guilty." I couldn't let the idea that I was missing a big part of the picture go. "I don't know how I feel about any of this right now."

"I don't either, but I want you safe," Landon said. "What are your plans for the rest of the afternoon?"

"I'm going to the festival."

"Anywhere else?"

"No, Mr. Bossy Pants."

"I hate to say it, but you really are getting more and more like Aunt Tillie."

"Just for that, I'm eating bacon without you."

"Oh, don't be that way."

"I'm going to get all hopped up on grease and you won't be around to enjoy it."

His eyes narrowed. "That's the meanest thing you've ever said to me."

I couldn't stop myself from smiling. "I guess that will teach you a lesson, huh?"

LUNCH DONE, I HEADED to the festival. For every one story about murder and mayhem in Hemlock Cove I write ten festival stories. We have one almost every weekend. The only money coming into town comes from the tourist industry, so that's simply become a fact of life.

The festival was hopping for so early in the day. The town was crawling with witches, so it was an eclectic bunch. I greeted a few faces I recognized – while steering clear of Hazel – and was almost to the ice cream truck for a treat when I caught sight of Masterson.

He wasn't alone. There were two witches, one I didn't recognize and the other I did, flanking him. The blonde on his right wore a shirt with a plunging neckline that put her ample assets on full display. The other woman was Evie, and she seemed determined to snag the board member's attention all for herself as she kept trying to box the blonde out of the conversation.

I stared so long I lost track of time. Masterson shifted his gaze, as if sensing someone was watching him, and focused on me.

"Hello, Bay." He lifted his hand in greeting.

I made a big show of shaking my head to cover my actions. I didn't want him to know I was aware of his relationship with Lorna … at least not yet.

"Sorry." I offered up a bland smile. "I was just running through a mental to-do list and lost my train of thought."

"Happens to me all the time." His grin was welcoming. "I love this festival, by the way. I hear a lot of this week's guests are staying at The Overlook. That must be fun."

As far as I could tell, only a good fifty percent of the women claiming to be witches were the real deal. Of those, only ten percent had noticeable power … and Hazel was one of them. In truth, I hadn't paid them much attention. Adam's death was my primary concern. Still, sometimes white lies are the easiest way to go.

"They're tons of fun, but I've had only one meal with them so far," I replied. "I don't live in the inn. I live on the property, but I'm not there for every meal." Almost every meal, but he didn't need to know how deep my culinary laziness ran.

"That's great." He flashed me one more smile and then turned back to his friends. It was clear he believed the conversation was over. That was just as well. I wasn't sure I wanted to directly accuse him of having an affair with Lorna or wait it out. For now, I was content to let him do his thing … which apparently included looking down any shirt within close proximity. He wasn't even sly about it.

"What a pig," I muttered as I turned to leave. I pulled up short when I caught sight of Nick Harris. I recognized him from the photos Lorna showed me when I was at her house earlier in the day. His hair was longer now and his gaze was sharp and focused … directly on Masterson.

I sensed trouble, so I intercepted him when it looked as if he was going to approach the board member, flashing a bright smile that probably looked ridiculous to anyone who knew me. "So … how about some ice cream?"

Nick blinked several times in rapid succession. It was obvious he didn't expect to be interrupted. "What?"

"Ice cream," I repeated firmly. "I think you could use some … and I know I could."

Bewildered, Nick glanced around. "Are you talking to me?"

"I am. Do you know who I am?"

"You're the chick who runs the newspaper."

"Oh, that's sweet." This time my smile was genuine. "I haven't been called a chick in years. It makes me feel young at heart again."

"I … don't … understand."

I wrapped my hand lightly around his wrist. "I still think you should come with me. Trustee Masterson isn't going anywhere. I want to talk to you before you say anything to him."

Nick narrowed his eyes. "How do you know I was going to talk to him?"

"I know a great number of things, and some of them are even useful. Come on. Ice cream is always a good idea."

Doubt returned, clouding his glassy eyes, but finally he nodded. "Okay, but I don't need any ice cream. I'm not a little kid."

"Ice cream isn't for little kids. It's for those who enjoy a tasty treat. I don't think there's an age limit on that."

HE OPTED FOR BLUE MOON WHILE I ordered chocolate, with hot fudge, whipped cream and a cherry. It wasn't bacon, but I would make sure to rub it in with Landon later.

"See. It's better."

Nick's expression remained dour but his lips were blue from the ice cream he'd been shoveling in. "It's good," he conceded. "I just … don't know that I have much of an appetite."

He'd already eaten half of his bowl, so I didn't believe that. Still, he was in mourning. It was best not to push him too far. "I'm sorry about your father," I offered. "I genuinely liked him."

"He was murdered."

"I know."

"You were the one who went in after him, weren't you? You and your cousin. The one with the green hair."

"It's blue this week."

"Oh. I liked it green." He looked momentarily wistful and then stabbed his ice cream. "I can't believe he's dead. I mean … it doesn't feel real. I keep wondering if it's a dream. I want to wake up if it is."

"I think that's normal whenever anything bad happens," I said. "When I was a little girl – much younger than you – my parents divorced and I kept hoping it was a dream for weeks."

"This isn't a dream."

"No, it's not."

He abandoned his spoon in his dish and focused on me. "Do you know who killed my dad? I asked my mother, but she's kind of lost. She doesn't really want to talk to us right now."

"That's not true." I immediately started shaking my head. "She wants to talk to you. It's just … people react in different ways when they're grieving. Right now, it's hard for her to wrap her head around what happened. She can barely keep her own head up. Helping you guys probably feels overwhelming."

"She just sits in her bedroom and cries. I hear her through the door."

"I'm sorry about that." I meant it. "I was with her this morning. I thought she was holding it together relatively well."

"Well, she's not holding it together now. She's all over the place … and I can't stand it." His eyes took on a hint of malevolence as he stared at Masterson. "It's all his fault."

Oh, well, that answered that question. It was obvious Nick was aware of his mother's relationship with Masterson. Did that mean he knew about Lisa, too? It was likely. I didn't want to be the one to drop that particular bomb on him.

"What's his fault?" I asked feigning ignorance.

"He's been with my mom," Nick growled. "They've been together for months. She doesn't think I know … but I know."

"Does that bother you?"

He shot me a "Well, duh" look. "What do you think?"

"I think you have a right to be bothered," I replied evenly. "I also think sometimes things happen in a marriage that don't make a lot of sense. I know you're angry with your mother … ."

He cut me off with a firm shake of his head. "I'm not angry with my mother. I mean … I'm not happy with her, but I'm not angry with her. I'm angry with him. He … *seduced* … her. I think that's the word, right?"

Sure, if this was the *Dynasty* era. "I don't know that I believe that. Have you talked to your mother about this?"

"I'm not talking to her about it." His cheeks flooded with color, the teenager he was on full display. "No way."

"Okay. I probably would have issues doing the same if I were in your position. What were you going to say to Masterson?"

"I was going to punch him in the face for killing my dad."

"You think he killed your dad?"

"Who else? He was dating my mother and my father wouldn't let her have a divorce. It's the only thing that makes sense."

I had news for him. He'd gotten some parts of the story wrong. Still, it wasn't my place. "I think you should talk to your mother before you do anything. You don't want to make matters worse."

"How could I possibly make things worse? My dad is dead."

"Things can always get worse. You really should talk to your mother. It's important."

"I don't know." He shook his head and rubbed his chin. "I don't think I can do that."

"You should try," I insisted. "I guarantee approaching Masterson is a bad idea. It won't end well."

"How do you know?"

"I come from a long line of impulsive people, and it very rarely ends well when we melt down in public. There's a better way to handle this. Talk to your mother."

"I need to think about it."

"Good. Do you want more ice cream while you do your thinking?"

"I guess it couldn't hurt."

FIFTEEN

I greeted Landon with a choice when his shift ended.

"We can either go back to the festival and you can eat so much bacon that you get the sweats again or we can head to the inn and eat pot roast and red velvet cake. Your choice."

Landon's mouth dropped open in mock horror. "It's like *Sophie's Choice*."

I smirked. "I don't care either way, but if we eat at the inn we'll be close to home ... and bed."

"Are you anxious to be close to our bed because you're feeling tired or frisky?"

He wasn't going to like my answer. "Well ... ."

His fingers were gentle as they brushed my hair out of my face. "I'm tired, too. I didn't realize how tired you looked until just now. Do you want to tell me about your day?"

"Can it wait until we're on the way home?" I cast a glance over my shoulder to make sure no one of consequence was listening. "I just want to get out of here."

He nodded without hesitation and pulled me to him. "Yeah. We'll eat at the inn. I can have pot roast sweats just as easily as bacon sweats."

I snickered. "Good to know."

We walked to his Explorer in silence. He loaded me in on the passenger side — taking the time to open the door for me and fasten my seat belt — and then hopped behind the steering wheel. He didn't press me for details as we drove to the inn, which I appreciated. Still, it was better to get it out of the way now.

"So ... I saw Nick Harris this afternoon."

Landon's forehead wrinkled as he stared out the windshield. "That's the dead guy's son, right? Why is that important? Did something happen?"

"The whole thing is a mess." I stared out the window as the foliage blurred. "He knows about his mother's affair, but as far as I can tell he doesn't know about his father's relationship with Lisa. That seems weird because Dani brought up her father's relationship."

"Maybe neither one of them said anything to the other because they didn't want to upset anybody."

"Maybe." I chewed my bottom lip. That was always possible, but it felt unlikely. "The thing is, when Clove, Thistle and I were kids we told each other everything. We couldn't wait to gossip about our mothers. Like the time we thought Twila was messing around with the guy who drove the bus – who also dressed up like a clown in his free time – we couldn't wait to share that information."

Landon shuddered at mention of a clown. "Not all kids are the same. Maybe Nick and Dani aren't close."

"I guess." I leaned my head against the glass and thought about our conundrum. "I researched harbingers today. There were things I didn't know, but I'm not sure anything I found helps us."

"I'm not going to lie," he started as he pulled into the guesthouse driveway. Apparently we were walking to dinner. "I find the bird thing creepy. I never really paid birds much heed until we saw that flock circling over Lorna last night. That was all kinds of weird."

It was definitely weird. "I don't know what to make of it. I just ... feel out of my depth."

"Have you considered bringing up the topic over dinner? You'll be surrounded by witches. Maybe one of them knows more about the subject."

I wasn't sure if I liked or hated the option, but it was something to consider. "You're smarter than you look sometimes."

"That's impossible. I look like a genius."

Actually, he looked like a male model. I decided to keep that observation to myself, though.

CLOVE, THISTLE, SAM AND MARCUS WERE ensconced in the library at the inn. Thistle hovered by the glass door, watching the other witches enjoy drinks in the lounge, her eyes speculative.

I met Clove's gaze, hoping she would volunteer the pertinent information without me having to ask, but she and Sam were too wrapped up in one another.

"What are you doing?" I asked, glaring as Sam pressed his hand to Clove's abdomen. She sat on his lap, their heads bent together, and they whispered and giggled. It was a sweet scene ... that almost made me sick to my stomach.

"Stop that!" I slapped Sam's hand away when he held it flat against her midriff again. "Do you want to tip them off about what's going on?"

Sam lifted his head and gave me a lazy smile. "There's a baby in there. Are you telling me you don't find that miraculous?"

Oh, geez. "Not really. Babies have been hanging around in places like that since the dawn of time. It's nothing new."

"I see you're in a crabby mood," Clove complained, shooting me a dubious look as Landon moved to the drink cart. "Why are you so unhappy?"

"I'm not unhappy."

Clove didn't look convinced. "Landon, why is she so unhappy?"

"She doesn't like the birds," he automatically answered, his eyes going to the open doorway when he heard familiar snorting. "Hello, beautiful." He beamed at Peg as the pig wandered in. She was back in her tutu and looked thrilled to see him. "How's my favorite girl?"

The question, although seemingly innocent, was enough to irritate me. "Seriously?"

Landon realized his mistake too late. "I didn't mean that the way it sounded." He was sheepish. "I just ... she's very cute. Everyone knows you're my favorite girl, Bay. Peg has low self-esteem. She needs me to bolster her ego."

I rolled my eyes and flopped on the couch, leaving Landon to play with his favorite girl while Thistle snickered and Marcus shot me a sympathetic look.

"You look like you've had a rough day," Marcus noted. "Didn't you sleep last night?"

"Actually, I didn't sleep all that well," I admitted. "I had a weird dream."

"About what?" Thistle asked, tearing her eyes from the activity. "By the way, have you noticed that Aunt Tillie is hiding behind the potted plant and spying on all the other witches? She's not even being stealthy about it."

I craned my neck to see, laughing when I realized she wore a hat that had fake palm fronds jutting from the top of it. "Where did she get that hat?"

"I think she made it," Clove replied. "She thinks no one can see her if she doesn't move and hides behind the plant."

"She's like a cat that way," Thistle agreed. "A moronic cat, but a cat all the same."

I elevated my feet on the coffee table and rubbed my forehead. "So ... about that dream." I told them the story, from beginning to end, and then frowned when Thistle's eyes lit with annoyance. "What?"

"You didn't mention the dream when you were doing research earlier," she complained. "You just said you saw the birds hanging around Lorna ... and making a spectacle right before Adam died. Why did you leave out the dream?"

I shrugged. "I don't know. I didn't really think about it. Do you think the dream is important?"

"I would say so. You're growing more and more powerful with each passing day. I think there's a reason for that dream."

"I think so, too." Landon looked up from the floor, Peg giving him sloppy kisses, and held my gaze. "I think you need to stay away from Lorna. Leave the investigation to Chief Terry and me from here on out."

I was flabbergasted. "Excuse me? That's not what you said this morning." My tone was shriller than I intended. "You said we were stronger together and we would solve this as a team."

"We are part of the same team." He feigned patience as he rolled to a sitting position. "You're always going to be the most important member of my team."

Something had obviously changed. He'd just said as much. "But you want to cut me out of the action."

"I didn't say that." He held up a finger and wagged it. "Don't put words in my mouth. I want you safe, Bay. I don't like the birds. They creep me out. When you couple that with the ghost with his lips sewn shut I can't help worrying about you. Sue me."

"Wait ... what ghost had his lips sewn shut?" Clove forgot about flirting with Sam and swung her head in my direction. "You didn't mention a ghost with his lips sewn shut. How does that even happen?"

"I forgot with all the Aunt Tillie hoopla," I muttered. "It was at Lorna's house."

"Was it Adam?" Thistle folded her arms across her chest and rested her hip against the door as she regarded me. She seemed to be standing guard ... although I had no idea against what.

I nodded. "He looked like a man who was tortured and had his lips stitched together with a very heavy thread. The thing is, other than the stab wounds and some dirt, he looked normal when we found him. That obviously wasn't done to him in life."

"Which means someone managed to do it in death," Thistle noted, rubbing the back of her neck. "I don't even know what to make of that."

She wasn't the only one. "He couldn't speak. He looked really upset. We need to find a way to unbind him."

"That's easier said than done," Clove pointed out. "We've never been very good with spells like that."

"We'll have to figure out a way to get better at them. I can't help but think that Adam is key."

"You're a necromancer," Thistle pointed out. "Can't you force him to rip out the thread?"

I found the notion appalling. "Why would I do that?"

She shrugged. "I don't know. He's a ghost. It's not as if he can feel pain."

Landon looked intrigued at the prospect. "Is that possible? Can you do that?"

I hadn't really considered it before now. The more I thought about it, the more uncomfortable I was with the prospect. "I would rather not do that unless I have no other choice," I countered. "It makes me feel ... mean."

"Mean?" Landon arched a speculative eyebrow. "Since when does anybody in this family care about being mean?"

"Since now. I don't want to use this new magic for anything bad. I already screwed with those three other ghosts. I would like to refrain from doing that again if I can help it."

"What new magic?" a voice asked from the other side of Thistle, who had forgotten to watch for interlopers because she was caught up in questioning me.

When I jerked my head in that direction, I found Hazel watching us with curious eyes. Well ... crap on a cracker.

"I'm sorry to interrupt," she said, her expression conciliatory. "I couldn't help but overhear, and I'm intrigued."

"You couldn't help but overhear?" Thistle's eyes flashed with annoyance as she regarded the woman. She and Aunt Tillie agreed on very little, but their dislike of Hazel was well matched. "You would've had to have been on top of us to hear a single word we said."

"Believe it or not, your entire family has voices that carry," Hazel replied brightly. "It's good to see you again, Thistle. You look exactly the same now as you did then ... other than the hair. This suits you much better. But I'm talking to Bay now."

And just like that, Thistle had been dismissed. Hazel turned her full attention to me. "What new powers have you been manifesting?

You'll have to forgive my question if you find it invasive, but I've always had a certain fascination with you, Bay. I can't help myself."

Landon finally separated himself from his lovefest with Peg and joined me on the couch. There was something mildly aggressive about the way he positioned himself between the two of us. "Bay is the most fascinating person I know," he agreed. "I don't know that I think this conversation is appropriate for the dinner hour, though."

"Really?" Hazel looked amused rather than put off. "The inn is full of witches. We all understand about magic. Quite frankly, we understand about loyalty, too. Certain factions of the Winchester household have always been secretive, but that's no reason to make Bay suffer."

"Bay isn't suffering," Landon countered. "She's just hungry. It's pot roast night. We all love pot roast night."

I wanted to laugh at the way he delivered the statement. There was a certain amount of insolence in his drawl, but there was a pointed admonishment in his eyes when Hazel held his gaze. He was sending a warning. I couldn't help but wonder if she would back down.

"I don't know you very well, Mr. Michaels," Hazel started. "You seem like a good man. A little intense, perhaps, but I have a feeling that goes with the territory as it pertains to your occupation. I've known Bay for a very long time — longer than you, in fact — and I think I know her better."

"I wouldn't count on that," Thistle muttered, her forehead creasing. "Landon and Bay have been in each other's lives for a long time. Granted, we were forced to hang out with you at gatherings over the years when we were children, but we were hardly bonded to you."

"I blame Tillie for that," Hazel replied evenly. "She was always determined to keep you away from outside influences. She insulated you because she thought you would be powerful. I recognized your power before she did."

Her tone rankled. "You recognized our power?"

"Yes. You're a fearsome threesome. Real power comes in threes. You know that. With Bay as your ringleader, you could do almost anything."

Thistle was outraged. "With Bay as our ringleader? I'm the ringleader. Me!"

Hazel shot her a hilarious look. "You're one point of the triangle. Depending on the direction you're looking from, you could be the top or one of the bottom corners. You've always been a bottom corner. There's no shame in that."

Thistle's mouth dropped open. "Did you just call me a bottom corner?"

"Batten the hatches," Landon muttered, sliding his arm around my shoulders. "Hurricane Thistle is about to reach land."

"Shut up, Landon," Thistle snapped, her eyes glowing with potential mayhem. "This is serious. I'm the ringleader of our group. *Me*." She thumped her chest and looked to Clove for confirmation. "Tell him ... and her. Tell everybody."

"Well ... ." Clove was obviously uncomfortable as she shifted on Sam's lap. "I don't know that I would call you the leader. I don't really think we have a leader."

That was a good answer. Would it be enough to placate Thistle? "Clove is right. We don't have a leader."

"Yes, we do. I'm the leader." Thistle refused to back down. "I'm serious. Everyone knows I'm the leader. Bay can't be the leader simply because she's the oldest. That's not fair."

"It's not about being the oldest," Hazel countered. "It's about power ... and level-headedness. You can't lay claim to either."

Oh, good grief. This was going south ... and fast. "Thistle can be the leader," I said hurriedly. "I'm fine with it." The last thing we needed was a meltdown at this juncture. "It doesn't matter who's in charge."

"Of course it does." Hazel wrinkled her nose. "You're the leader. You're in charge of your trio. It is what it is."

I wanted to dig a hole and crawl inside to avoid Thistle's hateful glare. "It doesn't matter. I ... Aunt Tillie!" I'd never been so excited to see anyone in my life. Sure, my great-aunt was wearing a hat that had palm fronds sticking out of it and a pair of green leggings that featured tree branches creeping into a very odd – almost obscene, really – place, but if anyone could make Hazel back down, it was Aunt Tillie.

"Why are you yelling my name, Bay?" Aunt Tillie asked distastefully as she strolled into the room. "I may be old, but my hearing is just fine."

"It's not about being old." I offered her a cutesy smile that felt out of place. "We missed you. You know how much we love you."

Suspicion flitted across Aunt Tillie's pinched features. "What are you up to?"

"I was just explaining to the girls that I've always been interested in their development as witches," Hazel volunteered. "They're amazing women. I'll wager they've turned into amazing witches. I can't wait to see their magical display at the gathering."

Hold up. This was the first I heard about that. "What magical display?"

"Your mothers have signed you up for a spell performance," Aunt Tillie replied, her gaze never leaving Hazel's face. "They capitulated to peer pressure, even though I told them it was ridiculous."

"We're not performing a spell." I was firm. "It's just not going to happen."

"Definitely not," Thistle agreed. "We're not dancing monkeys."

"You have one way to get out of it," Aunt Tillie countered pointedly, her gaze bouncing between us. "You have a built-in excuse if you just own up to the secret you've all been keeping."

It didn't take a genius to figure out what she was referring to. "I don't think that's necessary. In fact ... ." I trailed off, uncertain. Honestly, I had no idea what more I could say.

"We're not using that as an excuse," Thistle shot back. "We'll just tell our mothers we don't want to do it. Stop being ... well ... you."

"Keep pushing me, mouth," Aunt Tillie warned. "You won't like what happens. I have enough on my plate without having to worry about you."

Thistle rolled her eyes. "And here we go."

For her part, Hazel seemed more intrigued at the mention of a secret than anything else. "What excuse do you have built in to get out of the ritual spell?" she asked, her eyes keen as she looked between us. "The only thing I can think of is … ." Realization dawned on her face and I recognized we were in real trouble a split-second before she started screeching.

"Oh, you're pregnant!" She swooped in on me and grabbed my hands. "That's such wonderful news. How great for you."

"I'm not pregnant." I jerked away from her. "I'm not stupid enough to forget how birth control works."

"Thanks, Bay," Clove snapped, her eyes filling with tears. "As if I wasn't feeling bad enough."

"Oh, don't be that way. That's not even you talking. It's the hormones. I … ow! What?" I turned away from Clove and focused on Thistle as she viciously tugged my ear. I was about to drag her into the other room and make her eat dirt when every pleasant thought I'd ever had fled.

There, standing in the open doorway, were my mother, Twila and Marnie.

"Uh-oh," I whispered, my mouth going dry. "This isn't good."

"Definitely not," Thistle agreed. "Do you think we can play Aunt Tillie's cat card and be really still? Maybe they won't see us."

"Yeah. I don't think that's going to work."

SIXTEEN

"Explain yourselves."

Mom, Marnie and Twila dragged us into the family living quarters, which were separate from the rest of the inn, so they could scream at us without garnering attention from the guests. It was bad enough that they'd found out, but the pitying look Hazel shot us before we disappeared into the house was an added smack in the face.

Speaking of that, I wanted to smack her in the face … with a brick. I knew that she hadn't planned any of this, but if she'd just kept her mouth shut none of this would've happened.

"I think she's talking to you, Clove," Thistle noted, throwing herself into one of the comfortable easy chairs.

Clove looked terrified. I thought she might actually pass out. She was so pale I could practically see through her. To his credit, Sam stood between her and our mothers. He was trying to be a wall, but all he was doing was making himself a target.

"Don't yell at her," he ordered, his hands clenched into fists at his side. It wasn't that he was going to punch anyone as much as he was obviously trying to bolster himself. I felt bad for him. "She can't take it."

"She can't take it?" Marnie arched an eyebrow. As Clove's mother, it was her job to deliver the ultimate diatribe. She looked as wan as her daughter. They were carbon copies of each other, so she painted an interesting picture. "Well, perhaps she's not the only one who can't take it. Maybe I can't take it either."

Oh, that was a huge load of crap. "Nothing has happened to you," I volunteered, drawing three sets of furious eyes. "You're not pregnant so ... why don't you get over yourselves?"

Thistle's eyes went wide with amusement as Landon sidled closer to me.

"Sweetie, now might not be the time for you to pick a fight," he offered. "I mean ... I'm not telling you what to do or anything, but I'm not sure I can take all three of them."

I shot him a quelling look. "I've got this." My words were bolder than my courage. "Clove is pregnant. There. It's out of the bag. You know and everybody can calm down and accept it."

"Accept it?" Marnie's voice was unnaturally shrill. "What if I don't want to accept it? Have you considered that?"

Ugh. She was being purposely obnoxious. "It's not about you," I shot back. "It's about Clove. Why can't you guys just be supportive and give her the encouragement she needs? There's a reason we were trying to keep it secret."

"And just how long were you planning to keep it secret?" Mom challenged, her eyes a fascinating mixture of fire and ice. If I didn't know it was impossible, I would think she was about to combust. "Were you going to hide Clove from us for six months and then magically show up with a baby?"

"Don't be ridiculous. Besides, she's a lot further along than that. You really only have four and a half months to adjust."

Marnie's mouth dropped open. "Four and a half months!" She swiveled on Clove. "How are you that far along?"

"I think the better question is: How did we not notice she was that far along?" Twila countered. She seemed to be taking the news best. That was hardly a surprise. She might've been the flighty one — and that was putting it mildly — but her nature allowed her to roll with changes much more seamlessly than my rigid mother and Clove's dramatic maternal figure. "Why didn't you tell us, Clove?"

"That's what I want to know." Aunt Tillie, cookie in hand, plopped herself on the couch and smiled. She seemed to be enjoying the spectacle. I wanted to shake her. I knew her finding out about the baby would screw us. Still, I figured she would be able to hold out for a few days. "We're not ogres. Well, Winnie is an ogre, but she's not your mother. Why not just gather your courage and tell us the truth?"

Clove frowned. "I just ... I was afraid. I knew you guys would yell. I hate it when you yell."

"What makes you think we're going to yell?" Marnie shrieked.

"Perhaps because you're yelling," Sam shot back. "I wanted to tell everyone from the start, but Clove refused. She's terrified ... she hasn't been sleeping. You all should think long and hard about that. She shouldn't be this afraid."

He wasn't wrong. "That's a very good point," I said. "Do you want us living in fear? I mean ... that's ridiculous. We're not kids anymore; we're adults. There's no reason to freak out about this."

"Oh, really?" Marnie shot me a look that could've melted a cauldron. "You don't think that being married is a necessity when one is pregnant?"

"No," I answered without hesitation. "I don't believe that. You were all married when you had us and look how that turned out. None of the marriages lasted, but we're fine."

"Are you blaming that on us?"

Well, that was a thorny question. "It takes two people to break up a marriage," I answered carefully. "You can't deny that our fathers felt overwhelmed by this family. They shouldn't have left. That's on them and they'll have to live with the repercussions the rest of their days. That doesn't mean Clove has to be married to be a good mother."

"Of course not," Mom interjected. "That's not what we're saying. You aren't little girls any longer. You're not teenagers with rampaging hormones. Why couldn't you wait until after the wedding, Clove?"

Still behind Sam, Clove peeked out, sheepish. "It's not like we did it on purpose. It was an accident. We thought we would have more time before it happened. That doesn't mean we're not excited about the baby."

"Nobody says you can't be excited," Marnie shot back. "I just ... I didn't expect this from you. Thistle, yes. I thought she would be the bad one."

I pressed my lips together to keep from laughing at Thistle.

"Hey! I'm not the one who's baby crazy," Thistle snapped. "Clove was dying to be a mother. I guess she got her wish."

"I guess she did." Marnie was prim. "Well, what's the next step? What do we tell people?"

I felt as if I was mired in conversational quicksand ... fifty years ago. "Why do you have to tell anyone anything? It's nobody's business."

"Besides, Sam and Clove are going to be married in, like, two days," Thistle pointed out. "After that, will anybody really care?"

"Frankly, I don't understand why anyone cares now," Landon noted. "I mean ... are you not going to love this baby because Sam and Clove weren't married when it was conceived? Try as I might, I can't imagine that. I think this is going to be the most spoiled baby on the planet."

"And who doesn't love babies?" I added.

Thistle and Aunt Tillie raised their hands, earning a dark glare from me. They weren't helping.

"What?" Thistle made a face. "They're messy poop machines. It's not like they're all that great."

Marcus shot her a look. "You're going to be a fabulous mother someday. I can't wait to see you holding a baby and going gooey all over."

"We've already talked about this," Thistle warned. "I'll have one ... maybe two if the first one is really quiet. Once I pop them out, you're responsible for all the diapers and midnight feedings. I need my beauty sleep."

She was a bold talker, but nobody, including Marcus, believed her.

"It will be fine," he reassured her. There's nothing to worry about."

"Definitely," I agreed. "There's absolutely nothing to worry about ...

so stop worrying. This isn't a big deal. Clove is financially stable. She and Sam have an awesome house. This baby will be loved and there's a wedding in a few days. Stop your bellyaching."

For the first time since the baby bomb dropped, my mother and aunts looked almost happy.

"It is kind of neat," Mom said after a beat. "I mean ... I'm not thrilled about how it happened, but having Annie here so often has made us realize how much we missed having small children under the roof. It might be fun."

"Yes, and this will be a small child who won't be able to talk back for years," Marnie noted. "Those are the best kinds of children."

I rolled my eyes but maintained my composure. "See. This is a good thing. We're expanding our family."

"Yeah." A genuine smile spread across Marnie's face. "I hope it's a girl. Do you know yet?"

Clove shook her head. "We're waiting until the birth."

"Why?" Aunt Tillie made a hilarious face. "It's a girl. You know that. It's always girls in this family ... and the babies keep the Winchester name." She said the last part for Sam's benefit, but the look on his face told me that despite the healthy level of fear he kept in reserve for our tempestuous great-aunt he was having none of it.

"The baby's last name will be Winchester-Cornell," he corrected. "We've already talked about that."

"No way!" Aunt Tillie leaned forward. "That's not how it works in this family."

"That's how it works now," Clove corrected, firm. "It's not fair for Sam to be cut out."

"Besides, we had different names when we were kids," I added. "You changed them only after the divorces."

"That's neither here nor there. All babies born to this family are Winchesters."

"The baby will still be a Winchester," Thistle offered. "It will be a Cornell, too. There's no reason to get your panties in a bunch."

"Okay, mouth, you've done it this time." Aunt Tillie's face flushed with annoyance. "You're on top of my list. Congratulations. You managed to supplant Hazel and Margaret. That's truly miraculous."

"Oh, curse me," Thistle shot back. "I don't even care."

"You should. Besides, I'm not wearing panties. They don't look right with these leggings, so I'm going commando. That means there are no panties to get into a bunch."

I had to bite the inside of my cheek to keep from laughing at the pained look on Landon's face. Apparently he could've gone his entire life without having to envision the picture she was painting.

"Let's focus on the important things," Mom suggested. "Clove is pregnant and she's getting married. I don't think we have time to worry about trivial stuff when we have that on the agenda."

She wasn't wrong. "Yes. Let's focus on that. I mean ... you guys are all going to be grannies and grand-aunties. That's got to be exciting."

The smiles that had been on their faces died.

"I didn't think about that," Mom muttered.

"Yeah, I don't want to be a granny." Marnie was firm. "I need to come up with something different for the kid to call me. This granny thing won't cut it."

Ah, well, one crisis averted.

LANDON WAS SO DETERMINED TO KEEP ME from having nightmares he practically dragged me on top of him to sleep. At first I thought it would be impossible to drift off. I was wrong.

"How did you sleep?"

His eyes were the first thing I saw when I woke. He was staring directly into my face, and he looked worried.

"Fine." I smiled as I ran my finger over his stubbled chin. "Everything is fine."

"You look better rested than yesterday, that's for sure. Still ... if you had a bad dream I want to know about it."

"Well ... I had a dream about Mom, Twila and Marnie wearing shirts with the word 'Grandmother' on them and they were crossed out with those big circle things with the lines through them. Aunt

Tillie was trying to strap the baby to her chest and ride around on her scooter. That wasn't exactly a good dream. It wasn't a bad one either."

"I can't help you there. That's simple anxiety ... though the big conversation went down better than you led me to believe it would. They weren't nearly as furious as I expected."

"There's no reason for them to be furious. I mean ... Clove and Sam are getting married. Even if they weren't, this is hardly the end of the world. Most of the time I think of our mothers as progressive. On some things, though, they have an antiquated belief system."

"Yeah ... although I prefer we're married before having kids."

I shifted, mildly uncomfortable with the direct way he addressed our future. "Oh, yeah?"

His smirk was mischievous. "Are you not okay with that?"

"I don't know. We haven't really talked about it that much."

"That's not true. We have talked about it. You know I believe you're my future, right?"

It had taken a great deal of time and comfort, but I did know that. I couldn't see myself with anyone else, and I knew he felt the same. "I know. Still, I was kind of hoping we could wait a bit before we have to worry about that."

"I wholeheartedly agree. Your powers being what they are, I don't think it's safe to add a baby to the mix now."

I hadn't even considered that. "A baby would probably be afraid of ghosts."

He pursed his lips, cocking his head as he thought about the statement. "I don't know. Were you afraid of the first ghost you saw?"

"I'm not even sure I realized it was a ghost. I mean ... I probably saw ghosts long before I could comprehend what they were. I'm not even entirely sure when I came to the conclusion that I was actually dealing with a ghost."

"Good point. What are the odds any child we have will see ghosts?"

That was the question. "I don't know. It's not a very common — or comfortable — gift. It runs in families. I got it because Aunt Tillie can see them. My mother can't, but ... it's possible that one or more of our children could see ghosts."

"Then we'll deal with it." He was matter-of-fact. "It'll be easier for our child because you'll understand what's happening. It had to be difficult for your mother when she couldn't see what you were seeing."

"Yeah, and I figured out early that it wasn't a good thing to tell her. She got frustrated. Plus, well, I didn't want her to send me away, so I stopped telling her about what I could see for a long time. We'll have to make sure that doesn't happen with our kid."

Landon looked pensive. "Why did you think she would send you away?"

I shrugged. "It just seemed a possibility. My mom and aunts watched a lot of those Lifetime movies and they were always talking about sending crazy people away. I was convinced I was crazy for a long time."

"I'm sorry." He pressed a kiss to my forehead. "You shouldn't have had to go through that. You won't ever again. Our daughter won't either."

"What if we have a son?"

He smirked. "I have pretty much convinced myself that we're going to be blessed with girls. I'm fine with that, by the way. I don't care what we have as long as he or she is happy."

That was exactly what I wanted to hear. "Same here."

He gave me another kiss. "How about we shower and head up to the inn? I'm hungry and I want to talk to Terry. We need to come up with a plan on how we're going to greet the day ... and start chasing down leads. So far, we're doing nothing but chasing leads that circle and die quickly."

"Are you including me in that 'we'?"

He shrugged. "Maybe. It depends on what we plan. Let's play it by ear for now. What I really want to do is eat some bacon, and torture your mother and aunts about being grannies and grand-aunties."

I smirked. "You're going to give them a ton of grief about this, aren't you?"

"Oh, you have no idea."

SEVENTEEN

Landon and Chief Terry had met with Landon's boss, who wanted an update on the case. They couldn't very well take me with them, so I took advantage of the situation and headed to the office. I had some things to do — including okaying the layout for the week's edition — and I couldn't shirk my duties no matter how much the birds bothered me. Investigating murder wasn't my primary job, but the way things had gone the past year and a half I probably should've considered heading to the academy for proper training.

Viola was waiting for me. "Where have you been?" She was positively apoplectic.

"Around," I replied, furrowing my brow. "Why are you so worked up?"

"Why do you think?"

I had no idea. Viola was tempestuous in life. She was even worse in death. For some reason, though, I enjoyed her company. She reminded me of Aunt Tillie in a way, even though they were bitter enemies. She often said idiotic things that made me laugh, and because she was dead she had a lot of time on her hands to spy on others. Occasionally she came up with a good gossipy tidbit, so I tried to appease her as often as possible.

"I don't know," I answered. "Why don't you tell me why you're upset and we'll tackle the problem from there??"

She shot me a withering look right out of my mother's playbook. "Don't handle me. I can't stand it when people handle me."

"I'm not trying to handle you. I'm just trying to figure out why you're so worked up."

"Them." She gestured vaguely at nothing.

I glanced around, confused. "What?"

"You know." She leaned forward so we were in a conspiratorial huddle. "*Them*."

I had no idea if that was supposed to mean something to me. "I need more information."

"Oh, geez. I can't believe I have to spell this out for you. Them. Them. Them!" This time she waved her hand toward my office window.

I looked through the glass. There was nothing out of the ordinary happening. In fact, all I could see were festival shenanigans. "The witches?" I asked finally. "Is that who you're talking about? I thought you were looking forward to them visiting."

"That's exactly who I'm talking about." She bobbed her head. "How could you invite them here? And excited isn't the right word. I'm hypervigilant because they need to be watched."

"I didn't invite them." It was my mother and aunts who decided to resurrect the gathering. This was on them. "I'm just covering the event."

"Well, they're evil."

"Why?"

"All witches are evil."

"I think you're preaching to the wrong choir there," I argued. "You know I'm a witch?"

Viola's "Well, duh" look was right out of a slapstick comedy. "You're not an evil witch, though."

"You just said all witches are evil."

"I wasn't talking about you ... or your mother and aunts, for that matter."

"What about Clove and Thistle?"

"Clove is a sweet girl. Nobody could ever consider her evil. As for Thistle ... I think the less said the better."

I smirked. "Probably. What about Aunt Tillie?"

"Is that even a serious question? Of course she's an evil witch. I mean ... her photo is on Wikipedia next to the evil witch entry. No joke. I put it there."

"After you died?"

She nodded. "I'm getting better at affecting the physical world. It took me an entire night, but I managed to load her photo."

Not that I didn't believe her, but I had to check. I logged onto my computer, briefly shoving Viola's witch hysteria out of my mind. When I navigated to the page in question, I found she was telling the truth.

"Wow." Without thinking, I took a screenshot so I could forever remember this moment ... and share it with Clove and Thistle. They would get a kick out of it. "I can't believe you managed that. I'm impressed."

"Yes, well, I'm impressive." She made a big show of sitting in one of the chairs across from me. She was a ghost, so she didn't need to sit, but she'd held on to many of her mannerisms from life. I found it comforting to know that her mind was still intact ... especially after she died directly in front of me from a gunshot to the head. "You need to get over the witches," I suggested, shifting the conversation back to the original topic. "There's nothing you can do about them, so there's no point in getting worked up about something you can't change."

"Of course you would think that. You like the witches."

"I don't particularly like or dislike them. I am curious about why you're so anti-witch. I mean ... other than Aunt Tillie. I know she gave you grief the course of your life, but you're hardly alone in that."

"I told you that I don't like any witches."

I decided to let the indirect dig go. "Okay ... but why?"

"This town has always been crawling with them."

That was news to me. As far as I knew, we were the only real witches who lived in the area. "You know that most of the people in this town aren't real witches, right?" I couldn't be sure that Viola's knowledge base extended that far. "The people here just pretend to be witches for the tourists."

"Are we really having this conversation?" She flicked me between the eyebrows, and she was strong enough that I felt it.

I reared back, surprised. "You really are getting better at that." I rubbed my forehead. "That was ... wow."

"Yes, I'm gifted." Viola rolled her eyes. "I need you to focus. Those witches out there are dangerous, especially given what's going on with the birds."

The statement was simple enough, but it set my teeth on edge. "You've seen the birds?"

"Have you?"

"Yeah, I've seen them." Oddly enough, even though she was a kvetch of the highest order — something Aunt Tillie had been telling me for years — Viola was actually circling an important topic. "What do you think they mean?"

She shrugged. "How am I supposed to know? I'm not a bird expert ... but I have found that they sense ghosts and don't like us one bit. I can change their flight path if I'm feeling feisty, although that's sort of lost its luster."

I filed away that tidbit for later. "You're not a bird expert, but you seem to believe you have some knowledge about witches. The birds have been a thing since Adam died."

"Yeah, that's sad." Viola worked her jaw, her eyes trained on the window. "He was a good man. I never understood why he married Lorna."

"Do you know something about Lorna?"

"Just that she's a witch."

Viola could've knocked me over with a harbinger feather I was so surprised by the statement. "How do you know she's a witch? I've been around her numerous times and I've never gotten that vibe."

"Well, maybe she's not the same sort of witch you are. Have you ever considered that?"

"What other kinds of witches are there?" I genuinely wanted to know.

"Evil witches."

"But ... ." This conversation was going nowhere. When Landon mentioned earlier that the investigation kept circling and dying, that's how I felt about my interaction with Viola. "Let's start from the beginning." I forced a smile for her benefit. "Tell me why you think Lorna is a witch."

"I don't have any concrete knowledge that she's a witch," Viola admitted after a beat.

"Then why did you say that?"

"Because her mother was definitely a witch."

I leaned back in my chair, conflicted. "I don't remember Lorna's mother all that well. She died a good fifteen years ago or so, right?"

"That sounds about right." Viola nodded as she did the math in her head. "Maybe it was closer to twenty now. It's hard for me to remember now that I'm dead. Time doesn't pass the same way."

"I can look up her date of death," I offered. "I was a kid when she died. I remember it was big news around town because it was some sort of weird accident. Mom didn't think it was a good idea to take us to the funeral because we were too young.

"I remember being interested because everyone was whispering about the death," I continued. "It was some sort of freak farm equipment accident or something. She fell in a thresher, I think."

"That was one hunch," Viola confirmed. "There were whispers that it was something else, though."

"What sort of whispers?"

"People said that Diane's ghost killed her."

Now I was really lost. "I'm sorry... who is Diane?"

"You know ... *Diane*."

It took everything I had to keep my temper in check. Having a linear conversation with Viola was often a fruitless endeavor. "I still don't know who Diane is."

"Lorna's sister."

I racked my brain. "I didn't know Lorna had a sister," I said finally. That seemed like something I should know. "She's lived in Hemlock Cove her entire life. She was born back when it was Walkerville, but I was under the impression that she'd never left the area."

"That's true."

"So ... how do I not know about her sister?"

"She disappeared when you were still a kid," Viola replied. "Lorna and Diane were eleven months apart. They were the sort of twins who weren't really twins."

I knew what she meant. There was a name for siblings born within a year of each other: Irish twins. "What happened to her?"

"Nobody knows. Diane was the older sister and was closer with the mother."

"What was the mother's name?"

"Leslie Merchant."

I nodded and typed the woman's name into the newspaper archives. I found her obituary relatively quickly. "She died nineteen years ago, which would've made me eleven. It looks like there was a police investigation at the time because Lorna was home when the incident occurred."

I typed in Diane's name. There was less information on her. "It says here that Diane ran away."

"That was the assumption. She was always a wild child. She had crazy dark hair, like Clove, and she was rail thin. She had a face like Thistle, though."

"What is that supposed to mean?"

"Like she was always smelling something nasty." Viola mimicked the face in question and I couldn't swallow my chuckle. I very much doubted Thistle would appreciate Viola's imitation of her.

"Was Diane a witch?"

"The whole family was rumored to be witches, with Leslie the queen of the coven. Lorna was considered the quiet one. People had high hopes for her ... but now I have to wonder if she was simply better at hiding her true nature."

"I don't understand."

"I'm saying that Lorna probably killed Adam. That's what everyone in town is whispering about anyway. I heard Margaret telling her little flying monkeys about it yesterday. She's telling anyone who will listen that Lorna is guilty."

That didn't surprise me. "Mrs. Little should keep her mouth shut about things that aren't fact," I said. "This isn't the first time this week that she's been spreading absolute nonsense. She told me that Sheila Carpenter was having an affair with Adam and that turned out to be total nonsense because she just wanted to pay me back for stealing the campground property and pay Sheila back for not allowing her to deliver a sermon at church."

"Yeah, that sounds just like her," Viola agreed. "But I don't know that she's wrong about Lorna. Even Margaret is occasionally right."

"Well, there's no proof that Lorna is guilty." I thought about the bereaved woman I'd spent the previous morning with. "She's mourning hard. I know that doesn't necessarily mean anything — it could be remorse if she did kill him — but I'm not prepared to declare her guilty based on rumor and innuendo."

"I'm just telling you what I heard."

"What about the sister? How did she disappear?"

"It was in the middle of the night," Viola replied. "She was supposedly in bed sleeping when Leslie turned in for the evening and was gone by the time she woke. Lorna and Diane shared a room. Lorna swears she didn't hear anything."

"Were any of Diane's belongings missing?"

Viola shrugged. "I have no idea. It was a long time ago. If I were you, I'd ask Tillie. She helped search for the girl. They never found her."

Even though I was fed up with Aunt Tillie's antics and attitude, that's exactly what I planned to do.

SHE WASN'T HARD TO TRACK down. As was her everyday routine of late, she was dressed to impress — the dragon leggings I knew for a fact had been chucked more than once covering her legs — and zipping around the sidewalks on her scooter.

"I'm thinking of giving the scooter a name," she announced when I flagged her down. "What do you think about Monster?"

"As a name for your scooter?"

"Yeah. I'm riding my Monster. I think it has a nice ring to it."

I honestly didn't care. "Go nuts."

"I might paint flames on it, too."

"That sounds like a surefire way to make Mom's head implode ... so go for it."

She grinned. "You're still mad about last night, aren't you? I know things didn't go how you expected, but it's better that the news is out. Lying is always a poor way to improve familial relations."

That was rich coming from her. Still, a niggling suspicion cropped up at the back of my mind. "You didn't purposely arrange it so the information came out that way, did you?"

"What a horrible thing to say about your favorite aunt. I can't believe you would even go there."

That wasn't a denial, but because things had worked out — er, well, mostly worked out — I was willing to let it go. At least for the time being. "Nobody likes a fink," I reminded her. That was a mantra she'd preached constantly when we were kids and she was trying to keep us from tattling on her. "I need to ask you about Diane and Leslie Merchant. What do you know about them?"

"Why are you asking about them?"

"I just had a very long conversation with Viola."

"I'm sorry." Aunt Tillie was solemn. "Do you want me to put you out of your misery now? I'm sure you want to die after having a conversation with that woman."

I ignored the dig. This was not the time for one of Aunt Tillie's petty fights to derail me. "She claims Leslie was a witch and she passed on her magic to Lorna and Diane."

Aunt Tillie snorted. "Oh, please. Leslie was not a witch."

"Why does Viola think that?"

"Leslie pretended to be a witch ... and before it was considered cool in this town. She didn't have any magic. She was a fair potion maker. That was basically her claim to fame."

"And what kind of potions did she concoct?"

"The usual. She made healing potions, claimed she could cure alcoholism ... which was a steaming pile of crap. She also made love potions and peddled them to the women in town so they could snag a husband."

That was hardly the first time I'd heard a similar story. Women of a certain age, when they had children to provide for, were called witch and worse when they thought outside the box. "What happened to Leslie's husband?"

"Drank himself to death. He was a mean cuss. Nobody mourned his death ... including Leslie and her girls. It was almost a relief when he died."

That was interesting. "So the husband died of alcoholism ... and the mother died in a weird farm accident ... and the sister disappeared. That's a lot of odd happenings around one woman."

"Are you thinking Lorna took all of them out?"

I wasn't sure what I believed. "I don't know. That's a lot of coincidences. Viola said you helped search for Diane. Do you believe she ran away?"

"I don't know. I didn't know her all that well. She was a mouthy girl — and I didn't want her hanging around your mother and aunts because they were mouthy enough — but I often thought she was misunderstood more than malevolent."

And that right there was why you could never fully write off Aunt Tillie. Buried deep down — extremely deep down sometimes — was a good heart. She probably searched from sun-up to sunset looking for that girl ... and for days.

"No sign of her was ever found?"

"None."

"Did she take any of her belongings from the house?"

"As I remember it, some clothes and a bag were gone, but that doesn't necessarily mean she packed that bag. If someone wanted to cover up a death, that would be an easy way to do it. Especially years ago. Cops didn't worry about missing teenagers back then like they do today."

"Yeah." I rubbed the back of my neck. "Do you think Lorna could be a witch?"

"I don't think her mother was a witch so I doubt she is. Still, now that you mention it, death does seem to follow her. But I'm not sure I believe she's capable of the mayhem you're suggesting."

"I'm not sure I believe it either. Still, I have to check."

"Well, have fun with that." She tossed her cape over her shoulder and narrowed her eyes as they landed on Mrs. Little. "Now, if you'll excuse me, I've got a different sort of witch to burn at the stake."

I could do nothing but shake my head. "Don't do anything that could open you up to a lawsuit. Mom will be mad."

"I'm not afraid of your mother ... but don't tell her I said that."

I grinned. "It will be our little secret, even though you are a fink."

"Watch yourself. You don't want to join your cousin at the top of my list, do you?"

"Go forth and wreak havoc."

"That's the plan."

EIGHTEEN

I was still bothered by the witch rumors regarding Lorna's family when lunch time rolled around. I met Landon and Chief Terry at the diner, but my mind wasn't on the casual conversation and food.

"What's your deal?" Landon asked after we placed our orders.

"What?" I drew my eyebrows together. "I didn't say anything."

"Exactly. You haven't said more than two words since you joined us." He gave my hair a light tug and smiled. "I like my women chatty."

"Oh, geez." Chief Terry rolled his eyes. "If this is going to turn into a scene from *The Flirting Game,* I'm out of here."

"I'm just worried," Landon countered. "What are you thinking?"

I couldn't quite wrap my head around the news and needed an outside opinion, so I filled them in on my morning. When I finished, Chief Terry spoke first.

"I remember that," he nodded while fiddling with the straw wrapper on the table. "I was in the academy when Diane disappeared."

"Did you know her?" Landon leaned back and rested his arm on the back of the booth. I took the opportunity to slide closer to him, absorb some of his warmth. I had a few ideas, none of them good, which was making me cold all over.

"I knew of her. I wasn't really her speed. She was wild, liked to party and hang out with a rough crowd. Even back then I was kind of a goody-goody."

"I like that you're a goody-goody." I patted his hand and smiled. "If you weren't such a good guy, Aunt Tillie would've completely skewed my moral compass when I was a kid. You saved me."

"Oh, that's kind of cute." He beamed at me. "It's a load of hogwash, but cute."

"Now I'm going to puke," Landon lamented, shaking his head. "I hate it when you guys do that surrogate-father-and-daughter thing. It makes me uncomfortable."

"The only reason it makes you uncomfortable is because I know what a filthy mind you have and how you point it at my sweetheart."

Landon was smug. "She's my sweetheart now."

"She'll always be my sweetheart ... and don't make that word perverted. I don't like it." Chief Terry shot him a warning look and then focused on me. "What do you think it means?"

"I don't know." That was the truth. "I was just surprised. I never gave much thought to Lorna's family. I had no idea they were rumored to be witches. I thought that distinction belonged to my family alone."

"Well, to be fair, the term 'witch' has been thrown around as long as I can remember," Chief Terry countered. "Margaret is responsible for some of that. She thinks she can isolate and alienate people by calling them names."

I could see that. "Do you think Leslie Merchant was a witch?"

"I ... don't know." Chief Terry hesitated before finishing. "I always found her weird. I would be lying if I said otherwise. I don't know that I believe she was a witch. That's hard to wrap my head around."

"Yeah." I tapped the side of my glass and leaned back in the booth. "What about the farm equipment accident?"

"That was before I was on the force here. I was still serving in Traverse City at the time."

"You must've heard something about it." I refused to let it go. "I'm not asking for the gory details, but Viola made it sound as if there was a possibility it wasn't an accident."

"Viola was always prone to histrionics," Chief Terry muttered, shaking his head. "As far as I know, it was ruled an accident quickly. Leslie was in the field — they had a huge cornfield at the time — and the story goes that she thought she'd put the harvester in park and moved ahead of it to check something. The brake failed and ... she was killed quickly."

I was horrified at the thought. "That's just ... not the way I want to go."

"You're going to live forever," Landon countered, his hand moving to my back. "I get what you're saying. Did a mechanic prove the brake failed?"

"If I remember correctly he said that it stuck and then unstuck randomly. People believed she thought it was in park but it was really stuck, and that's how she was caught unaware."

"That's just a terrible way to go." I shook my head and pressed my eyes shut. "I don't like that at all."

"Join the club." Landon was squeamish about certain things and that was on full display now. "I'm curious about the witch rumors. Can witches call birds?"

It was an interesting question. "Witches can use animals. We don't. We tend to stay far away from animals. Chief Terry got us Sugar when we were kids and we loved him dearly until the end. Other than him, the only other pet we've really had is Peg and she's a recent addition."

"You don't control your animals," Landon pointed out. "Someone is controlling these birds. My guess is that it's Lorna."

"She's the obvious choice," I agreed. "I want to be sure, though. I just don't feel certain that we're on the right track. Something feels off."

"How will you ascertain you're on the right track?"

"I have no idea. I need to think about it ... and do a little research. I bet there's more news to dig up on Diane."

"I can run a search on her, too," Chief Terry offered. "It's possible she only hid her location when she first ran away. Maybe now that decades have passed she's gone back to living in the open."

"You're assuming she's alive," I pointed out. "It's possible she never went missing. She could've been killed and dumped somewhere. We can't rule out that possibility."

"No, I guess we can't." He rubbed his chin. "I'll still see what I come up with."

"It can't hurt," I agreed. "What was your meeting with Steve about? I figure it had to be big for him to come to town the way he did."

Landon frowned and shifted on his seat. It was obvious he was uncomfortable with the question. His boss, Steve Newton, allowed him plenty of leeway when it came to doing his job.

"What?" I was instantly alert. "What happened?"

"I'm not supposed to tell you, but ... screw it." Landon glanced over his shoulder to make sure nobody was eavesdropping. "Steve came to warn us that a formal request had been lodged with the home office."

"I have no idea what that means," I admitted.

"It came from Masterson. He requested that any questions be asked in a private location."

"But ... ." I was officially flabbergasted. "I didn't think you guys had questioned him yet."

"We haven't. Apparently he figured out it was only a matter of time and decided to head us off. Now we're limited as to when we can approach him. We have to call his office and arrange a time convenient for all parties."

The way his lips curved down told me what he thought of that suggestion. "So Masterson knows that you're looking at him."

"He at least knows that we'll have to question him," Landon corrected. "His relationship with Lorna puts him in a precarious position. He's trying to make sure that he controls the information as best as he can. We were also warned that it would be unwise to spread the nature of his relationship with Lorna around town."

"How is that supposed to work?" I challenged. "You guys are hardly the only ones who know."

"He doesn't realize that. My guess is he thinks he can keep this under wraps."

"Good luck with that." I sipped my iced tea and stared out the window. "Still ... everything we have seems to lead back to Lorna. I have trouble believing that's a coincidence."

"You're not the only one," Landon admitted. "We're calling her in for a formal interview after lunch. We have no other choice."

"What do you think she'll say?"

"Probably nothing, but we have to do it."

They did, and the fact that Lorna would be away from her home for an extended period gave me an idea about something I had to do.

ONCE I LEFT THE DINER, I HEADED to Lorna's house, parking a full block away and behind a neighbor's hedge so there would be no chance of her seeing my vehicle. Then I waited.

She left not long after. She was in her vehicle and didn't as much as glance in my direction as she left. As soon as I was certain she was gone, I hopped out of my car and headed for the house. I had no idea if Nick or Dani was inside but I was determined to get close enough to figure it out.

"What are you doing?" Thistle stepped out from behind a bush just as I was about to head up the driveway, causing me to rear back and make a strangled sound deep in my throat.

"What are you doing here?" I challenged, my voice raspy as I fought to recover. "Were you hiding in that bush?"

She smirked. "Aunt Tillie sent me."

"Aunt Tillie sent you here? Why?"

"She figured you were about to do something stupid ... and she wasn't wrong. You're going to break into Lorna's house, aren't you?"

I hated that Aunt Tillie knew me so well. "That's the plan," I admitted, rolling my neck. "I have to make sure Dani and Nick aren't inside first."

"They're not. I saw them both leave from where I was hiding. We have a clear shot."

"*We*?" I couldn't help being dubious. "Why are you coming with me?"

"You need backup and I'm as curious as you are. Aunt Tillie gave me a brief rundown before sending me after you. She mentioned something about Lorna possibly being a witch and you being an idiot who can't keep your nose out of Lorna's business. Then she said she had to keep stalking Hazel and we were on our own."

That sounded just like her. "Well ... awesome." I flicked my eyes toward the empty house. "You're sure Dani and Nick aren't here?"

"I saw them leave myself."

"Then I guess we should get to it."

"Absolutely," Thistle agreed. "Let's invade Lorna's privacy and find out if she's calling birds to kill people for her."

"I don't think the birds are killing people."

"Close enough."

That wasn't even remotely true, but I was too keyed up to argue. "Let's go. The faster we get in, the faster we can get out."

THIS WASN'T the first time we'd invaded someone's home in an effort to get information. Yes, we knew it was wrong and there was every chance we could get caught — and good luck explaining that — but that didn't stop us.

"Where should we start?" Thistle kept her voice low even though we were relatively assured we were alone.

"Probably Lorna's bedroom and any office we can find are the safest bets," I replied, glancing around the kitchen. I was hopeful Adam would return, but he didn't seem to be hanging around today. "I doubt Lorna would keep anything in a high-traffic area, because people have been stopping by to share their condolences."

"Good point."

By tacit agreement, we headed toward the second floor. It took a moment to sort through the rooms, but it became obvious relatively quickly what we were dealing with.

"There's no office," Thistle noted. "There are two adult rooms."

"His and hers," I agreed. "Lorna and Adam weren't sharing a bed. They were separated."

"I thought maybe that was a lie, but I guess not." We headed toward the master bedroom. "This looks like Lorna's room."

I nodded, my lips pursed as we invaded the mourning woman's personal space. At first glance, the bedroom appeared normal. There wasn't much furniture to riffle through. Basically a bed and dresser and that's it. But for some reason, something beckoned me to the back corner of the room, where the closet was located.

"What is it?" Thistle asked when she saw me crossing.

"I don't know." My heart started pounding harder the closer I got to the closet, and when I finally arrived — after what felt like years rather than seconds — I took a long, steadying breath before throwing open the door.

There, eyes wide with fear, was Adam's ghost. He huddled in the shadows looking terrified.

"I was wondering if I would see you again," I said as I took him in. "I think you're what I've been looking for."

Adam's gaze was earnest. The way he moved his chin told me he was trying to speak. The thread — or whatever it was — holding his lips together was too strong.

"Can I look?" My hands shook as I raised them and I felt Thistle move in at my back.

"Who are you talking to?"

"Adam," I replied, frowning as my fingers went through him. He was a ghost, for crying out loud. How was I supposed to touch him and make things better?

"Is his mouth still sewn shut?"

I nodded, frustration rearing up. "It is, and I don't know what to do about it. It's not as if I can pull out the thread. It's not really there. In fact ... I just don't know."

Thistle shot me a quelling look before moving closer. "I wish I could see him. Obviously, because his mouth is sewn shut he can't talk. I won't be able to hear him."

"Nobody will be able to hear him." I hated how petulant I sounded, but I couldn't stop myself. "This is the worst."

"It is the worst," Thistle agreed. "But why can't you just remove the thread?"

Apparently she'd decided to play deaf and dumb today. "I just told you that I can't touch him. There's no way I can remove the thread."

"I didn't say you could. Can't you force him to remove it? You can't touch the plane he lives on. He's caught between two worlds. It seems to me that the only way to save him is to force him to save himself."

"But ... how?"

She shrugged. "You're the necromancer. You figure it out."

That wasn't what I wanted to hear. "But ... ." I frowned as I regarded Adam. He looked so fearful, pathetic even. "I guess I could try."

I shot him an encouraging smile. "This won't hurt." At least I hoped that was true. "I'm just going to ... ." I had no idea what I was going to do. This necromancer thing was new enough that I constantly felt lost. Still, I recognized I needed to try ... so that's what I did.

The magic unfurled like a fern tendril in the spring. It was slow, felt mildly tedious, but there was strength in the attempt. Energy sparked in the back of my brain and before I realized what was happening I'd managed to make a connection.

"Can you hear me?" I asked without actually uttering the words. I was piping them directly into Adam's brain.

He nodded, his eyes going wide enough to make me fear they might pop out of his head.

"Then here is what I need you to do."

It was difficult to convince Adam to remove the thread. He fought the effort, but I exerted as much control as was necessary. I felt guilty about it — and then some — but he was the only one with answers. Finally, he managed to remove the thread, leaving gaping holes on his ghostly flesh. He gasped at the sudden freedom, and then looked at me appraisingly.

"How did you know I could do that?" His voice was dry and rasped.

"I played a hunch." I glanced toward Thistle and she nodded at the unasked question. She could hear him. My powers allowed that if she was close when I questioned a ghost. "We need to know what happened to you, Adam. It's important."

"I ... ." The sound of a door closing on the main floor drew everyone's attention.

"What was that?" Thistle hissed.

I hurried out of Lorna's bedroom and into the hallway, racing toward the end of the stairs and positioning myself so I could look down without drawing attention. Dani was back, and heading toward the stairs.

Well ... crap.

I hurried back into Lorna's room and pointed to the window. It opened out near a huge maple tree. That was our only chance of escape.

Thistle immediately started shaking her head but she knew as well as I that we had only seconds to act.

"I hate you for this," she muttered as she tugged up the window and dislodged the screen. This was hardly the first time we'd been forced to sneak out a second-story window. "I mean ... I really hate you for this."

I didn't blame her. I turned to tell Adam to go to The Overlook — it seemed a safe place to meet — but he was gone. Apparently his fight-or-flight response kicked in and he took the opportunity to vanish. I couldn't really blame him. I would've done the same if I could.

Ah, well, I would have to worry about it later. For now, the only thing I could do was escape.

Thistle climbed into the tree first, and I made shooing motions to get her to drop to a lower branch so I could follow. She did, but she wasn't happy about it. Very carefully, very slowly, we made our way to the ground. Once our feet were firmly planted on solid earth, I turned to her ... and whatever I was going to say died on my lips.

The sound of birds assailed my ears and a shudder ran up my spine. Thistle jerked her head at the noise, her eyes going wide as a clutch of crows – five or six of them at least – swooped from the sky directly toward us.

"Run!" I shoved her as hard as I could. "Don't look back. Just … run!"

"I really hate you!"

NINETEEN

Thistle was furious by the time we reached downtown. She rode with me because she'd walked to Lorna's house, and I had to hear her nonstop diatribe about what an idiot I was for the duration of the trek.

"You're being a baby," I complained, studying my arms and glaring at the scratches I found. Landon wasn't going to be happy when he heard I'd had yet another run-in with the birds ... and that this time it got physical. "We're fine. Probably." Something occurred to me. "Birds don't carry rabies, do they?"

Thistle's glare was withering. "You are the absolute worst."

"I thought you reserved that honor for Aunt Tillie."

"Which should tell you how far you've fallen in my estimation."

I ran my tongue over my teeth and tamped down my irritation. She'd been at the house in the first place because she was worried about me. She had a right to her anger ... mostly. "How about some ice cream?" I decided to switch topics. "That might make you feel better."

Even though she was angry I could practically see the gears in Thistle's mind working. "It had better be good ice cream."

"They have double chocolate chip and hot fudge at the festival truck."

"Fine. We should probably grab Clove. If we go for ice cream without her she'll be ticked."

On that we could agree.

It didn't take long to talk Clove into closing the store for forty-five minutes — the tourists would return later; they were something of a captive audience — and we ordered heaping bowls of ice cream and settled at a picnic table to talk.

"I can't believe that happened." Clove's eyes were wide. "Why didn't you invite me?"

"I think we're telling the story wrong if you feel you've been left out," Thistle replied darkly. "Besides, we had to jump out the window and climb down a tree. That's probably not safe given your condition."

Clove jutted out her lower lip. "It's still not fair. I don't want to be left out of everything just because I'm having a baby."

"Oh, don't worry," I said. "I'm sure the birds will be back. You can dodge them with us the next time they attack."

Clove frowned. "I don't like birds."

"Nobody does," Thistle muttered. "They're like Aunt Tillie ... small, evil and they want to peck you to death."

I pressed my lips together to keep from laughing, the expression quickly fleeing when I saw Landon and Chief Terry cutting through the crowd. "Oh, geez."

"What's wrong now?" Thistle zealously guarded her ice cream bowl, as if I was trying to distract her long enough to steal her treat.

I inclined my chin toward the men. "They're going to be angry."

"That's your problem." Thistle made a face. "I hope they ground you to within an inch of your life."

"They can't ground me." I was mostly certain that was true. "I'm an adult."

"Let's see what happens, shall we?" Before I could register what she was doing, Thistle raised her hand and waved to get their attention. "We're over here! Hey, Chief Terry! Come over here."

Several sets of eyes drifted in our direction, causing me to hunch my shoulders. "Why don't you just take out an advertisement in the newspaper or something?"

"Why would I do that when I can embarrass you in person for free?"

She had a point. I kept my gaze on my ice cream, refusing to look up as they approached. I could sense the moment Landon finally got a clear view of me. His reaction was swift.

"What happened to you?" He slid onto the bench next to me and immediately grabbed my arm to study the scratches. "Bay ... ."

"It's nothing," I reassured him quickly, forcing myself to be bold rather than shrink in the face of what I knew would be righteous fury. "We're fine."

"Speak for yourself," Thistle countered. "I'm thinking of going to the health clinic because now I can't get the notion that birds have rabies out of my mind. I don't want to be foaming at the mouth at Clove's wedding. That's Aunt Tillie's job."

I pinned her with a furious look. "Birds don't get rabies." At least I hoped they didn't. "Besides, they barely broke the skin."

"Birds?" Just as I expected, Landon's countenance darkened. "What did you do?"

I balked. "What makes you think I did anything? Isn't it possible that I was minding my own business and birds attacked out of nowhere?"

"No."

"Well ... ." I didn't want to admit what we'd done. He would be angry. And, worse, he might arrest me. He hadn't done it yet – he'd watched others do it a time or two – but I couldn't shake the feeling that it was only a matter of time before he lost his temper and shoved me in a cage.

"We broke into Lorna's house looking for proof that she's a dark witch, but we ran into a few issues," Thistle volunteered, ignoring the fury I directed toward her. "The good news is that Bay managed to free Adam from whatever spell had been cast on him. Or, rather, he freed himself. She commanded him to remove the thread keeping his lips sewn together. The second that happened, we were interrupted and had to jump out of a second-story window."

Landon started to stand and then immediately sat again. "You jumped out of a second-story window?" His voice carried under the right circumstances ... which apparently included ice cream time at a festival. "What is the matter with you?"

"You're not my parent," I reminded him. "You can't yell at me. I did what I felt I needed to do and I'm not sorry about it."

Chief Terry cleared his throat to get my attention. "I may not be your parent, but I'm close. I hate to agree with Landon, but ... that's two moronic things you've done in less than a week. Perhaps some ramifications need to be introduced here so you'll finally learn."

I worked my jaw. "Fine. Arrest me. Knock yourself out."

His glare never wavered. "Don't tempt me."

"And don't push me," Landon added. "I'm angry, Bay. Like ... really angry. I don't understand why you did this."

"I was hoping to find proof that Lorna is a dark witch. At least then we would have a direction to look."

"And did you find that proof?" Chief Terry asked. "Was it worth risking your entire future? I mean ... that's what you did, young lady. Had Lorna caught you, what do you think would've happened?"

I'd given careful consideration to that question and come up with ... well ... nothing good. "We weren't caught."

"You were almost caught."

"By Dani. We could've bamboozled her."

"Oh, well, you could've bamboozled her. How great is that?" Chief Terry folded his arms across his chest and stared at the sky. His anger was palpable. "I just don't understand you sometimes. You're supposed to be smarter than this.

"I expect Tillie to pull these kinds of shenanigans," he continued. "Even Thistle to some extent. You, however, are my good girl. You were always a good girl. You make me want to ... ." He broke off and mimed throttling an invisible person. He put a lot of effort into it, to the point his mime would've been funny under different circumstances.

I was debating how to respond when Aunt Tillie swooped in. She clearly hadn't gotten the hang of using the scooter's brakes because she careened into the table without slowing, offering up a loud "oomph" as she fought to keep from landing in Thistle's ice cream.

"What the ... ?" Chief Terry grabbed her arm to keep her from falling. "Speaking of people who think before they act. We were just talking about you. Were your ears burning?"

"I was burning rubber," Aunt Tillie responded, her face flushed with what could only be described as excitement. "Margaret was trying to catch me, but I left her in the dust. I think she's still back there sputtering."

Chief Terry looked like a man who had been saddled with babysitting several of the most obnoxious children in the history of mankind. "Do I even want to know what you did to Margaret?"

"Probably not." Aunt Tillie's smile was bright. "What have you guys been up to?"

"Oh, well, I'm glad you asked." Chief Terry launched into the tale before I had the chance to put my unique spin on it. By the time he was finished, Aunt Tillie was cackling and rubbing her hands together.

"That's awesome," she enthused. "What kinds of birds were they?"

"What does that matter?" Thistle asked blankly.

"The sort of birds being controlled have a direct link to the witch controlling them, mouth," Aunt Tillie fired back. "I'm trying to help you morons. By the way, here's a free tip on that front: Don't admit to 'The Man' when you break the law. These two might be pushovers, but there will come a point when they arrest you. Trust me. I know."

I frowned. It was true that she'd been arrested — and more than once — even by Chief Terry.

"You had that arrest coming," Chief Terry warned. "I'm not sorry about it."

"You really did have it coming," Thistle said. "I, however, was just trying to protect my cousin. At your behest, I might add. I'm totally innocent here. See ... I'm eating ice cream. Only the innocent can eat ice cream."

Landon leaned around me and flicked her ear. "Just shut up for once. This is serious."

I needed this conversation to move away from laws that were broken and focus on the problem at hand. The birds were becoming a real issue. "Ravens and crows," I replied to Aunt Tillie's earlier question. "They were mostly ravens and crows, although there were a few others thrown in for good measure. They came toward the tail end of the … attack."

"Like what?"

"Um … ." I was hardly an ornithologist.

"There were a few sparrows and what looked to be a duck," Thistle volunteered. "We didn't spend much time hanging around to identify them."

"A duck?" Aunt Tillie made a face. "That makes sense. They're pretty much jerks ninety percent of the time. The only time they're not is when they're freshly hatched."

"This is a fascinating conversation," Landon drawled. "What does the type of birds have to do with anything?"

"I just told you." Aunt Tillie's tone was withering. "The types of birds called to a certain energy identifies the energy."

"And what do these birds tell us?"

"That we're dealing with a dark witch." She delivered the line as solid fact. "I wasn't certain before — I thought Bay was just being Bay — but now I'm convinced that we're dealing with a dark witch. My bad."

My bad? I wanted to strangle her. "I told you we were dealing with a dark witch from the start."

"And you turned out to be right. Fancy that." Aunt Tillie reached for Thistle's spoon, but Thistle smacked her hand away. "I'll remember this moment," Aunt Tillie threatened. "You're dead to me."

"I'm crushed," Thistle said. "Go back to the birds. We need information and apparently you have some … even though you were pretending otherwise until three minutes ago."

"I wasn't pretending otherwise," Aunt Tillie countered. "I just didn't realize how serious the situation was. I thought Bay was being Bay."

"Stop saying that," I growled. "That's not a thing."

"Oh, it's totally a thing," Thistle countered. "I mean ... you're not as bad as Clove, but you're a total whiner."

"Says the woman who thinks she got rabies from the birds."

"Hey!" She extended a warning finger in my direction. "Birds are horrible creatures. They're dirty ... and nasty ... and they make weird sounds. Sometimes they look at me funny. I hate that."

I rolled my eyes. "Whatever. Can we get back to the important part of the discussion? What do we do about the birds? And how do we figure out who the dark witch is?"

"It's Lorna," Aunt Tillie replied simply. "She's the only one who makes sense. You said yourself she came from a dark witch and has been using her powers under the radar ever since."

I pinched the bridge of my nose to ward off an incoming headache. "You said that Leslie wasn't a dark witch, that she just made potions."

"I didn't say that."

I was incredulous. "You did."

"I did not."

"You did so."

"I did not. I would remember saying that."

"That did it." I moved to stand, thoughts of wrestling her to the ground and making her eat dirt flitting through my head. I didn't get a chance, because Landon grabbed my shoulder and forced me to sit.

"I don't think that's a good idea," he supplied. "There are witnesses here and I will have no choice but to arrest you if you commit murder out in the open."

I pouted. I couldn't stop myself. "Well ... that's no fun."

He didn't smile like he normally would, which told me I was still in trouble. Ah, well, I would have to wear him down with kisses later. If that didn't work, there was always bacon. I'd purchased a nightgown from a novelty store online two weeks before — it made me look like a strip of bacon … with some rather impressive cleavage — and tucked it away for the next time I was in trouble. It looked like I would be using it sooner rather than later.

"The birds are relics," Aunt Tillie volunteered. "They're kind of like spirit animals. The person doing this is calling to the darkest creatures in the vicinity. That just so happens to be birds in this case."

"Relics?" I furrowed my brow. I vaguely remembered reading about them when Aunt Tillie was trying to enforce regular magic classes when we were kids. "That means they're more powerful than regular birds."

"Pretty much," Aunt Tillie confirmed. "Our witch is imbuing them with power. Until she's destroyed — or locked up and removed from temptation — those birds will continue to grow in number and power."

That was not what I wanted to hear. "Well ... crap." I moved to scratch at one of the marks on my arm, but Landon stopped me.

"We need to clean these," he said after examining the wounds. "I don't think you have rabies or anything, but I don't want to risk an infection."

"We've got stuff at the store," Clove offered. "I'll clean them both up when we finish our ice cream."

Even though he was clearly still angry, Landon took a moment to order my hair. "I would hate for your arm to fall off or anything."

"Yeah. That would suck." I rubbed my forehead. "What do you think we should do about Lorna? I mean ... she's the obvious choice as our dark witch."

"She is," Landon agreed. "We don't have proof of anything, though. In fact, as far as the investigation is concerned, we're standing in the middle of a clue-barren desert. We have nothing. Lorna was seen outside the blacksmith shop at the time the medical examiner set for Adam's death. If she killed him, it was in a unique way."

"Huh." Well, that put us in a pickle. "So ... what do we do?"

"You don't do anything," Landon shot back. "You're done for the day. You're going to Hypnotic to clean those cuts and scratches, and letting the professionals do their jobs."

That sounded unlikely, but there was no way I would argue with him in front of an audience, especially when his temper was so close to the surface. "I already planned to go to Hypnotic," I promised. "You don't have to worry about me. I've had my fill of birds for the day."

"We all have." Thistle ran her hand over her forearm. "Besides, we have to get ready for the ritual gathering tonight. We're supposed to do a blessing ... although I think our mothers have backed off on that now given Clove's pregnancy. That did turn out to be a convenient excuse."

I frowned. "That can't be right. The ritual isn't happening already, is it?"

"It's not the big ritual," Clove replied. "Hazel is hosting tonight. It's supposed to be a pre-blessing, to make sure the bluff is ready for the solstice celebration and wedding tomorrow. She arranged it with our mothers."

"Which means that we should all avoid it," Aunt Tillie suggested. "If Hazel arranged it, it'll be boring."

I was maudlin. "It'll be boring," I agreed. "But we can't ignore it. If we do, our mothers will melt down."

"So what?" Aunt Tillie was full of bravado. "Let them melt down. We should present a united front and let them know we mean business. If we do, they won't be able to boss us around ... like ever."

"And why would we present a united front with you after the way you turned on us over Clove's pregnancy?" I challenged. "You were a fink. You told us never to ally ourselves with finks."

"It's true," Thistle said sagely. "You did teach us that."

Aunt Tillie's expression was dark. "I am not a fink. You take that back."

"If the fink hat fits ... ."

Landon made an exasperated sound, interrupting us before we could launch into a petty argument. "You're all going to the ritual and you know it. As for Lorna ... leave her to us. I don't want you guys finding trouble. We'll handle this case going forward."

He was stern enough that all I could do was swallow hard. I hated being left out of things, but it was obvious he was in no mood for an argument. I could hardly blame him.

"We'll focus on the ritual tonight," I promised.

"And you'll stay out of the investigation," Landon prodded.

"For tonight," I agreed. "As for tomorrow ... well, that's a new day."

"Ugh." He dropped his head and stared at the table. "This is what I get for falling in love with a mouthy woman who has her own ideas. I just ... why can't you ever do things my way?"

"I do. I just can't this time. We're in this. But for tonight we'll leave it alone. Besides, I need to research relics before I decide on my next move. That'll take time."

He grabbed my half-eaten ice cream and started shoveling it in his mouth. "You make me tired, Bay."

"I know, but I'm worth it."

"You still drive me crazy."

"Just think how boring your life would be if I didn't."

TWENTY

I conducted research all afternoon. The information on relics was interesting ... and yet limited.

"They're definitely harbingers," I noted as I stretched my arms over my head. I sat on the couch in Hypnotic and I hadn't moved for hours. "But they're more than that. Supposedly the individual calling to them can invade the animals with a sliver of human soul. That's what makes them malevolent."

"Really?" Clove made a face. "I don't like the sound of that."

"How does it work?" Thistle asked. "Doesn't the witch in question have to fracture her soul to carry out something like that?"

"Pretty much." That had been the part bothering me, too. "That's why only dark witches can do it."

"Well, that's awesome." Thistle's distaste was evident. "And here we thought the worst thing we would have to worry about was a killer with sexual motivations."

I frowned. "How do you figure that?"

"Well, our suspects are a wife who was thrown over for another woman, the other woman who couldn't get the man she was in love with to divorce his wife, and the wife's boyfriend, who wants to keep his sexual involvement with a married woman on the down low. Those are all sexual motivations."

Huh. I hadn't really thought of it that way. She was right, though. "Well ... I need to think about that. Birds aren't known for being sexual. They externally fertilize eggs."

"True, but certain birds — like peacocks, for example — preen and present themselves to garner favor from the opposite sex."

"That's a male thing."

"And warlocks exist. We haven't crossed paths with many of them, but they're real."

"I guess. I ... ." Wind chimes over the door sounded to alert us to the presence of customers.

"Oh, no," Clove fretted as she stood. "I should've locked the door sooner. If we don't leave in the next five minutes we'll be late."

"You're already technically late," Mom drawled from the doorway, catching me by surprise. She was dressed in a purple robe rich in color and a little frayed around the hem. It looked old, which was probably because it was practically ancient ... at least by our standards. I hadn't seen her dust it off in more than a decade. Behind her, Twila and Marnie wore identical robes. "Why are you guys still loafing around? The ritual starts in twenty minutes."

I was beyond confused. "Why are you guys in town?" It's not like they never came to town. They attended festivals and enjoyed the occasional gossip fest at the coffee shop. They stocked up at the store at least once a week. At this time of day, though, they were normally knee deep in dinner preparations. It was odd for them to change their schedule.

"We're here for the ritual," Mom replied, her eyes flashing. "Have you suddenly gone deaf?"

"But ... ." I shifted my eyes to Thistle. "I thought you said the ritual was on the bluff tonight."

"That's what I was told," she replied with a shrug.

"The ritual was scheduled for the bluff," Mom agreed. "After Hazel visited, however, she agreed that the magic out there was already primed and it was unnecessary to mess with the energy. She decided to move the ritual to the town square because she believes Hemlock Cove is inundated with negative energy right now."

Oh, well, that was interesting. The fact that Hazel had picked up on that made me realize that she was an untapped resource. As much as I disliked her, as nervous as she made me feel, she was a fountain of witchy information. "That sounds good." I stood with determination. "I just need to tell Landon I won't be going with him. I don't want him looking for me."

"Landon is already out there," Mom countered. "Hazel is showing him around and explaining things."

I was definitely out of the loop on this one. "Oh, well ... ." I caught Thistle's cloudy gaze. She was obviously as confused as me. "Then I guess we should head out for the ritual."

"We don't have to wear those ugly robes, do we?" Clove asked, wrinkling her nose. "I just mean ... the color isn't flattering and they're kind of shapeless."

Mom rolled her eyes. "The robes are for those already inducted into the coven. Things broke apart before you guys reached the age of maturity. You don't get the robes unless you officially join the coven."

"Which we have no intention of doing," Thistle mused. "Great. We're excited for the ritual ... and the fact that the food trucks will be close if we get bored. This really is the best of both worlds."

"We're expected to fast through the night," Twila argued. "That makes the solstice celebration pure."

"It also makes us hungry," Clove complained. "I can't fast for the next twenty-four hours. That's cruel and unusual punishment. I'm nourishing a human being here." She gestured toward her stomach. "I can't go without dinner."

"And we're standing in solidarity with Clove," Thistle added. "We can't go without dinner either."

As ridiculous as I found the argument, there was no way I was joining the fasting witches. "Yeah. I think we're going to watch and enjoy the ritual, and then eat a healthy dinner with our significant others."

"Do what you want." Mom's tone was airy. "If you don't want to take this seriously, you're not required to join in the fasting. After all, you're not full coven members. It's not required."

I could tell she was disappointed, but there was nothing I could do about that. Going without food wasn't an option. I couldn't help thinking they were to blame for our gluttonous behavior. If they weren't such good cooks we wouldn't be so food-oriented.

"Great." I forced a smile for her benefit. "Let's ritual the night away."

Thistle waited until Mom and the aunts disappeared through the door. "That was the geekiest thing you've ever said."

"I heard it the second I said it."

THE TOWN SQUARE WAS DECKED OUT WITH twinkle lights and small candles. They'd been placed along the ground, in the shape of a pentagram, and glinted against the dimming light in a fantastical way. Honestly, it was breathtaking.

"Do you think I'll get in trouble if I have a snack before we get started?" Clove asked, rubbing her stomach. "The baby is hungry."

"That baby is going to turn out to be a convenient excuse," Thistle noted. "You'll be able to eat whatever you want for the next few months and no one will be able to say a thing about it."

"That means we can eat whatever we want, too," I noted. "I mean ... Clove is forcing us to bend to her emotions."

Thistle brightened considerably. "Now that right there is genius thinking. Why wasn't your brain firing on all cylinders like this earlier?"

That was a good question. I had another. "None of them know about the other new development," I offered. "They don't know that Clove is controlling us with her emotions ... at least sometimes."

"It's probably best they don't know that," Thistle argued. "If Aunt Tillie finds out our link is so strong — and thus our individual minds so weak — that we're allowing her to influence us, then she's going to melt down."

"True story." I heaved out a sigh. "Let's try to keep this particular secret to ourselves for the foreseeable future, huh? I think that will be best for everybody."

"I can get behind that."

We split up to find our respective significant others. Sam was stress eating at the bacon truck with Landon. With the wedding arriving the following day, nerves were apparently getting the better of him. I couldn't blame him. Landon didn't even have that excuse and he was shoveling it in.

"Hello, Bay." His tone was cool as he regarded me. "How was the rest of your afternoon?"

I knew exactly what he was asking and I didn't like it. "Fine. How was your afternoon?"

"Productive."

"Really?" Hope surged in my chest. "What did you find? Do you have enough to arrest Lorna?"

He slanted his eyes in my direction. "I'm afraid that I can't talk about an ongoing investigation with a civilian. I don't make the rules, but I do have to follow them."

Oh, well, now he was just punishing me. "Fine." I turned to storm off but he caught my arm. "I'm not in the mood to fight with you right now," I warned. "I get that you're angry, but you can't be mean just for the sake of being mean."

"I'm not being mean." His tone softened. "Dammit, Bay, I love you. Do you not understand why I'm upset? For crying out loud, you could've been killed. You could've been caught and then I would've been forced to arrest you. Do you have any idea how hard that would be?"

"It wouldn't exactly be a picnic by the lake for me either. I did what I had to do. I can't take it back ... and I wouldn't. Adam is out there now, and he's free. I'm hoping when he regroups that he'll be able to find me. If he does, we'll have the answers we need. Isn't that the important thing?"

"*You're* the important thing," he countered. "*This* is the most important thing." He collected my hand and pressed it to his chest. "Don't you understand that I can't make it without you? I believe in your autonomy. I want you to be who you are. Fear is a funny thing, though. It doesn't care about being rational."

He was so open, so earnest, that I couldn't help taking pity on him. "I'm sorry." Despite my earlier words, I meant it. "I didn't mean to hurt you. I never want that. I just ... I had to know. I figured that Lorna being with you gave me an opening. We were supposed to get in and out. Dani coming home was a surprise."

"That wasn't a true apology," he countered.

"That's because I'm not sorry for doing what I did. I am sorry for causing you to worry ... and I admit I could've thought things out better. I am sorry about that."

"Ugh." He groaned and rolled his eyes. "You are so much work. I should stay angry at you just for the sake of being right. That's the Winchester way, after all."

I grinned and leaned closer. "I'll wow you tonight with the bacon negligee I bought and was keeping for a special occasion if you promise to let this go."

He straightened, surprise flitting across his handsome features. "Bacon negligee? Does that mean you look like a slice of bacon?"

"Yes."

"That shouldn't be hot, but what I'm picturing in my head is hot."

Somehow I knew he would say that. I leaned close and lowered my voice to a conspiratorial whisper. "I probably shouldn't tell you this because you might get over-excited, but it's also scented."

"Does that mean you're going to smell like bacon?" He practically had little hearts dancing in his eyes.

"Yes ... and it's the best of both worlds, because unlike Aunt Tillie's curse, I can take the nightgown on and off."

"You're the only one who ever wants the bacon smell to go away." He slid his arms around my waist and tugged me close. "Fine. I declare this fight over. I don't want you to think I'm calling it off because of the bacon negligee, though."

"Why are you doing it?"

"Because I honestly don't want you to change. It's just ... there are times I'm afraid, Bay." He rested his cheek against my forehead.

"Somehow you've become my life. Your family has become my family. Your happiness and safety is more important than anything else.

"I get that you're brave ... and your powers are expanding ... and you come from a bold line of empowered women who don't believe anyone should be able to tell them what to do," he continued. "When we have a daughter of our own, I want her to be just like you ... other than the constantly finding danger thing. That freaks me out."

"You're not going to be a helicopter parent, are you?"

"I don't know what that is, but I'm guessing no. But if it's something I find cool, I reserve the right to change my mind."

I smiled into his shoulder. "I am sorry about making you worry." I meant it with my whole heart. "I didn't think things would go the way they went."

"You never do."

"Can we just put this behind us for now? I need to focus on this ritual. Supposedly it's going to be a big deal."

"We can let it go ... for now."

"Great." I pressed a kiss to the corner of his mouth. "Are you going to meet me at home or what?"

He pulled back, his eyebrows drawn. "Why would I meet you at home?"

I was taken aback. "You're staying?"

"Yeah. I want to see what all the hoopla is about."

"But ... it's a bunch of witches. We're just going to be chanting and calling to the four corners. It's nothing you haven't seen."

"Maybe, but I still want to be a part of it. This life is our destiny, Bay. Any children we have — whether it's one or ten — will have one foot in the magic world. I need to understand everything I can, and not just for them, but for you, too."

"You've been talking about children a lot lately," I said. "It makes me kind of nervous. I don't think we're ready for that step."

"We're not," he agreed without hesitation. "It's a natural progression, though. We'll get there eventually. As for mentioning it ... I guess I've got it on my mind. Ever since Aunt Tillie sent us to the future and we saw those kids ... ." He left it hanging.

"Those kids weren't our kids," I cautioned him. "They were figments of Aunt Tillie's imagination. What we saw wasn't real."

"I know." He said the words, but I wasn't sure I believed them. "First, I would never name one of our children Sumac."

He laughed at my serious expression. "I'm not attached to that part. I wasn't even attached to that girl. It was the one in the field." He turned serious. "I know I shouldn't get attached, but I can't stop myself. I liked her ... and she was this perfect little mix of you and me.

"Even if we don't get that exact girl, it doesn't matter," he continued. "We'll get another just like her. I want to understand the world she comes from. I don't think that's unreasonable."

"It's not. I just didn't realize you were interested. You try to avoid the bluff rituals as often as possible."

"That's because those rituals turn into drunken revelries of nakedness ... and you're never the naked one."

His dour response caused my grin to widen. "I want you to be involved. I do. You've earned it."

"*We've* earned it," he corrected, cupping the back of my head. "I know we've only been together about a year and a half, but the time has flown. It's been wonderful, and I want more.

"Going forward, it's going to happen just as fast," he continued. "We have a lifetime in front of us, but it's going to feel as if it passes in minutes. I don't want to miss anything ... and I definitely don't want you risking yourself and cutting that time even shorter."

"That's fair. I don't want anything to happen to you either. But you're an FBI agent and danger comes with the territory. I took that on when I took you on. You have to do the same for me. When you came back, you said that you were in it for the long haul and that you were fine with the witch stuff. You can't go back on your word."

"I have no intention of going back on my word." He captured my lips and gave me a lingering kiss. "We'll work this out. We always do. I don't want you to worry ... and I'm sorry about being snarky earlier. That wasn't fair."

"Snark is the name of the game in the Winchester world."

"Yeah, well ... we're fine. I'm not even angry any longer. I just want to watch the ritual and then eat my weight in bacon.."

"I think that can be arranged."

"Yeah, well ... ." He trailed off, turning his head to the left. "It got really quiet."

I didn't realize until he pointed it out that I was thinking the same thing. When I turned to the square, I found a multitude of eyes focused on us. Mom looked disgusted. Aunt Tillie looked amused from her spot behind Mom ... so that, at least, was something.

"If you're ready," Hazel intoned. "We're about to begin."

"Sure." I rapidly separated from Landon. "We're definitely ready. We're looking forward to it."

"Totally," Landon echoed. "I love a good ritual. As long as you all don't get naked I think it'll be a great night."

The gazes darkened as Landon shrank next to me. "That probably wasn't a smart thing to say," he murmured.

Aunt Tillie responded before I could, shooting her thumb in the air and doing a little dance. "Way to go, Landon. Every time I think I'm going to ruin an event, I know I can always count on you to make me look good."

I pursed my lips and slid him a sidelong look. "It's fine."

"Let's hope so. Now I feel as if they're the birds and I'm on the dinner menu."

TWENTY-ONE

Hazel strode to the center of the square, her robe a shiny silver and gleaming against the lights as she took her spot.

Aunt Tillie bitterly complained the entire time. "Do you know who wears robes? Cults. She's trying to build a cult and I'm the only one who sees it."

I slid her a sidelong look as Landon shuffled closer to me. He was obviously curious about the ritual, but he was the sort of man who would protect what he loved … even if he didn't know what he was fighting against. That's simply who he was.

"I once heard about a cult that ate nothing but oysters," Aunt Tillie continued, ignoring the dark look Mom shot her. "Do you know why?"

"Probably something about oysters being aphrodisiacs," Landon replied without hesitation.

The look she shot him was withering. "Why am I not surprised that you're up on all things perverted?"

Landon's grin was toothy. "Perhaps I'm gifted."

"Yeah, yeah, yeah." She moved to my left. "This is going to suck."

It wasn't odd to see Aunt Tillie out of sorts. This situation, however, was vastly different from her usual meltdowns. "Are you jealous?" I asked finally.

Her eyebrows, shot through with gray, flew up her forehead. "Excuse me?"

I was calm as I regarded her. "Jealous," I repeated. "I mean ... Hazel is getting the attention usually reserved for you."

"I am most certainly not jealous." She turned haughty. "The fact that you could even suggest that makes me sick to my stomach. I am not the jealous sort."

"No?" I knew that wasn't true, but it hardly mattered. Hazel had started calling to the four corners, her face serene.

"I call upon the wardens of the north," she began. "We beseech you to stand as our strength."

Aunt Tillie's frown only deepened. "That's not how you do it," she argued. "That didn't even rhyme."

I risked a glance at Landon and found his shoulders shaking with silent laughter. I didn't want to follow suit — the odds of her taking it well were slim — so I focused my attention forward. Hazel droned on (and on and on and on) as she called to the corners. Her acolytes joined in, whispering in her wake.

"You know, they kind of do sound like a cult," I muttered.

"I told you." Aunt Tillie's eyes were dark as she folded her arms over her chest and glared at Hazel, who was now doing a little spin in the middle of things. "I don't like her."

Landon grinned as he cocked his head to the side. "She has pizazz."

"Don't make me curse you," Aunt Tillie shot back. "I'm not above doing it."

"Can you make it the bacon curse?" Landon's eyes lit with anticipation.

"No, the bacon curse is a way to punish Bay. You need punishment."

"If you punish me that way I'll spend the entire day smelling myself," Landon admitted.

"You'll probably be doing a few other things to yourself, too, since you're a pervert," Aunt Tillie said darkly. "Why is she still babbling?"

At the center of it all, Hazel raised her hands to the sky as she exalted the Goddess, and then she announced, "Clove Winchester, would you please join me?"

I started forward on instinct as Landon held out his hand to stop me.

"What are you doing?" he whispered, confused. "You're not Clove."

"Yeah, but ... what is she doing?"

"Let's watch and find out."

That was easy for him to say. He was comfortable with the ritual, amused even. I didn't like this most recent part one little bit. "But ... ." I frowned as Clove reluctantly approached Hazel from the other side of the square. She'd been standing with Thistle, happy to be outside of the circle. Now she was directly in its center.

I caught Thistle's eye and it was obvious she was as annoyed with the change of events as I was. "We should get Clove out of this," I suggested.

"Oh, when it's Clove you want to do something," Aunt Tillie sneered. "When Hazel was bothering me it was all, 'Shut up and suck it up.'"

"I'm pretty sure that's not how I phrased it."

"And yet that's what I heard. Go figure."

"You are an absolute delight," I muttered, shaking my head. "I mean ... an absolute delight."

"Shh." Landon pressed his finger to his lips to admonish us. "I'm trying to listen. This is obviously a big deal. I mean ... she's wearing robes. That's straight out of Harry Potter."

It took everything I had not to laugh, even as worry continued to scratch at the back of my brain. Clove nearly trembled as Hazel drew her into the circle.

"My sisters — and several brothers — I bring you good tidings," Hazel announced, causing my stomach to squeeze. "New life calls to us on the threshold of tomorrow and it wants us to bless the path ahead."

Oh, well, crud on a cracker. "Son of a ... !" I swore viciously under my breath as Landon slid me a sidelong look.

"Wow. How do you really feel?" he asked.

"I really feel Clove doesn't want to be the center of attention ... at least not for this."

"Well, is there anything you can do about it?"

"No, but that doesn't mean I have to be happy about it."

"Fair enough." He held up his hands. "I wasn't trying to annoy you or anything."

And yet he'd managed to carry it out with minimum effort. How awesome for him. I kept my snarky comments to myself and focused on Clove. "If I don't like this, I'm shutting it down," I announced. "You've been warned."

Landon was confused. "Why wouldn't you like this?"

"Because Hazel is the Devil and the Devil is evil," Aunt Tillie automatically answered for me. "We don't want her touching our baby."

Landon's forehead wrinkled. "Am I missing something?"

"Oh, all manner of things," Aunt Tillie muttered. "It's too late to fix that now, though. You're the pretty sort who gets through life on his looks. You're not expected to use your brain."

"And I'm done talking to you," Landon groused, his expression narrowing. "I don't know why I put up with this abuse."

"Because you're addicted to me," I replied, my eyes never leaving Clove. She looked a nervous wreck.

"I *am* addicted to you," Landon confirmed, grinning. "That was a really good answer."

"Yeah, yeah. We'll play your special bacon game later. Right now, I want to focus on this."

"I'll make you sizzle with desire," he whispered, using his most seductive voice.

Honestly, my nerves were so heightened that it didn't do a thing for me. "Sure. I'll roll around and pretend I'm sizzling. Whatever you want."

Landon's smile slipped. "You're not playing the game right."

"That's because this isn't a game." I lost my temper and glared at him. "This is my cousin, who is pregnant and afraid. She's been called out in front of everyone, and it's not okay."

Landon's expression was hard to read as he looked me up and down. "Are Clove's nerves making you act crazy again? I mean ... I get it. For some reason, her pregnancy is causing her emotions to fly out of control. That's normal. What I don't get is how she's influencing you and Thistle."

Well, if I didn't want to strangle him before ... . Slowly, deliberately, I tracked my gaze to Aunt Tillie. The look on her face was a mixture of triumph and annoyance.

"I knew it!" She jabbed a finger in my direction. "I knew you were holding something else back."

Landon's expression fell. "Oh, crap. I thought all the secrets were out in the open."

"Not quite." I pressed the heel of my hand to my forehead and applied as much pressure as possible to ward off the oncoming headache. There had to be a way to shut this down ... or maybe that was just wishful thinking. "Aunt Tillie, we have everything under control. This isn't a big deal."

"No big deal! Your cousin is controlling your mind."

"Not our minds," I shot back. "She's controlling our emotions. There's a big difference."

"In what world?"

"In this one." I was determined to hold it together even though I could sense several interested parties turning their attention from the ritual to our argument. "We need to delay this until later. I need to focus on Clove. She's afraid."

Sympathy pooled off Landon as he rested his hand on my shoulder. Instead of being amused this time, he was grim. "If you want me to collect her, I will."

"I ... ."

"Collect her," Aunt Tillie ordered. "While you're up there, flash your badge and scream 'witch' a couple of times for good measure. That should go over swimmingly."

Landon glared. "You make me so tired."

"Right back at you."

I ran my tongue over my lips and debated my options. "Let's just wait it out. She might not do anything."

"What do you think she's going to do?" Landon asked.

"I don't … ." I really had no idea. It was Clove's fear fueling me. I hadn't considered it at the start — I was still getting used to our new reality — but once Landon suggested it, I realized that's what we were dealing with. The knowledge didn't put me at ease.

"I don't know. I just want to watch."

"Okay." He moved his hand to the back of my neck and rubbed. "She'll be okay."

My mind recognized that was true. Hazel would have to be an idiot to hurt Clove in the middle of such a huge group … and with Aunt Tillie ready to strike out at her. Clove's emotions were a minefield, though, and she couldn't control them. That meant I couldn't control them either. "I'm sure it will be fine."

Concern etched lines in Landon's face but he didn't say anything because Hazel was speaking again.

"Our lives revolve around various things, including resurgence," she offered. "We find our power in the rolling fields … and the twinkling stars … and the intertwining roots of our past and present. We are more than one thing. We are many things … and yet the source of our power comes down to the same thing: love."

At the last word, her expression softened and she dropped to her knees in front of Clove.

"The Winchesters will welcome a new life soon," she explained, her hands going to either side of Clove's belly.

"Oh, well, I don't like that." Aunt Tillie moved to storm across the clearing, but Landon snagged her by the back of the cape before she could get away from us.

"You stay here." He tugged her until she was settled in at his right, making sure he could grab her again should she decide to make a scene. "I want to see what happens … and I don't want you making things worse."

Aunt Tillie made a protesting sound with her tongue. "I don't make things worse. Not ever."

"Yeah, right."

I tuned out their banter and focused on Clove, who was unnaturally pale. I could see her hands shaking from here.

"This baby is the future of the Winchester clan," Hazel intoned. "The pecking order of the family will change. This baby will be the first of the new breed, the alpha."

Something niggled in the back of my brain and I frowned. "I didn't think about that," I muttered.

Landon was obviously curious. "What?"

"Clove's baby will be the new leader."

Landon frowned. "Why? Because she's the first one having a baby?"

"Yes."

"Isn't that assuming the three of you have only one baby each? What happens if you have three babies, Clove has three babies and Thistle has three babies? Will that mean three different circles?"

That was also something I hadn't thought about. "I don't know that I want three babies."

"We had three babies in the future."

"Yes, but that wasn't the real future." I scorched Aunt Tillie with a dark look. "I blame you for this. He's obsessed with those kids we saw in the future, and even though I've told him they're not real he won't listen."

"Who says they're not real?" Aunt Tillie challenged.

"Common sense. There's no way I would ever name a kid Sumac. It's simply not going to happen."

"The names might not be real, but that doesn't mean the kids won't be."

"Ugh." I pinched the bridge of my nose. "I can't even … ."

"I like the name Sage," Landon offered. "I think it's cute. Sage Michaels."

"Sage Winchester," Aunt Tillie corrected. "I don't know why you people insist on trying to change tradition."

"Oh, it's going to happen." Landon was firm. "Do you want to know why? I'll tell you."

I shut out what he was saying. I couldn't focus on it. Instead, I lifted my eyes to the sky as the telltale sound of birds assailed my ears. It was dark enough that I couldn't see them ... but I recognized they were coming.

"We need to get inside," I murmured, my full attention on the screeching as it started drowning out the rest of the conversation. They were growing closer at a fantastic rate. "We need to get inside right now."

"What?" Landon looked confused as he turned his eyes to me. "I'm arguing with Aunt Tillie. I'll get to you in a moment."

"Whatever. Take your argument inside." I gave them a solid push.

"What are you freaking out about?" Landon demanded.

"Can't you hear it?" I jabbed my finger toward the sky. "The birds are coming."

All the annoyance drained from Landon's face as he abandoned his argument with Aunt Tillie. "Get inside," he ordered, moving to grab me. "I'll get everyone else out of here. You need to run."

"I'm not going anywhere without Clove." I was firm as I stormed toward my cousin.

Hazel's expression was full of befuddlement as she turned to look at me. "What's going on, Bay? Nothing bad is happening here. I hope you know that."

I ignored her and grabbed Clove's arm. "Things are about to get very bad here. In fact ... ." Before I could lay out the problem, someone started screaming.

"Harbingers! We're under attack!"

I had no idea who uttered the words but it didn't matter. They were enough to send the gathered witches screaming ... and running.

On impulse, I closed the distance to Clove and covered her to protect from what was about to come. Thanks to the panicking women, there was no way we would be able to take cover before the birds reached us.

Thistle, clearly having the same idea, appeared on the other side of Clove. "We need to throw up a shield spell," she said grimly. "We haven't done that since that time we were kids and Aunt Tillie kept launching water balloons at us. This is a little direr."

She wasn't wrong. "I … ." When I lifted my head I found Landon joining us. "Get inside," I ordered. "You won't be a target as long as you're away from us."

"Shut up, Bay." He was firm. "We're doing this together. You can't get rid of me, so don't even try."

"What are we going to do?" Tears filled Clove's eyes, making my throat ache.

"We're going to … ." I wasn't sure at first, my mind a blank. Then I had an idea … and I was absolutely certain what we should do. "Hold on." I closed my eyes and extended my magic, the voice in my head bellowing in a deafening tone.

The birds arrived at the same moment as the ghosts I called. The undead spirits shimmered an unnatural color, almost green, and formed a circle around us. I didn't recognize any of the faces, but it didn't matter. This time I called to the freshly dead on purpose. They were to act as a shield and I would release them the moment I could. As far as I could tell, that was our only option.

Aunt Tillie beamed when she glanced around the circle, pushing between Thistle and Clove so she could add her magic to the mix. "This is awesome."

"What is that?" Landon's mouth opened as he glanced around, his eyes wide. "Are those … ?" He didn't finish the question. Apparently he couldn't.

"You can see them?"

He nodded, his hand moving to grip mine. "What are they doing?"

"Protecting us."

"Will it work?"

"We're about to find out."

He moved his arm over my head as the birds zeroed in on us. I heard the other witches screaming as they fled. I had no idea if they were under physical attack or simply freaking out. There was nothing I could do for them, so I focused on the problem at hand.

"Stay close," I instructed. "This could get hairy. I … ."

The birds struck the ghosts and drowned out the rest of what I was going to say. Even though I was convinced I'd done everything I could, there was a chance they could fly through the ethereal circle. Instead they bounced off the ghosts, as if repelled by some unseen wall. As they pinged back, the birds spiraled out of the square and back toward the sky.

"How is that happening?" Aunt Tillie asked, obviously confused.

"One guess," Thistle said grimly, inclining her chin toward the space behind us.

There, our mothers stood in a line, their hands clasped. They chanted at the birds as they attacked, never once ducking or moving to protect themselves.

"We need to pool our magic," Aunt Tillie ordered. "We can take them all down if we work together."

That made sense, but I wasn't sure we could carry it out. "Let's do this. I'm sick to death of these birds."

"We all are," Landon agreed, his eyes still on the ghosts. He looked absolutely entranced. "This is amazing, Bay."

"No, what's amazing is what is still to come. Hold it together. This is going to be loud and bright."

"I'm with you." He moved his eyes to me. "Forever. Do your thing. I'll be right here."

And, because he was, I managed to tamp down my anxiety and release enough magic to cause a small explosion of feathers. It was going to work. It had to.

TWENTY-TWO

The magic of five witches — and one determined FBI agent — turned out to be the stuff of legends. When funneled through Aunt Tillie, who was apparently not a big bird fan, the energy we created was enough that the ghosts went on a tear and started shredding through the birds. We didn't kill them, mind you, but despite being controlled by another, the birds still cared more about self-preservation than they did attacking us.

Once we finished and the birds had fled, Landon made a big show of wiping his brow. "Whew. That was something, huh?"

Mom shot him a fond look. "It was," she agreed. "It was definitely something."

I rubbed my forehead and wondered if I would end up with a magic hangover before remembering Clove. When I turned my attention to her, she looked fine, serene even. "Are you okay?"

She nodded without hesitation. "I am. I knew the second we all joined together that those birds were toast."

I smiled because I could feel the confidence coursing through her. Apparently this empathic thing she had going for her covered more than just negative emotions. "We're pretty tough," I agreed, blowing out a sigh.

"I think we're the only tough ones," Thistle noted, her gaze dark as it moved around the now empty town square. "Everyone else scattered, leaving us to clean up the mess."

"What did you expect?" Aunt Tillie challenged. "I know you all look at Hazel as if she's some wonderful witch, but she's a big nothing. She wants to be queen, but everybody knows I'm the queen."

"You're not the one who controlled the ghosts," Landon pointed out. "That was Bay. I think she's queen for the day, especially since the ghosts scared off the birds."

Speaking of that ... . I glanced around to make sure none of the ghosts remained. I'd freed them the moment the birds dispersed because I didn't want them to undergo even one extra moment of emotional torture. It looked as if they'd all scattered the moment I released them.

"I aimed the spell," Aunt Tillie argued.

"Bay supplied the power." Landon refused to back down. "She gets to be the queen today. My big, bacon-y queen."

I shook my head. I could practically see the image dancing through his mind, and it was filthy. "Yes, I'm the queen. It doesn't really matter who controlled the spell. What matters is that we're okay ... and these birds are getting out of control."

"It's Lorna." Aunt Tillie was certain. "We need to take her out."

I balked. "We can't take her out without proof."

"What more proof do you need? Her mother was a dark witch. People around her keep dying. Let's smite her and call it a day. The wedding is tomorrow. We need to get this out of the way before Clove walks down the aisle. It's happening during the sunset solstice ceremony for a reason. We're only going to get one shot at making the ritual perfect."

At my core, I understood that, but I wasn't going to sacrifice Lorna just because Aunt Tillie had a hankering. That's not the way I operated. "We'll have time to figure it out in the morning. As for tonight, I think we'd all do better with a good night's sleep."

"I agree." Mom bobbed her head, her expression leaving little room for debate. "We'll regroup in the morning."

"That sounds like a plan." Thistle turned her gaze toward the end of town where the converted barn she shared with Marcus was located. "I'm heading home. I'll talk to you guys tomorrow." She made to start out, but Clove cleared her throat. "What?"

"You're not spending the night at your place. You're spending it at the Dandridge with me. It's already been decided."

I stilled. Uh-oh. "Wait ... ."

"Oh, yes." Clove was adamant as she nodded emphatically. "You, too. You both agreed to spend the night before my wedding with me. We're going to make chocolate martinis and reminisce ... and talk about the future. I can't have any alcohol, but I can still watch you two get tipsy."

Landon slanted his eyes toward me. "You're spending the night with Clove?"

I'd forgotten about it. It didn't seem like such a hardship when she first raised the idea. Now, though ... . "I'm sorry." I couldn't back out. It wouldn't be fair to Clove. She asked very little of us. "I know we had plans, but I promised."

"No, no, no." Landon's handsome face twisted into an exaggerated pout. "You promised me bacon games."

"I know, but ... I promised Clove first."

"Ugh!" Landon glared at Clove. "How does Sam feel about having to share in a sleepover? I'm sure he would prefer Thistle and Bay spend the night in their respective beds."

Clove was having none of it. "He's booked at the Dragonfly," she said, referring to the inn our fathers owned. "This has been planned for weeks. We're not supposed to spend the night together before the wedding. It's bad luck."

"We were just attacked by a flock of angry birds," Landon pointed out. "I think that's our bad luck for the night."

"I don't care." Clove folded her arms over her chest. "I want to spend the night with Bay and Thistle like we used to. This will be our last chance to ... do anything that doesn't involve toting around a baby. I'm going to be left out after that."

My heart went out to her. In truth, no matter how hard we tried to include her, our lives were about to inexplicably change. There was no getting around that. "Clove is right." I was firm when I pinned Landon with a quelling look. "We're spending the night together. I'll make it up to you tomorrow night ... after she's left on her honeymoon and we're both drunk because this bird disaster is behind us."

He didn't look convinced. "This sucks. I don't want to sleep alone."

"Maybe Aunt Tillie will loan you Peg."

I meant it as a joke, but he brightened considerably. "Yeah." He swiveled to Aunt Tillie. "Can I have Peg?"

She nodded. "Sure. I would hate for you to cry or something because you can't be alone. I'll loan her to you so we don't have to watch you fall apart. A grown man crying over sleeping alone is pathetic."

Landon ignored the dig. "Okay. I'm fine with this. Have fun." He gave me an absent kiss before separating. "I'll see you in the morning, sweetie ... I'm going to pick Peg up at the inn."

My mouth dropped open as he practically skipped away. "Well, I guess I know where I rank."

Mom unsuccessfully attempted to smother a chuckle. "There, there." She lightly patted my arm. "Think of it as a dry run for when you have children and you're not the most important person in each other's lives."

That didn't make me feel better. "I definitely need a chocolate martini."

"You and me both," Thistle added. "This has been a crazy night."

And it was likely to get crazier.

WE SETTLED IN AT THE DANDRIDGE, slipping into pajamas Clove supplied. They were new, a gift she'd purchased for us, and we all matched. The look on Thistle's face when she realized we were in identical pink pajama sets was worth the entire ordeal ... and so was the photo I snapped when she wasn't looking. It would make good blackmail material for years to come.

Thistle and I each indulged in two chocolate martinis, but that was the limit. We wanted to be well-rested for the next day, especially if we would have to engage in a fight. Clove insisted we all sleep together in the living room — she claimed the couch, leaving the floor for Thistle and me — but we didn't argue.

The martinis hit me harder than I expected. My eyes were so heavy I could barely keep them open as I slid into my sleeping bag on the floor. I dreamed almost instantly … and it was beyond odd. In the dream, Aunt Tillie was in the room with us and she carefully picked her way through the mess on the floor until she was next to Clove. She placed her hand on our cousin's head and then muttered a spell I didn't recognize.

"Happy wedding," she whispered before total blackness overcame me.

After a brief respite, the dreams came fast and furious.

There was the time we got Sugar for Christmas.

I stilled. "I … who are you?" I had trouble putting a real face with the voice and beard. "I know you."

"Of course you know me," the man said. "I'm Santa Claus! You don't believe in Santa Claus, though, do you?"

"No … yes … maybe … ." I didn't know how to answer. "If you're Santa Claus, did you bring me a gift?"

"I did."

"What is it?"

"You can't have it until I'm sure you believe in me. Those are the rules."

I narrowed my eyes. "Who makes these rules?"

"My elves."

"Aren't you the boss of your elves?"

"I'm not the boss of anyone. It seems everyone tells me what to do and I do it."

"That doesn't seem like a very good job," I said.

"It's the best job in the world," he countered. "I'm Santa Claus. I bring joy to the world, even if you don't believe in me."

"Maybe I do believe in you. I … ."

"If you believe in me, you have to say it."

"I believe in you," I mumbled.

"I can't hear you."

"She said she believes in you," Clove yelled.

"Thank you, Clove," he said. I knew now, in the dream world, that it was Chief Terry. Back then I didn't recognize him completely. "I know you believe. Your present will come as soon as Bay tells me she believes."

It was the moment of truth. I knew it. Everyone in town knew it. Now I only had to admit it.

"Fine," I said, crossing my arms over my chest. "I believe in Santa Claus."

"I still can't hear you," Terry said, staring me down. "You need to say it louder!"

"I believe in Santa Claus!" I practically screamed the words and Terry broke into a huge grin.

"That's better," he said, leaning over and rummaging in the bag at his feet. When he turned around, he held a puppy. The black menace had a huge bow tied around its neck and it wriggled crazily.

My eyes widened and my heart leapt as I took another step forward. "Is that for me?"

"That's for you, Clove and Thistle."

Tears threatened to overwhelm me. "Thank you."

"You have to take care of him. You girls have to feed him and walk him and love him. Do you think you're up to the task?"

"You bet we are," Clove said, rushing to my side to pet the puppy. "Wow!"

"How did you know to get us a puppy?" I asked.

"One of my elves told me."

"How did the elf know?"

"Your Aunt Tillie has a huge mouth," Terry replied, smiling at me one more time before turning his attention to the rest of the children. "Who wants presents?"

. . .

And the time we told Clove that Bigfoot was haunting the area around the Dandridge when we were spying on Sam.

Clove hadn't stopped whining since we'd left Hypnotic and the sound of her voice was starting to mentally chafe.

"This isn't hiking," Thistle grumbled. "This is walking from the car to the lighthouse. It's, like, half a mile."

"That's hiking," Clove complained.

"Hiking is climbing up a mountain or traversing the wild terrain of Alaska," Thistle countered. "A half a mile is not hiking."

"'Traversing the wild terrain'?" I raised an eyebrow as I glanced at her.

"I was watching Finding Bigfoot the other night," Thistle replied absently. "They're a little dramatic."

"That's something we should do," I said. "Look for Bigfoot."

"We would be awesome at that," Thistle agreed.

"Camping in the great outdoors, following tracks – it sounds fun," I laughed. "We would need to bring Aunt Tillie. Even Bigfoot would be afraid of her."

"We would definitely bring Aunt Tillie," Thistle agreed. "If she didn't scare off Bigfoot, at least she'd be slow enough to distract him while we got away."

"Bigfoot isn't real," Clove interjected knowingly.

"That's what people say about witches," Thistle replied.

"Bay, you don't think Bigfoot is real, do you?" Clove was now scanning the tree line worriedly, despite her bravado.

"I don't know," I replied truthfully. "Most of those old legends have some basis in fact. Bigfoot was sighted in this area for more than a century, if you believe the old stories."

"And that song," Thistle added. "What was it called? The Legend of the Dogman?"

"I remember that," Clove said suddenly. "It was a big deal when we were kids."

"It was just a radio gimmick," Thistle scoffed. "Every seven years or so they bring it back. Every group of kids thinks they're the first to hear it."

"But it's not true," Clove said, her eyes skittering warily around the dense foliage that surrounded us. "Right? It's not true?"

I glanced at Thistle, who wasn't even trying to hide the evil expression gracing her face. I had a feeling a plan was forming and the next solstice celebration was going to be a full-on Bigfoot extravaganza – just to torture Clove.

"I think you're safe," I replied. "If Bigfoot is real, he's probably more scared of us than we are of him."

"I doubt that," Clove said nervously.

"Don't worry, we'll protect you," Thistle teased.

There was the time we all worked together to save Clove from the man she'd dated before Sam, an individual who shook her faith in love. We created a wind monster that day that looked a lot like our dearly-departed Uncle Calvin. Landon was there. That's when he realized what we were.

"I'm the one in charge here," Trevor said angrily, worry on his face. "I'm the one with the knife."

"We don't need a knife," I said calmly.

"I call the winds of the north," Clove sang out from the far left, reaching her hand out to grasp Aunt Tillie's waiting hand. "Let's show Trevor here what he's worth."

"I call to the magic of the east," Thistle chanted from my right, reaching her left hand out to grasp my right hand. "This will let us punish this beast."

I gripped Thistle's hand harshly. "I call to the wardens of the west," I started. "For they always find what's best."

"What is this?" Trevor looked baffled. "Are you chanting? What are you guys? Witches?"

I felt my hand slip into Aunt Tillie's, unsure how this would end and curious at the same time.

"And I call on the power of the south," Aunt Tillie said, her eyes gleaming with rage. "Let's show this lout how to close his big mouth."

It wasn't our best rhyme, to be sure, but it was effective.

Nothing happened right away, and Trevor looked triumphant in the moment. Then the power surged.

"So mote it be."

I didn't have to look behind me to know that my mother and aunts had joined hands behind us, pushing their power into our spell to tip it over the edge.

The energy in the room exploded. There was another force present now, and it was bearing down on Trevor.

I don't know what he saw with that first glimpse, but the fear that washed over his face was more than enough to tell me not to look behind me.

There was a sudden roar and the wind spell that we'd conjured moved through us with such force it threatened to wrench my arm from Aunt Tillie's grasp. I didn't let it, though. I knew that our joined hands were driving the spell.

I risked a glance to my left and saw the monster move forward. The wind whipped through the room, driving my hair in front of my eyes. For a second, just a second, I recognized the figure in the wind – or at least I thought I did. I didn't have time to focus on that, though, because our spell was descending on Trevor – who was making a mad dash to flee from the room.

The wind monster reached out – yes, it had arms, though I had no idea where they had come from – and the ethereal fingers of death now had hold of Trevor. He tried in vain to stab the monster. You can't stab the wind.

Trevor's screams were more pitiful than anything else as the wind monster engulfed him. "Help! Please, God, help me!"

"There's no help for you here, Trevor," Aunt Tillie said coldly. "I'm the god here, and I want you out of my house!"

Trevor screamed again. I couldn't see his face. I didn't want to. The mewling sounds now emitting from his ravaged throat were enough for me to know that his face would be worse. However bad he was, however terrible he was, I didn't want to see this. But I couldn't look away.

"Holy shit!"

We hadn't heard the office door open. I swung in surprise when I heard the new voice and met Landon's stunned gaze from across the room. I let go of Aunt Tillie's hand. Thistle and Clove did the same.

The wind monster dissipated as quickly as it had formed. Within seconds, the room was empty, and Trevor was unconscious on the floor.

Landon stepped into the room, weapon drawn. He kicked Trevor with his foot and then turned to us anxiously.

"Is he dead?"

"No," Aunt Tillie said fitfully. "He only wishes he were."

Landon turned to me, sweat washing down his face. His eyes flashed in recognition and intensity. I don't know what I expected: questions, recriminations, outright denial? What Landon said, though, is something I'll never forget.

"Good job, ladies. Good job."

There were silly memories that involved threats to eat dirt.

There were heavy memories, like when Clove needed emotional bolstering.

There were also empowering memories ... and those were my favorite.

They cascaded one after the other for the entire night. My sleep was heavy even though my brain was busy. I might never admit it to Clove, but this was a really good idea. We needed the time together to re-forge bonds that could never be truly broken.

It was a good night.

TWENTY-THREE

I woke feeling rested, relaxed and a bit weepy. I found Thistle already awake and staring at me.

"Aunt Tillie," I said.

Thistle nodded. "She put us under a sleep spell. I thought it was weird that I passed out after two drinks. And I swear I thought I saw her when I was struggling to stay awake. Then ... after all those dreams ... I knew."

"Me, too." I glanced at Clove and found her still sleeping. "Do you think we should tell her?"

Thistle shook her head. "Let her figure it out herself. It was a wedding gift for her, after all."

That was true. "She'll be the most well-rested bride ever. She got a full night's sleep before her wedding, wasn't overtaken by nerves and had some pretty funny dreams."

"It was a gift for all of us," Thistle said whimsically before her lips curved into a frown. "I hate that old bat. She only did this to drive me crazy."

I arched an amused eyebrow. "You just said it was a beautiful gift."

"I didn't use that word." Thistle gripped her sleeping bag in her fists. "I hate it when she does things that make me like her."

I knew better. Thistle was all bravado and brashness. She loved Aunt Tillie as much as the rest of us. Sure, Aunt Tillie drove us all crazy, but she was still lovable ... deep, deep down.

"Well ... ." I was going to suggest we get up and shower so we could head out for breakfast when my phone started vibrating. I'd turned it to silent the previous night to make sure it didn't alert and wake Clove. I recognized Landon's number and smiled. "Did you miss me?"

"You have no idea." He sounded tired, as if he hadn't slept a wink. "By the way, Aunt Tillie is on my list. Yeah, you heard me. *My* list. I'm going to curse her into oblivion."

I was amused despite the early hour. "What did she do?"

"Do you know that Peg is up every two hours because she has to go outside? Did you know she squeals if you try to ignore her?"

"I didn't know that."

"Well, it's true ... and I'm annoyed."

I had to laugh. "Well ... I'm sorry your adventures with Peg weren't up to your lofty standards. I'm sure that was a disappointment."

The good news for both of us was that Peg interrupting his beauty sleep would give me a bit of breathing room before we had to tackle the dog issue. If we could make it through the summer that would be best for all concerned.

"It wasn't just Peg. I missed you."

He sounded morose, which gave me a small rush. "I missed you, too."

"I know we used to sleep apart a couple days a week, but I've become spoiled. I can't sleep without you snoring away next to me."

My smile slipped. "I don't snore."

"I missed the drool on my chest, too. Of course ... Peg drooled on my face so I wasn't completely drool-free."

"You let her in our bed?"

"It's not like it was a woman. It was the only way she would settle down. I think Aunt Tillie has spoiled her."

"I think you've spoiled her."

"Either way, I'm about to take her out again and then hop in the shower. Will you be back in time for breakfast?"

"Actually, I was hoping you would meet me in town for breakfast."

"Really?" He sounded surprised.

"I'm sure my mother and aunts will be overbearing with the wedding preparations, and I need to focus on our witch issue. Besides, before breakfast I thought we might interview Masterson."

There was silence on the other end of the call so long I thought I might've lost him. "Landon?"

"I'm here," he managed, although he didn't sound thrilled. "We can't interview Masterson without going through his attorney. I told you he called Steve and arranged for special treatment. We've been playing phone tag with his lawyer ever since. I'm pretty sure he's avoiding our calls."

I frowned. I had forgotten that little detail. "Okay, that applies to you and Chief Terry. It doesn't apply to me. We'll adjust our breakfast plans. I'll head to Masterson's place and meet you at the diner when I'm finished."

Landon balked. "I don't like that idea, Bay. What if he's our murderer?"

"Then I'll make sure he's well aware that you know where I am. I'll drop that in the conversation right away. He would have to be an idiot to trust me. Besides ... I don't think he's our guilty party. We're looking for a witch."

"I hate to be the one chastising you for being sexist, but men can be witches ... or warlocks ... or whatever a male witch is. You pointed that out one day when you claimed I was being sexist."

I hated that he had a point. "True. I don't think it's him, though. Why would he kill Adam?"

"Because he wanted Lorna for himself."

"Except by all accounts, Lorna and Adam were going to divorce in two years. Masterson seems to have a wandering eye. I don't think he's putting you guys off because he's guilty. I think he's putting you off to protect his reputation.

"My guess is that he's not in love with Lorna," I continued. "He was with two witches at the festival the other day – the one with the weird

Wizard of Oz name and another one I didn't recognize – and he was looking down their shirts. That's not a man in love."

"I hate to break it to you, Bay, but even men in love can be pigs."

"Are you saying you look down other women's shirts?"

"Of course not. I'm the sort of guy who only looks down one woman's shirt. That happens to be you ... and we're both happy with that scenario. Other guys don't have the same fidelity. Besides, you said yourself that you didn't question Lorna about her relationship with Masterson because you felt uncomfortable. Maybe it's not all that serious."

Ah, crap. He had another point. "I guess that's fair. I still don't think he's our guy."

"But you think Lorna is our gal."

"It makes sense," I admitted. "Her mother was reportedly a witch who died under mysterious circumstances. Her sister disappeared, and supposedly the mother preferred the sister. We saw the birds circling Lorna."

"I can hear a 'but' in there somewhere."

"But I'm not sure my gut believes Lorna is guilty," I admitted. "I need more information. Masterson is the logical next step."

"I don't know that I like you going there alone. Maybe you can question him and I'll sit outside."

"You've been warned to stay away," I reminded him. "If you go there you could be risking a formal reprimand at work."

"Maybe I don't care."

"You care." We both knew that to be true. "You just got that promotion so you could move in with me. What if your boss changes his mind because of this and tries to make you move? Then we're going to be in trouble."

"Then I'll quit."

I snorted. "You love that job."

"I love you more."

"It's far more likely that we'll do what you originally suggested and find a place to rent between the two locations. That will put off your plans to develop the campground property, because that's too far to commute daily."

He let loose a resigned sigh and I knew I had him. "Fine. I'll be at the diner. Make sure he knows I'm aware of where you are. If he lays a hand on you ... ."

"You do know that I've been taking care of myself for a long time, right?"

"I do. We're a unit, though. It's my job to beat up anyone who threatens you."

"Fair enough. At breakfast, we can talk about this looking down women's shirts thing. It sounds fascinating."

"Ugh. I just don't know when to keep my mouth shut."

"Oh, you're officially part of the family. That's a common problem with Winchesters."

"I've noticed. Don't spend too much time at Masterson's house. Ask your questions and get out. I don't know that I trust him."

That made two of us.

THISTLE VOLUNTEERED TO accompany me to Masterson's house, but I insisted she stay with Clove. Our cousin was bound to be a bundle of nerves when she woke — it was her wedding day, after all, and she'd been dreaming about it for years — and it would've been wrong to leave her to her own devices.

Thistle being Thistle was suspicious, of course, but could hardly argue. She was still griping about my escape an hour later when I slipped out the front door, Clove still snoozing.

Masterson's house was on the east side of town. It wasn't the ritziest section of Hemlock Cove, but it was hardly rundown. All the homes had perfectly manicured lawns and up-to-date siding. There was no garbage littering the grassy green expanses — an edict strictly enforced because of the importance of tourism — and all the vehicles parked in the driveways and on the streets were relatively new.

I parked in front of the house, making sure my car was visible, and then sprang up the front walk. There was no sense delaying this interview. I should've tracked him down and cornered him days ago.

I knocked twice and waited for someone to answer. Masterson lived alone — at least to my knowledge — and I doubted that Lorna was feeling up to overnight visits. At the very least, that would've looked bad to anyone who witnessed them engaging in a tryst so soon after Adam's death. That didn't mean Masterson didn't have another woman on the side, but I was willing to bet he was trying to lay low these days.

After another round of knocking I shifted my gaze to the driveway. His Range Rover was parked in front of the garage door. It was always possible he'd looked through the peephole and decided not to answer when he realized it was me. That didn't mean I was going to let him get away without grilling him.

I cut around the side of the house. I figured if I could catch his eye in a window he would have no choice but to at least shut me down to my face. When I reached the back of the house, I had to shield my eyes from the glare of the sun to see inside the sliding glass doors.

What I found there took my breath away.

Masterson was dead. I didn't have to break into the house to confirm that. He was sitting in a chair at the end of the rectangular table, his sightless eyes focused on me. Or, well, they would be focused on me if they were still in the sockets. They were missing, as if pecked out, and there were feathers from one end of the kitchen to the other.

He appeared to have a plate in front of him, what looked like a steak and potatoes on display. He hadn't eaten much before it happened because there was plenty left. Blood ran down his cheeks and his mouth was opened in a silent scream.

I fumbled for my phone and almost dropped it before recovering. My hands were still shaking when I found Landon's name on my contact list. He answered on the first ring.

"Did you change your mind about interviewing Masterson?"

The first time I tried to speak, nothing came out. The second, my voice was shrill. "I need you to come over here."

All traces of mirth left Landon's voice. "What is it, Bay?"

"It's Masterson. He's dead and ... it's not good. I need you to come here right now. I ... need ... you ... ."

"I'm coming, baby." There was strength in his tone as he reassured me. "Don't touch anything. I'll be right there."

CHIEF TERRY WAS THE FIRST to arrive. Landon had called him. He found me sitting on the back patio staring at my shoes.

"Are you okay?" He was the picture of concern as he closed in on me.

I nodded.

"Bay, look at me." His voice was gentle, as was the finger he placed at the bottom of my chin to tilt it up. "What happened?"

"I came to interview him," I replied woodenly.

"I know that. Landon called."

"He didn't answer the door."

"So you broke in?"

I sensed a lecture in my future and immediately started shaking my head. "I didn't break in. I didn't have to." I pointed toward the sliding glass doors. "He's kind of hard to miss."

Chief Terry kept his gaze on me for an extended moment and then looked in that direction, viciously swearing under his breath when he saw Masterson's body. "Well, that's just great."

I swallowed hard. "I haven't been inside. I didn't touch anything. You don't have to call me an idiot again."

He cast me a sidelong look. "You're not an idiot and I'm sorry if what I said after the fire hurt your feelings. You do occasionally do idiotic things, but you're a good girl for the most part. You're smart, too."

"Thanks."

"I still kind of want to shake you."

"I'm sure Landon will feel the same way when he gets here."

As if on cue, Landon appeared on this side of the hedge. He didn't even glance at Chief Terry before rushing to me. He dropped to his knees and gently pushed my hair out of my face. "Tell me you're okay."

"I'm fine." I felt stronger now. The initial vision of the body had shaken me, but I was starting to come back to reality. "I just ... it's bad."

"I'm sure it is." He pressed a kiss to my forehead and then turned to join Chief Terry. "Well ... holy bird feathers. That is ... really gross."

Chief Terry's stare was withering. "Is that your professional law enforcement opinion?"

"Pretty much."

"I hate to say it, but I agree with you."

"Do we think birds actually killed him?" Landon started for the door, slipping on a pair of rubber gloves as he went. "I mean ... that can't be the best way to go."

"I would say that's the absolute worst way to go," Chief Terry agreed.

"I still think sharks would be worse," I muttered.

Landon shot me a small smile, but it was muted. He was already on the case. "We need to get in there."

"I've already called the medical examiner," Chief Terry volunteered. "Let's take a look at what we've got first."

I remained where I was. They didn't need me mucking up the scene. Besides, I'd already seen everything I needed to see. After twenty minutes, they returned.

"The only marks on his body are from where his eyes were plucked out," Chief Terry explained. "I don't know if that's enough to kill a man. I mean ... if you believe horror movies, it's not."

"The medical examiner should be able to tell us," Landon noted.

"I don't think it was the eyes," I supplied.

"What do you think it was?" Landon looked genuinely curious. "It doesn't matter if you're right or wrong, just give me your best guess."

"I think it was a ritual. There was blood on his face. I'm willing to bet not much is found in his body."

"You think whoever did this took his blood?" Chief Terry was horrified. "I don't like the sound of that."

"I don't either," I admitted. "The thing is ... it makes sense. What happened to Adam was a brutal attack. Whoever killed him is feeling emboldened now. If he or she — and I'm leaning toward a she — is collecting blood, it has to be for a powerful spell."

"How do we find out?" Landon asked.

"I can think of only one way ... and you're not going to like it. Neither of you."

"Lay it on me all the same," Chief Terry instructed. "If you have a way to find answers, I want to hear it. We're running out of time before Clove's wedding. I want this handled before she walks down that aisle."

He wasn't the only one.

TWENTY-FOUR

The medical examiner, Dan Stevens, was prompt. He seemed as stymied by the scene as the rest of us.

"Did you find birds inside the house?" he asked, glancing around.

Chief Terry and Landon allowed me into the house as long as I promised to touch nothing, remain behind them and not draw attention to myself. I didn't want to get close to the body, so I was fine with that. Still, the second I walked through the sliding glass door I could feel the malevolent energy flowing through the room. The hate associated with it was staggering.

"There were no birds when we arrived," Chief Terry replied.

"What's she doing here?" Stevens inclined his head in my direction. "Is she a suspect?"

"No, she's not a suspect." Landon made a face. "She was here to interview Masterson. When he didn't answer the door, she walked to the back thinking he might be enjoying his coffee on the patio or something. That's when she saw him through the window."

As far as lies go, it was relatively smooth.

"What were you interviewing him about?"

"None of your business," Chief Terry answered for me. "She's not a suspect. When do you place the time of death?"

"I'm guessing sometime last night, probably around seven or eight o'clock."

"That would make sense since he died on top of his dinner," Landon mused. "Did you find anything but feathers? A dead bird anywhere?"

Stevens shook his head. "No, and I'm baffled." He focused on me. "Were the doors open when you arrived?"

"No. I wasn't even sure what I was seeing at first. The door was definitely shut."

"So how did the birds get inside?" Landon mused, more to himself than any of us.

That didn't stop Stevens from answering. "I figure that's your responsibility to answer," he said. "I'm just here to answer any questions you might have about the body."

"Okay, then answer a question," Chief Terry prodded. "Did losing his eyes kill him?"

"It's unlikely." Stevens lowered himself to stare at the body from below. "I've never seen anything like this. Birds are scavengers for the most part. I've seen bodies that birds have fed on, but all of that damage was done post-mortem. This is ... something else entirely."

That was putting it mildly.

"Would just losing the eyes be enough to kill him?" Chief Terry pressed.

"It shouldn't. It would have been horribly painful, but it shouldn't have killed him. What confuses me more is that there are no other marks on his body. If a bird attacks, would you just sit there and take it? He has no defensive wounds, no scratches ... so why was he just sitting there?"

I had a sneaking suspicion I knew why, but I couldn't volunteer my hunch in front of the medical examiner.

"I want to know how the birds got in and out," Chief Terry noted. "It's not as if they can open doors."

"Maybe someone has trained birds," Stevens suggested. "I've heard of stranger things."

"What have you heard that's stranger than trained birds attacking a guy eating a steak dinner?" I challenged.

Stevens merely shrugged. "The stories I could tell you."

"Some other time," Landon said dryly. "For now, we need to figure out where the birds came from and what killed him. I don't see much blood anywhere. There has to be another reason for his death."

"My guess would be some sort of poison," Stevens offered. "I'm far from an expert on birds, but for him to just sit there like that ... my guess is it wasn't that he didn't want to move. It was that he couldn't move."

A horrible notion crawled into my brain and took up residence. "Is it possible he was alive when this happened?"

"I guess it's possible," he shrugged. "He would have to have been injected with some sort of paralytic. I guess he could've ingested it in some way, but we won't know that until we note the contents of his stomach and look for injection sites."

"Make sure you look hard," Landon instructed. "Check between the toes and all that jazz."

"Do you have any idea who would want to do this?" Stevens asked. "This is a really weird death, even by Hemlock Cove standards."

"We're working on it," Chief Terry answered, pointing toward the door. "Make this your priority. The sooner we have answers, the better."

"I'm on it." Stevens mock-saluted. "This is the weirdest thing I've seen in years. I'm just as anxious for answers as you."

"I sincerely doubt it."

LANDON SECLUDED ME IN THE back corner of the yard.

"What are you going to do?"

On another day I might've actually feigned being upset by the question. Today, however, it seemed a wasted effort. "I'm going to gather Clove and Thistle — even though I wanted to keep Clove out of this — and head out to Hollow Creek."

Whatever answer he was expecting, that wasn't it. "Why?"

"Because I need to call some ghosts to me and that's the best place to do it. There are remnants of magic left out there from everything else that has happened. You heard the circus people. They could feel the energy."

"Yeah, but ... ."

"I also need to talk to them," I pointed out. "The ghosts, I mean. I need to do it in a place where people are unlikely to stumble across us. I'm taking Clove and Thistle so I won't be alone, which should appease you. We need answers."

Landon didn't look convinced. "It's not the ghosts I'm worried about," he admitted. "It's what you're going to do after you find the information you're looking for."

"I'm going to call you."

The look he shot me was dubious. "Please. If you find out who this witch is you're going to go after her alone. We both know it. You won't willingly put me at risk."

That was a fair point. "I won't purposely cut you out either. I'll at least tell you what's going on so we can deal with it together."

"Since when do you approach things that way?"

"I'm trying to grow here." I grinned at him. "We're a team, right? You're making a concerted effort to include me. I'll do the same."

He wasn't quite ready to let it go. "What do you expect to get out of this? You've pretty much decided it's Lorna."

"She makes the most sense," I agreed. "We need confirmation, though. We have a boatload of other witches in town. Maybe one of them is responsible."

"But Adam died the day before they arrived."

"He died the day before *most* of them arrived. Others were in the area. I remember Thistle mentioning it. None of them were staying at The Overlook, but if I was an evil witch visiting Hemlock Cove I wouldn't stay at The Overlook either."

Landon looked intrigued. "Why would a random witch attack the guy who owns the blacksmith shop?"

"That's what I intend to find out."

He blew out a sigh and dragged a hand through his hair. "Okay. Just keep me informed ... and be careful." He grabbed the front of my shirt and hauled me to my toes so he could plant a hot kiss on my lips. "I really did miss you last night."

I smiled. The naked emotion in his eyes was enough to warm me all over. "And I missed you. Although ... there's a funny story regarding Aunt Tillie I should tell you once we get a second alone to enjoy each other."

"Once we get a second alone to enjoy each other you're dressing up like bacon. That's all there is to it."

"Then after that."

"I can't wait to hear it." He stroked his hand down the back of my head and pressed a light kiss to my mouth. "I'll stick with this and see what we come up with. Maybe we'll have a meeting of the minds by noon and be able to put this behind us and enjoy the wedding."

"That would be nice."

"But you don't think it's going to happen."

"Oh, it's going to happen. Nothing is going to ruin Clove's day. Absolutely nothing."

"THIS IS STUPID."

Clove bitterly complained as she picked her way through the foliage separating the parking lot from the water at Hollow Creek.

"And here I thought you loved the great outdoors," Thistle drawled. "I'm shocked that you're not enjoying this."

"It's not about being outdoors ... although now I don't want to go anywhere that's not inside because I'm afraid birds will peck my eyes out." Clove wrinkled her ski-slope nose in dainty fashion. "Seriously, I could've lived my entire life without hearing that story, Bay."

"Hey. If I have to think about it, you have to think about it."

"Whatever." Clove wasn't happy when I'd returned to the

Dandridge to collect her and Thistle. She whined about wanting to stay behind and prepare for her wedding. I told her that was fine, that I would just take Thistle, and then I threatened I didn't want to hear a single word of complaint about being left out of our adventures. That was enough to change her mind. After all, we were just talking to ghosts. That was rarely dangerous.

"I still need to take a bath," Clove noted. "I got this special bath bomb that's supposed to make my skin as soft as dewy petals on a misty morning."

Thistle slowly slid her eyes to Clove. "I kind of want to punch you for actually uttering that sentence. I mean ... come on."

"You can't punch me." Clove extended a finger. "It's my wedding day. If you punch me, I'll send Aunt Tillie after you."

"And what makes you think she would care?"

"Because of the dreams she sent us. She cares."

"I didn't realize you were aware of what she did," I said as we arrived at the water's edge. "I thought maybe you were still in the dark."

"No. I knew when I woke up."

"She asked me about it," Thistle explained. "We were still talking about all the things she showed us when you called."

"With your horrible bird story," Clove added. "You know there are birds out here, right?"

"We don't have to worry about the birds." I was relatively certain that was true. "We're here to call Adam's ghost. Once we do that, you can head to The Overlook and start getting ready. I just didn't want to be alone for this."

"What are you going to do while we're at the inn?" Thistle asked, suspicion wrinkling her forehead. "Why aren't you coming with us?"

"I have to end this before the wedding."

"And you think Adam will tell you that Lorna is the one," Clove surmised. "Once he confirms it, you're going to head off to confront her."

"I don't know if I would phrase it that way, but that's basically it in a nutshell," I agreed. "If all goes as planned, this will be behind us in about two hours."

"From your lips to the Goddess's ears." Clove beamed as I focused on the water. "Let's get this over with. This is my wedding day. I'm supposed to be the center of attention, not an evil witch with a bird fetish."

"You'll be the center of attention no matter what," Thistle promised. "For the next few minutes, though, zip it." She ran her fingers over her lips for emphasis. "This is a serious situation and we don't need you spouting nonsense to distract us."

Clove lowered her head. "That's the meanest thing you've ever said to me."

"That's not even in the top hundred."

"Yes, but this is my wedding day. Everything is amplified. That means you're dead to me."

Thistle rolled her eyes until they landed on me. "Can you get this over with? I need to get back to the inn and start drinking."

There was something soothing about their banter. "Yeah, yeah, yeah. I'm on it." I raised my hands into the air, closing my eyes. I was getting better at calling ghosts.

When I first realized I could communicate with them I assumed they were in control of the interactions. That always left me feeling helpless, something I hated. Now, though, I understood I was in control. Sometimes I disliked the power at my disposal for entirely different reasons, but it was better this way.

When I opened my eyes, Adam's ghost was floating in front of me. He looked pained, as if he'd put up a fight – and lost – when I called to him. I couldn't help his discomfort. If all went as planned, he would be free to move on to the other side by the end of the day.

"I'm sorry I had to call you here like this," I started.

"Is he here?" Clove stared around blankly.

"No, Clove, she's talking to her imaginary friend," Thistle sneered. "Good grief."

Clove frowned. "It was just a simple question. There's no reason to be snarky."

"Hey, if I don't have snark to fall back on you might as well kill me now."

I admonished them both with a look and then focused on Adam. "I know you've been through an ordeal, but ... I need to talk to you. I freed you the other day. I'm not sure you remember. I made sure you could talk again."

It wasn't that I was expecting a "thank you" as much as I was trying to appeal to him. The look he shot me was anything but friendly.

"Saved me? Is that what you think you did?"

"Um ... yeah."

"He doesn't sound happy," Clove noted.

Thistle pinched her flank. "Shh. Let Bay talk to her ghost so we can get out of here. I bet they're drinking mimosas at the inn and we're missing out."

"I can't drink," Clove pointed out.

"That's your problem."

I ignored them both. I would've been better off doing this alone. "Your lips were sewn shut. I still don't know how that happened. I helped you break those chains."'

"You mean you forced me," Adam countered. "You made me rip that thread out. I didn't have a choice."

I was taken aback by his vitriol. "I don't understand. Are you saying you wanted to remain that way?"

"Of course not." Adam's expression was withering. "I didn't want any of this to happen. You're not some hero in this story. You made things worse."

I was taken aback. "Um ... ."

"Well, that's gratitude for you," Thistle said brightly. "I don't think he wanted you to free him from the shackles placed on him. Screw him. Let's go to the inn and drink mimosas."

That sounded preferable to what we had going on, but I was determined to get answers. "I need to know who killed you, Adam. I'm sure you don't want to dwell on it, but it's important. Once we have confirmation, we'll take her down and I'll send you on your way. It will be over relatively quickly."

"Are you an idiot?" Fury flared in the depths of Adam's ghostly eyes. "You can't free me. I'm tied to her forever. She told me that ... and I believe her."

"I can free you. I don't want to toot my own horn or anything, but I'm a necromancer."

Thistle shot me a sarcastic thumbs-up. "Way not to toot your own horn."

"I don't care what you are," Adam snapped. "You can't help me. You've made things worse. She's so angry now. Do you know what she's going to do? Do you have any idea who's next on her list? She won't stop."

"We'll stop her." I was firm. "You have nothing to worry about."

"That's easy for you to say."

"I can protect you from her." I was relatively assured of that. "Just tell me who did this. It was Lorna, right?"

"Ugh," Adam growled. "I can't answer your questions. Don't you understand? She's bound me to her. As long as she's alive, I'm trapped in this limbo. She won't have it any other way."

"I can break that tie."

"No, you can't."

"I can."

"No!" He practically screamed. "There's nothing you can do about this. It's done. It's ... over. I ... she's calling me again." He was grim. "She's demanding I go to her. Do you understand that she can force me to tell her about this? She'll know you're on to her. She'll kill you."

"I'll handle her," I promised. "This is almost over."

"It will never be over." With those words, he winked out of existence, leaving me with nothing but more questions.

"Well, that was helpful, huh?" Thistle clapped my shoulder. "We should get out of here. I can practically taste that mimosa."

Oddly enough, drinking was starting to feel like a feasible option.

TWENTY-FIVE

The mimosas were indeed flowing freely when we arrived at the inn. The schmaltzy lovefest you would expect before a wedding was not.

"You're late." Mom's expression was dark when it landed on me.

I was in no mood for her crap. "Why are you blaming this on me? There are three of us."

"You're the oldest. It's your job to get the others moving."

"Oh, well ... ."

"Leave her alone," Thistle ordered as she accepted the mimosa her mother handed her. "She's had a rough morning."

"Oh, geez." Mom rolled her eyes. "Are you going to whine like Landon about sleeping alone? I had to listen to him for twenty minutes this morning. It was ridiculous."

"He wasn't alone. He had Peg," I pointed out. "And, no, I survived the night without him just fine."

"Well, good for you." She absently patted my arm before sidling over to Clove. "It's your big day. Are you excited?"

"So excited." Clove started talking about her dress ... and her hair ... and the luxurious bath bomb she had stashed in her purse. She'd already moved on from Masterson's death and Adam's ghost. I was not that lucky.

I paced the kitchen, ignoring the mimosas my mother and aunts tried thrusting into my hand. I couldn't just let this go. We had hours until the sunset wedding. There was still time to work this out.

That's when I had an idea. "Where's Aunt Tillie?"

Mom's forehead creased and her expression darkened. "She's watching *The View*."

"And being a pain," Marnie added.

"When is she not a pain?" Thistle challenged. "Leave her in there. Mimosas are more fun without her."

"She's being a real pill," Mom complained. "She's got some weird vendetta against Hazel that I simply don't understand. She needs to let whatever grudge she's holding go. I can't even remember why she dislikes her."

"She hates her because Hazel wants to be in charge and everybody knows Aunt Tillie is in charge," I answered, making my decision on the spot. "I'll be back."

"Where are you going?" There was an edge to Mom's voice as it chased me. "You and Thistle are sharing maid of honor duties. There are things you are expected to do this afternoon."

"I'll be back." I escaped through the kitchen and into the family living quarters. Sure enough, Aunt Tillie was in her usual spot on the couch, Peg tucked in beside her, and she was yelling at the television.

"That's a load of crap," she exclaimed. "I can't believe they pay you idiots to spout your nonsense on television like this. I would be so much better."

I was used to the show, so I barely reacted. "You need to get dressed."

Slowly, Aunt Tillie tracked her eyes to me. "Excuse me?"

"You heard me." I was in no mood for her crap. "There's something I have to do, and because I can't do it alone you're coming with me."

Aunt Tillie didn't move from her perch. "Last time I checked, you weren't the boss of me. I'm the boss of you."

"It involves taking on an evil witch."

Aunt Tillie's eyes narrowed. "Hazel?"

Now I was the one who couldn't contain my eye roll. "No. She's a minor inconvenience. I'm talking about abject evil." I told her about Masterson's death, leaving nothing out. When I finished, she looked intrigued.

"Well, that is ... hmm." She stroked Peg's head as the pig stretched out beside her, obviously in heaven. "How did the birds get into the house?"

"Nobody knows. I don't even think that's important. What's important is that we have to end this before the wedding."

"Why? Do you think Lorna is going to take out someone else before tomorrow? If so, I can see going after her now. If not, we can wait. Once Clove is married and officially on her honeymoon, we can clean up the mess."

"I don't think that's going to be an option."

"Why?"

"Because Adam's ghost says he's being controlled by the witch who killed him. He couldn't even confirm it was Lorna. He made it sound as if he'll have to tell her we're on to her, which means she could send her evil feathered minions here."

"Well, with a suspect list of one I don't see that we need confirmation."

"I still want confirmation." I was firm on that. "I want to talk to her, lay everything out. If she denies it, we'll be able to tell that she's lying."

"You think she's going to admit it?"

"I think she wants to admit it," I clarified. "If you can do as much damage as she has in a few days' time, you want to take credit for it. She thinks she's stronger than us."

"You, maybe. She's not stronger than me."

I folded my arms over my chest and waited.

After holding my gaze for what felt like a really long time, she blew out a sigh and stood. "Fine. I'll go with you. I'm in the mood for a fight anyway. Your mother confiscated my scooter."

I would've been amused under different circumstances. "I can't believe you allowed that."

"I only allowed her to think she won. It's in the basement. I'll get it when I want it."

That sounded about right. "So ... you'll go with me?"

"I'll go with you. This witch needs to be put in her place."

"Then let's do this. I'm ready to enjoy Clove's big day."

"I'm ready to bug the crap out of Hazel. Different priorities, same outcome."

That was the only logical thing she was likely to say all day.

THE DRAPES WERE DRAWN TIGHT over the windows. Lorna didn't answer the door when we knocked. Her car was in the driveway, though, and I was certain she was home.

"I say we kick in the door A-Team-style and give her what for," Aunt Tillie announced. She was dressed for battle, combat helmet included, and her eyes were keen. She benefitted from a certain glow when a fight to the death was imminent.

"And I think we should knock again." I shot her a pointed look and made to rap on the door. It opened a split-second before I made contact, revealing Dani's curious face.

"Were you just knocking?" she asked. She looked confused.

"That would be us." I shifted from one foot to the other, suddenly uncomfortable. I didn't expect her to answer the door. "Is your mother here?"

"Yeah, she's just getting up." Dani pushed open the door so we could enter. "She's in the kitchen. I'm actually glad you're here. Maybe you can talk to her."

"What's wrong?" I was instantly alert, worry for Lorna's children bubbling up. "Is your brother all right? You look okay."

Dani arched a confused eyebrow. "I'm fine. My mother is the one falling apart. We're supposed to make plans for Dad's memorial service today, but she says she just wants to stay in bed. She thinks Nick and I should do it."

"By yourselves?" I was almost as offended by that suggestion as I was by the fact that Lorna was killing people. Hurting others was one thing. Emotionally abandoning her children in this manner was another. "Where are you headed?"

Dani clutched the over-sized purse she carried tighter. "To the funeral home. Nick doesn't want to go with me, so I guess I'm doing it myself."

I felt sorry for her ... and yet relieved. Dani wouldn't be in the house when we confronted her mother. "Where is Nick?"

She shrugged. "I don't know. He got a call from one of his friends earlier and seemed excited when he ran out. I don't know where he went."

"Excited happy or excited sad?"

"I don't know. Just excited."

I thought about the way Nick watched Masterson at the festival. I could guess which gossipy tidbit had garnered his attention. It was probably best that he was out of the house, too, even if he was being a ghoul.

"Well, I'll talk to your mother." I had zero expectations that Dani's life was suddenly going to improve, but I wanted to reassure her all the same. "I'll see if I can get through to her."

"That would be great." Dani sidled through the door, accidentally brushing against Aunt Tillie in such a way that she lost some color. "I'm sorry, Miss Tillie. I didn't mean to run into you. I know you hate being touched."

I cast Aunt Tillie a disdainful look. She was forever terrorizing the teenagers of Hemlock Cove. It was her way. "She's fine," I offered. "It was an accident. Don't worry about it."

"I'll give you a pass for today, but don't let it happen again," Aunt Tillie ordered. She offered Dani a wink before sliding in front of me. "As for your mother, we'll handle her. We have everything under control."

"I hope that's true. I don't think I can take much more of her."

After Dani left, I took the lead. I was more familiar with the house than Aunt Tillie. Dani had said her mother was in the kitchen, and that's where we found her.

Lorna looked rough. That was the only word I could use to describe her wan countenance. Her hair was greasy and piled in a messy bun. She wore the same pajamas she'd been in when I interviewed her for the article about Adam and there was a waxy texture to her face that didn't look entirely healthy.

"What do you want?" She looked despondent when she realized who was darkening her doorstep. "I told you everything I could for the story. Talk to other people if you need more."

"We're here to talk to you ... and not for a story," I countered. I gave the woman a wide berth as I circled the table and positioned myself opposite her. "Did you hear the news?"

Lorna's face was blank. "What news? I haven't had the television on. I've been ... busy."

Aunt Tillie leaned over so she was close enough to sniff Lorna – something I didn't think was safe – but I'd learned long ago that I had zero control over my tempestuous great-aunt. "It smells to me as if you've been busy drinking. And not the good stuff. That's bargain-basement whiskey if ever I've smelled it."

Lorna shot her a hateful look. "Well, if you don't like it you can always leave. In fact, I'm going to insist that you leave. I don't have the energy to put up with you right now. I'm expected at the funeral home to plan Adam's service, so I can't do ... whatever this is."

"We just ran into Dani," I argued. "She said she's dealing with the funeral arrangements."

The laugh Lorna let loose was hollow. "Of course she is."

"She said you insisted that she handle it," I added. "I know you're going through something, Lorna, but your children are struggling ... and badly. You need to step up for them." I was taking a circular route to my verbal assault.

"Well, if Dani said I told her to do it, then I did." Lorna leaned back in her chair, her eyes red-rimmed and puffy. "What do you want? I didn't invite you here. In fact, I don't want you here at all. I think you need to get out of my house."

"We're not leaving." I refused to back down and pinned her with my bossiest look. I learned it from my mother ... and Aunt Tillie ... and, well, Marnie and Twila. Actually, every woman in our family had a patented bossy look.

"I could make you leave," Lorna insisted. "I could call Chief Terry right now and have him haul you away."

"Good luck with that."

Lorna's expression was defiant for a full ten seconds ... and then her face crumbled. "What do you want?" She sounded exasperated, on the verge of tears. "I'm not joking when I say I'm in no condition to deal with whatever it is the two of you want. I'm at my limit."

I had trouble reconciling the woman I saw before me with the murderous witch I was picturing in my head. She was the only suspect, which meant she had to be a masterful actress. "Are you mourning Adam or Paul this morning?"

Confusion washed over Lorna's face. "I ... what do you mean?"

"Paul Masterson," I pressed. "He was found dead in his house this morning. It seems birds pecked his eyes out."

"What?" Lorna's eyes went wide. Yes, she was very good.

"No one knows how the birds got into his house. He was sitting in front of a steak and somehow the birds got in, ripped out his eyes and left him to die. I found him because I was going to question him about his relationship with you."

Lorna's hand flew to her mouth and the fright reflected back at me was heart-rending. Something was off about this situation ... other than the obvious, that is. "You're wrong. Paul isn't dead. I just talked to him on the phone last night.

"He said everything was going to be okay and not to worry about people finding out about our relationship," she continued. "He said he had Landon and Chief Terry in hand and they wouldn't be able to spread the information. I told him you knew, but he didn't seem worried that you would have the guts to print anything in the newspaper."

"I'm not generally a fan of salacious gossip," I countered. "I wouldn't print the details of your affair without reason."

"I'm guessing that Masterson's death is a good reason," Aunt Tillie noted. "I mean ... that's two men you've slept with who have died in the same week, Lorna. You're not having a good run of it, are you?"

"No. I ... ." She rubbed her forehead and then burst into tears. The torrent was so fierce I was caught off guard, forcing me to look to Aunt Tillie for guidance.

For her part, she looked equally perplexed. "Are you sure she's our evil witch?" she asked after watching Lorna's shoulders shake and her body convulse for a full thirty seconds. "She doesn't seem evil."

Oddly enough, I was having the same doubts.

"Witch?" Lorna sputtered, snot running down her lip. "You think I did this, don't you?"

I exhaled heavily and debated my options. Finally, I just went for it. We were out of time for subtlety. "Whoever is doing this is a witch. There's no doubt about that. We assumed because of your mother's background that you were the witch in question. Now, though ... ."

"If you're an evil witch, you should tell us now," Aunt Tillie commanded, her voice full of authority. "If you're not, we're genuinely sorry for your loss and hope you ascribe to the 'no blood, no foul' rule."

I wanted to sink under the table and hide. "Let's handle the witch question first," I suggested. "Are you controlling the birds?"

"No." She shook her head emphatically. "I don't understand why you would ask me a question like that."

"Before your husband's business exploded — something that has yet to be explained to my satisfaction — a flock of birds alerted over Hemlock Cove," I explained. "They're called harbingers."

"I know what harbingers are."

"Because your mother was a witch?"

Lorna nodded stiffly. "How did you figure that out?"

"It's common knowledge in certain circles. Some of the residents in Hemlock Cove have long memories."

Lorna's gaze moved to Aunt Tillie. "Like you? How long is your memory?"

"If you're asking whether I told her about your mother, I am ... to a certain extent," Aunt Tillie replied blithely. "It wasn't only me. There were others. I was always under the assumption that your mother was a witch for show and nothing more. If she had traces of the craft in her, they had to be minor. What's happening now isn't minor."

"It doesn't sound like it," Lorna agreed, a thoughtful wave washing over her twisted features. "My mother was a witch, but not the sort you're rumored to be. She didn't do evil things. I can promise you that."

"What about you? Do you do evil things?"

"Of course not."

"I saw you on a bench at the edge of the square the day after Adam died," I argued. "Birds were circling."

"They were? I don't remember that. I don't remember much about that night. I was drunk, if you want to know the truth. I've been drunk since Adam died."

"We can smell it," Aunt Tillie offered.

I pretended she hadn't spoken. "Birds attacked at the ritual last night, too. We managed to fight them off. Your mother died in a strange farm accident. Your sister went missing without a trace. All of those things put together make for a very dark story. I'm sorry, but ... I'm going to need more than your word that you're not a witch."

"Well, I don't have more than my word," she shot back. "My mother's death was suspicious to me, too, but there was no one else around. I have no proof it wasn't an accident. If I ever get proof, I'll go after the individual responsible. My mother was a good woman.

"As for my sister, well, Diane was always hard to contain," she continued. "She shared my mother's gift, though it seemed to be enhanced. When my mother tried to control her, shut down the spells she was casting, she ran away. She hasn't been back since.

"The magic skipped me. I'm not a witch. I don't have any power."

Aunt Tillie shifted on her chair. "Magic often skips generations," she acknowledged. "Or it will bless one child and leave another bereft. There's often no pattern or reason. That said ... what about your daughter?"

I jolted at the notion. I hadn't even considered Dani.

"My daughter is another story," Lorna acknowledged. "She's evil all around. She always has been. That one was born bad ... and there's nothing I can do about it. If you're searching for an evil witch, look no further, because she's the one you want."

Ugh. That was so not what I was expecting.

TWENTY-SIX

I couldn't comprehend what I was hearing.

"How long have you known that Dani is a witch?"

"Since she was five and set the curtains on fire when I wouldn't give her ice cream," Lorna replied, matter-of-fact. "That's why all the curtains are flame retardant now."

"But ... I've never seen her manifest." I ran through the brief conversation I'd had with Dani. "I've seen her around since she was a little kid. She's never exhibited any magical ability in front of me."

"Did you exhibit your magical ability in front of others?"

"No, but ... ." She had a point.

"I wanted her to be a good girl," Lorna offered. "I really wanted that more than you will ever know. I thought there was a chance I could fix things with her. Adam always refused to see what she really was, said I was overreacting and imposing my fears of my sister on her. But I always knew, deep down, that she was something to be feared."

I was utterly flabbergasted and didn't know what to say.

Aunt Tillie never had that problem. "What can she do?" She was all business. "You said she set the drapes on fire when she was a small child. Fire magic is rare in kids that age. Did your mother have fire magic?"

"I don't know much about witchcraft," Lorna admitted ruefully. "I was upset when I was a kid and realized that I didn't have any magic. Diane was always my mother's favorite because she was powerful.

"My mother didn't hate me or anything, I don't want you to think that," she continued. "It was simply inevitable that she bonded closer with Diane. They had more in common."

I stirred. "Why did Diane run away? You mentioned that your mother was trying to rein her in. That can't be the only reason."

"But it was." Lorna insisted. "Diane always thought she could do whatever she wanted, hurt whoever she wanted, claim whatever boy she wanted. If she couldn't do it with her natural charm she would use magic.

"My mother provided for us with her potions, love spells and the like. She understood that she was setting a bad example for Diane, but when you have children to feed, well, sometimes you have to make hard choices.

"She spent a lot of time talking to Diane, explaining the nature of magic and why it was never good to embrace the dark arts," she continued. "Diane would always laugh with me afterward — we shared a room and she liked to talk badly about Mother — and said that she was wasting her potential. She said she wouldn't be the same way.

"My mother made a few mistakes with Diane when she was small, laughing when she did something that wasn't so nice simply because she used magic to do it. She was often tickled by Diane's antics. As Diane grew older, she realized she'd created a monster of sorts and had no idea what to do about it."

"I remember your sister," Aunt Tillie offered. "She hid the fact that she had gifts well. I never saw anything in her that would suggest she was evil. I have to give her kudos on hiding her true nature."

"We were aware of you," Lorna explained. "Your family was held in high regard in some witch circles, including the coven my mother joined. Most witches knew enough to steer clear of you. The power that emanated from your family was otherworldly.

"Diane was a bit infatuated with you for a time, Miss Tillie. You probably don't remember. She followed you around to try to catch you casting spells. She never could. As for your nieces, there was a time she tried to befriend them. She wanted Winnie because she believed she was the most powerful, but she would've taken any of them.

"They were a tight-knit circle, though, and you couldn't separate them. Diane grew frustrated that she couldn't make inroads and eventually wrote them off. She said they were weak compared to you and not worth her time."

"It's not that they're weak," I countered. "They simply have other gifts. They prefer to nurture rather than tear down."

"Which is something that wouldn't have appealed to Diane, even on a superficial level," Lorna acknowledged. "She liked feeling powerful. She always wanted to be in charge."

"I'm starting to think that's a witch thing," I noted. "There are very few witches who don't want to be the boss. There's still a line that shouldn't be crossed, but she obviously crossed it. What was the final straw for your mother?"

"There was a boy ... Daniel Robinson."

Aunt Tillie stirred. "Wait ... the Robinson boy? Did she do that?"

I was lost. "Who is Daniel Robinson?"

"He was a classmate of your mother's," Aunt Tillie replied, her brow furrowed. "He was a nice boy. He had a crush on Marnie for some reason, even though she didn't give him the time of day. He asked her to some dance and she said yes because she felt sorry for him ... and, if memory serves, she wouldn't have had a date otherwise.

"The night before the dance, he was out running on the county highway," she continued. "He was a member of the track team. He didn't come home. When he was found on the side of the road, they thought he'd been struck by a vehicle, but there were no signs of that.

"They did an extensive autopsy. They could find nothing wrong with him. He simply dropped dead by the side of the road. Marnie felt horrible after, believed she should've been nicer to him. It was too late to give him the attention she thought he deserved."

Lorna nodded in agreement. "He was a nice boy. I had a crush on him. Diane decided she wanted him more and went after him. She asked him to that dance and he declined. She was jealous because he chose Marnie. She was convinced that he'd only pursued her because she'd cast a spell on him."

"Marnie would never do that." I was adamant. "That's not who she is."

Lorna held up her hands. "I'm just saying that Diane believed that's who she was. When Daniel died, my mother was suspicious. She questioned her. Of course, Diane denied it, but my mother wasn't so easily swayed.

"One day while Diane was at school, Mother collected all of her crystals and potions and destroyed all her books," she continued. "Then she tried to enforce a 'no magic' rule on the house. Diane was furious, fought with her, and then ultimately Diane left in the middle of the night."

"Did she leave a note?"

Lorna shook her head. "No, but she told me the previous day that she'd had it with the family, hated how weak our mother was, and refused to be the sort of witch she wanted her to be. She had grand plans to go to Salem, because that's where she heard all the best witches lived. I wasn't all that surprised when I woke and she was gone."

"Your mother looked for her," Aunt Tillie noted. "Your mother wasn't ready to let her go."

"No, and we looked for a long time. Finally, though, my mother admitted that Diane wasn't going to come back and she let it go. It wasn't something that came easily to her, but she was convinced that Diane would return one day. She didn't, not even when Mother died. I have no idea where she ended up."

I rubbed my cheek as I absorbed the new information. "Is it possible that Diane returned long enough to kill your mother?"

"I guess anything is possible, but I would like to believe she wouldn't do that. Even though Diane was angry ... she was still our mother."

"Yeah, well ... what about Dani? Did she know about Diane?"

"She did. When Dani got old enough to understand I sat her down to explain about her magic. When I related what had happened to Diane, she was excited. She wanted to track down Diane and learn from her. I knew then that there was no teaching her how to be a good person. You're either born good or bad. I firmly believe that."

"I don't," Aunt Tillie countered. "That's neither here nor there, though. If Dani killed Adam and Masterson, she's a danger to everyone in this community. Do you think she would go after you and her brother?"

"I think it's only a matter of time. The second Nick graduates, I'm getting him out of this town, out of her reach. It's the only thing I can do for him."

"Will she be satisfied with the two deaths she's already caused?" I asked. "Or ... will she want more?"

"I didn't realize she killed Adam," Lorna offered. "I really didn't. Now that I know, it makes a sick sort of sense. As for being satisfied, I don't think anything will satisfy her now. She probably won't ever stop."

"We have to find her. We can't let her carry on like this."

"Are you going to kill her?"

"Not if we can help it. We just have to find her. We have no choice." I flicked my eyes to Aunt Tillie. "You're in this to the end, right?"

She nodded, resolute. "To the bitter end. Let's find the girl and end this. We don't have any other options. Lorna is right, she won't stop. With each murder she'll get more powerful ... and she'll believe that she can't be stopped."

"WHERE SHOULD WE START LOOKING?"

For once, Aunt Tillie was calm and willing to seek direction.

"I don't know." I pursed my lips as I sat in the driver's seat of my car. We'd yet to leave Lorna's driveway.

"Where do you think she is?"

"I have no idea. You're supposed to be the head cowboy on this one. Take us to the rodeo."

It took everything I had not to roll my eyes. "Just once it would be nice if you talked like a normal person," I said.

"What's the point? That won't help us find her."

"No ... I ... ." Something occurred to me and I blew out a sigh. "We need to go to the police station before we do anything."

Aunt Tillie, as I expected, balked. "Why would I possibly do that?"

"We need their help. Also ... they need to be made aware of what's going on. They're operating under the assumption that Lorna is guilty."

"So?"

"So Dani is out there somewhere and she's evil. There's every chance she could realize what we were doing at her house this morning. She might be out for vengeance."

"So?"

I wanted to shake her until she absorbed what I was saying. "So what better way to hurt me than to go after them? Besides, if she's really evil, she might try to get them on her side or something. We need to make them aware. They're the sort of men who will rush to the aid of a teenager if they believe she's in trouble. If she's truly as powerful as her mother says and she puts her hands on them ... ." I purposely left it hanging because I couldn't think about the possibility.

"She could hurt or control them," Aunt Tillie finished, grim. "I didn't think about that, but you're right. They have to know."

"Mom and the others have to know, too," I pointed out. "Dani might be smart enough to go out there and play to their emotions. I mean ... everyone thinks Lorna is the witch. She might use that to her advantage."

Aunt Tillie started digging in her pocket and came back with her phone. "I'll call the inn, have them batten down the hatches. I hate to say it, but there are so many witches out there it might be better if

Dani heads that way. That's the best piece of land to defend against whatever she's going to do."

I hadn't really considered that. It made sense ... and yet the notion made my stomach jittery. "Let's just find her and go from there."

LANDON AND CHIEF TERRY WERE in the latter's office when we arrived at the police station. They looked surprised to see me ... and downright annoyed to see Aunt Tillie.

"Do I even want to know what you two are doing together?" Chief Terry whined. "You're supposed to be out at the inn doing ... women stuff."

Aunt Tillie's expression was hard to read. There was a hint of annoyance lurking in her eyes and mischief curling her lips. I expected her to say something awful. I wasn't disappointed. "What sort of women stuff?" she challenged.

"You know ... women stuff."

"Like menstruation? Did you think we were out at the inn menstruating together?"

I had to press my lips together to keep from laughing at Landon and Chief Terry's horrified expressions. This was not the time for fun and games, but Aunt Tillie wasn't going to back down until she had her way ... and it was kind of funny.

"I guarantee nobody thought you were doing that," Chief Terry fired back. "I'm talking about girl things, like ... hair ... and makeup ... and toenails." He waved at my head. "That's the sort of things women do before a wedding."

"I had no idea," I drawled dryly. "I didn't realize there were rules about what women could do before a wedding."

"Oh, don't you start." Chief Terry made a face. "I wasn't trying to be sexist. It's just ... you guys are supposed to be safe and out of trouble. Why are you out and about? This can't be good."

"It's not good," I confirmed. "I have something to tell you and you're going to be angry."

He slapped his hand to his forehead and growled as Landon slid his eyes to me.

"Do I need to sit down?" Landon asked.

I shook my head. "No, but ... we're in trouble." I laid it all out for him, leaving nothing out. When I finished, he looked more confused than edified.

"I don't understand," he said, shaking his head. "Are we really supposed to be frightened of a teenager?"

"She's not a normal teenager," I replied, frustration bubbling up. "You can't think that. She'll use your sympathy against you. You can't fall for it."

"Why are we taking Lorna's word for this?" Chief Terry challenged. "I mean ... she could've been lying to you. Maybe she's pointing the finger at her own daughter to save herself."

"It's possible, but I don't believe it," I argued. "You didn't see her. The story she told ... well ... it makes sense in a weird sort of way. I never got a hint of magic off Lorna. That's the thing that kept holding me back. There's a reason. She's not magical. All those surrounding her are magical."

"Bay, I don't want to tell you your business, but this is crazy," Landon supplied. "We can't just kill a teenaged girl because you say she's evil."

"I'm not saying we should kill her." Wait ... was I? She was definitely dangerous. Killing her wasn't an option unless she gave us no choice. I was firm on that. "We need to find her. We can't let her run all over town hurting people."

"I agree, but we can't exactly arrest her on the say-so of her mother either," Chief Terry insisted. "We can't put 'homicide by magic' on the report."

I got that — no, I really did — but that didn't mean I could simply walk away. "We have to find her. Odds are she knows we're on to her. We can't just let her run roughshod over the town. Besides, she's controlling the birds. She could do real damage with them if we're not careful."

"Just so I'm clear, why did she do this in the first place?" Landon asked. "Was she upset at her father for cheating on her mother?"

"I think that's part of it. The other part is that she likes it. She likes being in control. I think killing her father gave her a taste of something she'd never experienced and now she wants more. She killed Masterson because he was with her mother. I'm guessing that was a way to make her mother pay. I'm not sure she'll be all that discriminating going forward."

"Except there's one more person she probably has a grudge against," Landon noted.

"Who's that?"

"Lisa," Aunt Tillie answered for him. "She was involved in the affairs. I very much doubt Dani will just let her off."

I hadn't even considered that. "We have to get to her."

Landon and Chief Terry were already on their feet.

"We'll check on her," Chief Terry insisted. "You guys are done here. You can't be involved. You need to go back to the inn and get ready for the wedding."

That didn't sound likely in the least. "I can't stop until we have her. I'm sorry, but ... either I go with you or I go alone. I won't be cut out of this."

Chief Terry turned his expectant eyes to Landon. "Are you going to handle this?"

Landon shook his head. "She's earned the right to be part of it. Besides, I hate to admit it, but if this kid is as powerful as Bay says she is we're definitely going to need some magical help."

Chief Terry made an exasperated sound that reverberated through the room. "That's not what I want to hear."

"Oh, suck it up, big guy." Aunt Tillie patted his shoulder. "You'll be glad you have us with you when the evil witch hits the fan. I guarantee it."

TWENTY-SEVEN

The hunt for Dani was on and we made a fearsome foursome, even as we stopped at Lisa's shop and found it completely empty ... and devoid of bird feathers. We checked her house to ensure the same. She wasn't there, but she also wasn't dead. I was taking that as a good sign.

Of course, from the way Landon and Chief Terry reacted to Aunt Tillie leading the charge as we checked various locations it was obvious they didn't feel the same way. Still, I was glad to have her around ... simply because I figured she would come in handy if it came to a magical fight. Taking on a child would be difficult.

The next place we headed was the funeral home. Dani had announced her intention to arrange her father's memorial service. She wasn't there. The funeral director seemed puzzled by our presence. He said he hadn't set up a meeting with Dani, which meant she'd been lying from the start this morning. She was on to us … er, me.

That was hardly a surprise.

"Where would she go?" Landon mused as we climbed back into his Explorer.

I didn't know the girl well enough to answer. Instead, I started digging for my phone when it dinged in my pocket. "I just know that it's going to be Mom," I complained as I retrieved it. "She's probably mad we disappeared. Oh, I was right. It is her."

"Give me that." Aunt Tillie grabbed the phone from me, and for a moment I thought she was going to do something dramatic and toss it out of a window. Instead, she answered the call with a sickly-sweet voice that made me roll my eyes. "Hello, Winnie dear. It's a lovely day, isn't it?"

I sank lower in my seat because I could see my mother's face in my mind's eye. She was going to kill me.

From his spot in the driver's seat, Landon looked as if he was fighting off laughter but remained silent.

"I have no idea what you're talking about, Winnie." Aunt Tillie's inflection never changed. She remained calm. "That's a horrible thing to accuse your aunt of. I have never in my life been so offended. Bay? I'm not with Bay. I don't know why you would think that. Oh, this is her phone. How weird."

I slapped at Aunt Tillie's arm and reached for the phone. "You're making things worse. Give me that."

"Stop it!" Aunt Tillie extended a warning finger in my direction. "I'm in charge here. You have to do what I say."

That seemed unlikely. "That's my phone."

"I don't care. I ... what? Winnie, I'm not talking to Bay. I'm talking to myself. I'm old. I'm getting senile. Solo conversations happen all the time because my only friends are those I make up in my head."

"Ugh." I slapped my hand to my forehead. She only said things like that when it benefited her. Otherwise she claimed to be in her prime. This was spiraling ... and fast. "Give me that phone." Finally, I wrestled it away from her and pressed it to my ear. "Hello, Mom. You have nothing to worry about."

On the other end of the call, Mom was obviously dubious. "Why did you just disappear? We went looking for you because it was your turn for a pedicure."

"I know. I just ... there's a lot going on and I wanted to check on something. I figured I would be back by now."

"You can remedy that by coming home this instant."

She sounded so reasonable. I knew better. "I can't come home just yet. We have a situation. We know who killed Adam ... and Masterson ... and is controlling the birds. We're looking for her now."'

"You and Aunt Tillie?"

"And Landon and Chief Terry."

A moment of silence assailed my ears and when Mom spoke again her voice was lower. "Please put Terry on the phone."

Uh-oh. I sensed trouble. "Mom, this isn't his fault," I complained, cringing at a loud noise on her end of the call. "What was that?"

"Don't change the subject, young lady. You know I hate it when you do that. I'm not happy with you at all right now, Bay. This is Clove's big day. She needs you here. I ... what is that?" Her temper shifted from me to something happening at The Overlook. "How did that owl get in the house?"

My blood ran cold. That's when I recognized the noise I'd heard only moments before. "Mom."

She ignored me and continued yelling at those with her. "Keep him away from the eggs. I don't think he would want to eat them because that's kind of like cannibalism, but he looks rather aggressive."

"Mom."

I heard a loud bang somewhere near my mother and my stomach twisted.

"Mom."

"I can't deal with you right now, Bay," Mom shot back, annoyance evident. "You need to get back here right now. You're being rude to your cousin. I ... what now? Did a bird just fly into the window, Twila?"

Obviously she was no longer talking to me, but I screeched to get her attention all the same. "Mom! Do not hang up!"

She sounded absolutely exasperated. "What, Bay?"

"She's there. Dani is there. That's why the birds are attacking."

In the front seat, Chief Terry stirred and extended a finger toward the ignition of the Explorer. Landon turned the key without further instruction.

"Dani who?" Mom asked.

"Dani Harris," I replied, remaining as calm as I could. "Lorna admitted she's powerful and she's the one doing this. You have to find a place to hide, to shut out the birds. We're on our way back. You can't let her in the house."

"We won't let her in the house, Bay, but my guess is she's already on the property." Mom's voice was calm. "We'll fight her off. You don't have to worry about us. I don't think it's wise that you come here."

I was confused. "Why?"

"Because you'll be the ones who are vulnerable in that scenario." Mom said. "We're entrenched in the inn. We can keep her out indefinitely. We're not the only witches here."

The inn was full of coven members. In this particular instance that was good. "I'm still coming."

"You can't. If Dani really is as powerful as you're making her out to be you'll be vulnerable when you try to make it inside the inn. You'll be exposed. Landon, Terry and Aunt Tillie will be exposed, too. You're safer staying away."

That wasn't going to happen. "We're coming no matter what you say."

Impatience overriding her again, Aunt Tillie grabbed the phone and pressed it to her ear. "Don't even try to keep us away, Winnie. That won't work."

I couldn't hear Mom's response, but it didn't matter. Landon cast a worried look over his shoulder before pulling onto the highway, holding my gaze for a moment before focusing on the road.

"Bay, it'll be okay," he reassured me. "It won't take long to get there."

"I know." I stared out the window. "They're under attack ... and Dani will be positioned between them and us when we arrive. She has a lot of room to play with ... and she'll have the upper hand."

"She's still just a kid," Chief Terry protested. "We should be able to overpower her."

"Are you sure?" I certainly wasn't. "Will you be able to shoot a teenager if you get a clear shot?"

He balked. "Why are we shooting her? We'll just order her to stand down."

"I think what Bay is saying is that Dani is unlikely to back down," Landon replied quietly. "We might have to make some hard decisions."

"She'll stand down." Chief Terry sounded convinced. "She's a teenager. Self-preservation is the most important thing."

I could only hope that was true.

BIRDS SWARMED THE SKY ABOVE THE inn as we arrived at the Winchester ancestral property. Landon parked on the driveway instead of the lot near the hotel. We were clearly visible, but we weren't boxed in.

"Call Winnie," Landon ordered Chief Terry. "Find out where they are and make sure they're okay."

Chief Terry viciously swore under his breath as he fumbled with his phone. It was clear the birds made him nervous. "This is the creepiest thing I've ever seen."

I looked out the passenger window and found a huge bald eagle staring at me from a fallen tree. It was a large animal, majestic and beautiful ... and it looked aggressive. "Oh, geez."

Landon followed my gaze. "You have got to be kidding me. I didn't even know we had eagles in this area."

"I knew we had a few, but ... we can't fight that thing."

"No, we can't," he agreed. "It's against the law to hurt one of them."

I hadn't even considered that. "Well ... hopefully he'll stay over there." I focused on Chief Terry as he disconnected the call. "What did she say?"

"They're all safe in the dining room. There are no windows in that room, so the birds can't get in. They've barricaded the swinging doors. They're safe for now, but ... ."

"But they can't stay there forever," I surmised, rubbing the back of my neck as I scanned the property. "We need to draw Dani out."

"And then what?" Landon protested. "Are we just supposed to shoot her when she appears?"

"No." I would never expect that from him. "I'm going to talk to her, try to reason with her." *And, if that doesn't work, I'll be the one to take her out,* I silently added. I couldn't expect him to take out a teenager. It wasn't fair.

"You're going to try to reason with her, huh?" Landon made a face. "Look around, Bay. She's summoned hundreds of birds to attack the second you exit this vehicle. I don't think she can be reasoned with."

I was starting to fear that, too, but we didn't have many options. "What do you suggest we do?" I challenged. "We can't sit here while they hide inside a windowless room. Someone has to draw her out."

"That doesn't mean it has to be you."

Aunt Tillie, who had been quiet for a long time, stirred. "I think he means I should be the one to try to talk to her," she said. "He's willing to sacrifice me."

"I most certainly am not," Landon snapped, his eyes flashing. "I don't want anyone to be sacrificed. There has to be a way to keep everybody safe."

"Even if you shot every bird on this property, we wouldn't be safe," I reminded him. "Her powers don't simply revolve around the birds. She can do more … including set fires."

"So, what's the plan?" Chief Terry demanded. "We're going to exit the Explorer and try to get her to see our way of thinking after she killed her own father? No offense, but that strikes me as unlikely."

"We're not all leaving the Explorer." I was firm on that. "You three are staying here while I try to talk to her."

Landon balked. "Absolutely not. That's not happening."

"She's not going to talk in front of you," I pointed out. "She wants to talk to a witch."

"That's why it should be me," Aunt Tillie volunteered. "I'm the most powerful witch we've got. She'll respect me."

"She might respect your power, but anything you say to her will come off as out of tune and dated," I argued. "I'm at least closer to her age."

Aunt Tillie narrowed her eyes speculatively. "Are you saying I'm old?"

"I'm saying that in her eyes you're old," I answered. "She's a teenager. Anyone older than thirty seems ancient to her."

Aunt Tillie worked her jaw and I could see she was debating the merits of my suggestion. Finally, she nodded. "Okay. I'll be watching your back from here. If you have to run back … ."

"Then I'll run back," I reassured her. "It's okay. I'm our best shot of taking her down."

"And what happens when she doesn't want to be talked down?" Landon challenged, grabbing my hand before I could exit the vehicle. "I won't risk you, Bay. I … can't."

I shot him my most reassuring smile. "I'm the only option we have. You won't lose me. I promise."

"But … ." He changed course quickly. "Let me go with you. You'll need eyes in the back of your head with all those birds. If I'm with you … ."

"Then you'll become a distraction," I finished calmly. "You need to be here with the others, safe. That way my attention won't be split."

"I don't want you alone!" he practically exploded.

"I won't be alone." For some reason I was unnaturally calm as I regarded him. "You're always here." I moved his hand to the spot above my heart. "Besides, she might have an air force of birds, but I have an army of ghosts at my disposal. I think one will be scarier than the other when it comes down to it."

He didn't look convinced. "Bay … ." He almost sounded as if he was going to cry.

I leaned forward and pressed my forehead to his. "I'll be okay. Have a little faith."

"I have faith, sweetie. I just … I don't like being separated from you."

I could see that. "We don't have a choice."

"There's always a choice."

"And we have to make this one right now. I promise we'll be drinking ourselves silly on Aunt Tillie's wine and dancing under the full moon in a few hours. Just … let me do this. It's our best shot."

He blew out a sigh and then pressed his lips to mine. "Don't you leave me."

"I'll be back before you know it." I caught Aunt Tillie's gaze as I pulled away and reached for the door handle. "You know what to do?"

She nodded, calm. "Everything will be fine. Do what I did when you guys were teenagers. Talk big and scare the crap out of her. She'll fall in line fast enough if she thinks no boy will ever look at her again, so threaten her looks."

I was amused despite myself. "Do you think that will really work?"

"Teenagers are vain creatures. It always works."

MY PALMS WERE SWEATY WHEN I made it to the end of the driveway. I cast the eagle a leery look, but he didn't leave his perch. Slowly, I crossed in front of the Explorer and started plodding toward the house.

I heard the birds in the sky cackling as they circled — and momentarily I wondered if there would be a bird crap situation at some point — but otherwise I focused on the trees and bushes littering the yard during my approach. Dani was behind one of them. I was certain of it.

Sure enough, when I was almost to the small parking lot, she stepped out from behind a huge maple tree and blocked my path.

"I bet you're surprised to see me," she announced, grinning like a loon as she caught my gaze. "You had no idea it was me, did you?" She was obviously having a good time.

"Not until I talked to your mother," I admitted, stopping in my tracks. I didn't want to get too close to her. "She told us what you are ... but only after we informed her of Masterson's death."

"He had it coming." Dani's voice turned cold. "He was doing bad things with my mother and he totally deserved what he got."

She didn't seem remorseful in the slightest, which worried me. "I agree that he wasn't the best man," I hedged. "That doesn't mean you had to kill him."

"I didn't kill him." There was a hint of mischief flitting through her eyes. "I mean ... I heard that was a tragic accident. Birds somehow got into his house and killed him. You can't blame that on me."

I pointedly glanced around at the birds circling the inn. "Oh, no? Are you sure about that?"

"Very sure. I have it on good authority that I'm in the clear."

That was an odd thing to say. "Birds didn't kill your father," I pointed out. "You can't blame your feathered friends for that."

"No, Mr. Masterson killed my father ... and the birds paid him back for what he did to our family."

Now I was definitely confused. "Masterson killed your father? But ... why?"

"He was in love with my mother and wanted her to end her marriage. He was working with that horrible seamstress ... who is now hiding. She thinks that will stop me from finding her, but it won't."

Well, that answered that question. "Then you haven't killed Lisa?"

"I don't kill people. I have no idea what you're talking about."

I frowned as I glanced over my shoulder. Landon's Explorer was far enough away that I couldn't read his facial expressions. I could feel his anxiety, though. "I think the time for games is over, Dani," I started. "You need to stand down."

She snorted, disdainful. "And why would I do that? I'm the most powerful one here."

"No, you're not."

"Who else is more powerful? That crazy old lady on the scooter? She's not. I've been the one supplying all the magic to this town the past few weeks. Frankly, you guys have been a disappointment."

"Just because we don't constantly show off our magic doesn't mean we don't have it," I reminded her calmly. "You're in over your head here. Plus, well, you're woefully outnumbered. This place is crawling with witches. You picked the worst possible weekend to attack."

"Perhaps ... if I were alone in this. I'm not. I have a little backup of my own."

Even as I felt the shadow move in from my right, I realized the missing puzzle piece was finally visible … and I couldn't believe I hadn't realized it sooner.

Slowly, I slid my eyes to the familiar face joining the fray. She was a witch, and I wanted to kick myself for not grasping sooner how this was all going to play out.

"I guess I should've seen this coming."

"I guess you should have," Evie agreed, her eyes burning with malevolence. "You obviously weren't smart enough for that."

Obviously not.

TWENTY-EIGHT

Evie. The weird witch who was named after *The Wizard of Oz*. She seemed pleased with herself ... probably because I looked as shocked as I felt.

I glanced over my shoulder again and saw that Landon was moving to get out of the Explorer. Chief Terry wrestled with him in an effort to keep him inside, but he wouldn't be able to overpower him indefinitely. Recognizing that, I turned back to her.

"Aren't you going to say anything?" Evie challenged.

"I'm considering what to say," I admitted after a moment. "Why are you involved in this?"

Evie shrugged, noncommittal. "Why not?"

"Dani has a personal stake," I pointed out. "She has a reason — however convoluted — for going after Masterson. Her father is more of a curiosity, but at least I can see the rationalization, however weak. But you ... ."

"You think I have no dog in the show," Evie noted. "I guess, from your perspective, you would think that. You weren't even born when I left. Your mother, she knows me ... and yet she didn't recognize me when I checked into her inn. That was a little ... disappointing."

I couldn't hide my confusion. "My mother knows you?"

"She does."

"But ... ." And that's when things slipped into place. "Diane. You're Diane."

Evie's grin widened until it took over the bottom half of her face. "Very good. It took you longer than it should have — which means you're as slow as your mother — but apparently you're faster than Twila."

"How long have you two been in contact?" I glanced between them. Dani looked almost gleeful, as if she'd just won the lottery and was about to buy a castle. Evie's reaction was harder to gauge.

"I've been back in the area for years," Evie replied. "I don't live in Hemlock Cove, of course — that would've been too risky — but I live close enough to monitor the comings and goings of the area's most famous witches. Of course ... those accolades aren't exactly earned, are they?"

It didn't take a Mensa member to figure she was bitter. She had issues with the older generation of witches in our family. She felt slighted. That's what Lorna had said. She thought my mother and aunts should've embraced her, made her one of them, and instead they closed ranks. That was the Winchester way, but as an outsider she couldn't have known that.

"You're still angry they didn't want to play with you," I supplied finally. "You wanted to be one of them, but they didn't allow you to even serve as an alternate on the team. That must've been difficult for you."

Evie's gaze darkened. "I don't need to be one of them. I'm more powerful than all three of them combined."

I didn't believe that for a second. "Are you? How do you figure?"

"Look around." She gestured toward the birds. "I've got your mothers trapped in their own house. They can't leave unless I allow it. Me!" She thumped her chest. "I'm in charge here. I've set all of this up and I decide who plays on the team this time."

She was delusional. Had she always been that way? I couldn't help but wonder. It really didn't matter at this point. It was time to take her down. What about Dani, though? Was she aware of what she was doing? Did her aunt twist her? Was she just as evil as her aunt? I had to figure out those answers before I moved forward.

"Did you kill your father, Dani?" I focused my full attention on the teenager because I knew it would agitate her aunt. "Did you do this or did she?"

"What does it matter?" Dani puffed out her chest. "I was part of it. I knew what she was going to do. I put the butane in the workshop. I knew what would happen when it exploded. That was me."

That wasn't what I wanted to hear. Still ... knowing what was going to happen was different than participating. "How did you two meet? Did she contact you?"

Dani didn't get a chance to answer. Evie did it for her. She was too enamored with the idea of being the center of attention to cede it to anyone, including her student.

"I watched my sister for years," Evie volunteered. "I thought there was a chance she would manifest after Mother died. I figured she was holding Lorna back. I was wrong on that front ... sadly."

"You killed your mother," I surmised.

"I did." Evie's smugness made me want to wipe the evil smirk right off her face. "I came back to talk to her several years after leaving Walkerville. *Talk*, no more. I was having a rough time of it. I wanted to see if she would help me. It turned out that was a mistake. She said she wouldn't help unless I allowed her to bind my powers.

"She didn't recognize me at first, of course. I'd gone to great lengths to change my appearance for a very important reason. I didn't want anyone in this town — least of all your mother and aunts — to recognize me. Once she became convinced of who I was, things turned ... ugly.

"We argued and I told her she was missing out, that she wouldn't have to struggle to scratch out a living in a dying town if she would simply embrace what she was," she continued. "She didn't agree."

I could see that. "Your mother was a good person who fought hard to take care of you and Lorna. You never saw that because you didn't understand the benefit of hard work. You always wanted the easy way out."

"I'm a witch. If life was meant to be difficult for me I wouldn't have been blessed by the Goddess with so much magic."

I shook my head and tried to regroup. Everything I thought I knew was wrong. I had to line up my thoughts if I expected to get even a modicum of a happy ending. There was a chance — however slim — that Dani could be saved. Evie had unleashed all the evil magic. Dani could still learn ... maybe. "When did you approach Dani?"

"She was thirteen the first time we chatted," Evie replied. "I'd been watching her closely over the years. I was pretty sure she was gifted when she was seven and I watched her take down that horrible woman who owns the unicorn store."

"Mrs. Little," I volunteered. "She's earned a lot of takedowns."

"Yes, she's a horrible wench. Anyway, she sprayed some of the kids with a hose because they were on the sidewalk in front of her store. It wasn't unicorns at that point. It was something else ridiculously stupid. I watched Dani, saw how angry she was, and then wanted to clap when the hose sprang a leak and doused Mrs. Little while she was terrorizing the kids."

"You couldn't be sure just because of that," I noted. "That could've simply been a weak hose, one that sat out in the sun for too long and developed a hole or something."

"True, but I watched her more closely after that. I wasn't positive until she was thirteen and one of the boys was teasing her. She grew so enraged she tripped him with her magic. He went down, broke all his front teeth out and screwed up his face so badly I was certain he would be deformed for life."

"Mike O'Brien," Dani interjected with a grin. "He was always a jerk. After that, he never bothered me again. I don't know how, but he was certain that I did it. He was afraid of me after that."

"I remember the O'Briens," I noted. "They left town about two and a half years ago."

"Because Mike was afraid of me." Dani did a little dance she was so happy. "His grades fell and he was going to flunk out, so his parents moved him away."

"And that's when you had your first taste of power," I deduced.

"That's when you realized that you could make people do things that benefitted you."

"Pretty much."

I slid my eyes to Evie. "And that's when you decided to mold your niece."

"Pretty much," Evie agreed, smiling at Dani. "I started small. I approached her as a practitioner of Wicca from another town. I didn't push her too hard at first because I didn't want to frighten her. I played the long game."

"Eventually she found out you were her aunt."

"She did. About a year after I introduced myself to her. We bonded after that."

"And you never told your mother, Dani?" The question came out more accusatory than I intended, but my frustration was growing with each word. "Didn't you think you should tell your mother what was going on?"

"Why would I?" Dani snorted in derision. "My mother wasn't a witch. She didn't understand the power I had at my disposal. She was just a weak woman in a bad marriage. I didn't want to be like her, so why would I tell her?"

I pressed the heel of my hand to my forehead and tempered the anger that was thudding in my chest in time with my increasing heart rate. "I'm guessing you found out about your father's affair first and confided in your aunt."

"Actually, I had no idea. Aunt Evie told me."

Of course. That made more sense. "Your aunt told you about your father because she wanted to stoke your rage."

"I don't know about that, but she thought I would want to know. I was angry at first and started following him because I didn't believe her. I was a naive idiot back then, but I saw them together a few times and knew she was telling me the truth. I hated her for it … at first."

"Which you expected," I said to Evie. "You knew she would be angry and need time to adjust. That was all part of your plan."

"It was," Evie agreed. "She came around much more quickly than I expected. I let her vent to me for months before suggesting we teach him a lesson. At first, we teased him ... gave him indigestion after a big meal, a minor problem here and there in the bedroom.

"Then, one night Dani heard her parents arguing and realized they were going to divorce and she flipped out," she continued. "She wanted to protect her mother. I was aware of Lorna's relationship with Masterson at that point, but I didn't think it was wise to gum up the works of what I had planned."

"Of course not," I said. "You wanted to make Lorna suffer because that's your way. You couldn't take her out too quickly. You wanted to take everything she loved instead."

"She ended up with everything," Evie argued. "She ended up with what should've been mine, including Mother's house and land. I was completely cut out of the will."

Ah, well, that was another piece of the puzzle. I'd wondered what final straw got her to cross the line to darkness. Apparently it was greed. I shouldn't have been surprised. "You thought you would get money once she was dead. I bet you were bitterly disappointed when that didn't happen."

"Shocked is more like it. I kept waiting for a call from the attorney, but it never came."

"Yes, well ... how terrible for you. All that murder and you didn't even benefit."

Her eyes flashed with annoyance. "I deserved something from that woman after what she did to me."

"You mean when she tried to turn you away from dark magic?"

Evie let loose a laugh so hollow it sent chills down my spine. "There is no such thing as dark and light magic. There is only magic. That's something your family has never learned."

"Actually, I think that's something you've never learned," I countered. "There is a vast difference between the two ... but I think you'll find that out soon. It will be a lesson you should've learned a long time ago."

"Oh, really?" Evie didn't look worried in the least. Of course, she didn't know what I knew. "Are you going to take out both of us? I've drawn protective circles all over my body, tattooed them in myself with the blood of the fallen. You can't touch me."

My stomach rolled with unease. She really was dedicated … and deranged. "You won't be allowed to leave this land."

"You didn't answer my question. Are you going to take both of us on yourself? You'll fail."

"Then I guess it's good I won't be doing anything myself. When you use light magic, you're never alone."

"Oh, that was so ... ridiculous." She rolled her eyes. "I don't even care about you, if you want to know the truth. I want to see your mother. She's the one I owe. I was close to making inroads with Marnie after I failed with her, but she ruined it. She always ruined everything.

"Of course, losing you will be a payback of a different sort," she continued. "I guess that will be worth it."

I opened my mouth to respond, but I didn't have to. My mother was taking control of this conversation. All the witches inside the inn had poured out through the front door when they saw me conversing with Evie. They'd been listening the whole time.

"If you want me, Diane, I'm right here," Mom called out.

Evie jolted at the voice, and when she turned I didn't miss the way the color briefly drained from her features. She didn't allow the fear to take over for very long. She was back to bluster and false bravado within seconds.

"I was wondering how long you were going to hide inside," she said, that malevolent grin back. "I would've been disappointed if you allowed your daughter to fight your battle alone."

"She was never going to be alone." Mom moved to the front of the witch horde and joined hands with Marnie and Twila. They were earth witches, but that didn't mean they were unschooled in battle. "Let's do this."

"Oh, let's do this." Evie lifted her hands to the sky. I knew she was going to call the birds to strike. That seemed to be her only move.

I risked a glance at Dani and recognized that she was no longer having fun. Perhaps she thought this would be a verbal standoff and nothing more. Perhaps she really had no idea how all this worked because Evie had warped her mind in ways she didn't even realize.

Ultimately, it didn't matter. I would protect Dani to the best of my ability because I believed she could still be saved. Evie was a lost cause. She took the blood of her enemies and tried to protect herself with it. That was as dark as it got.

I mimicked her stance and raised my hands, earning a snicker as the birds started to descend.

"You can't wrest control of them from me," she gloated. "I'm stronger than you."

I held her gaze. "You might control the birds, but I control something else."

I briefly closed my eyes and called to every ghost in the area. I had no idea how many there were, but Viola was the first to pop into existence and let me know my spell was working.

"What's going on?" she asked, glancing around. "I ... ." When she saw the birds, her eyes went wide. "Oh, well, this is new."

"Take them out," I ordered as a host of other ghosts descended upon the parking lot, the shimmering light of their anchored souls twinkling across the landscape. "Turn them away. Kill them if you have to ... but try to keep the eagle alive. He's endangered, after all."

Viola nodded in a perfunctory manner. "I'm on it. You can count on me." Then, just as I expected, she acted as a general for the amassing ghosts and shouted commands. "Charge!"

That was a little over-the-top, but it ultimately wasn't important. Evie couldn't hear her anyway.

She realized something was happening. She couldn't see the ghosts, though, so all she knew was that every frontal assault was being turned back by an unseen force. For the first time since she'd crawled out of the shadows, I sensed real fear from her.

"That was pretty good," Aunt Tillie noted, appearing at my side. Landon and Chief Terry were with her, and Landon's face was flushed with exertion. "Your boyfriend had a meltdown, by the way. Terry threatened to lock him in the trunk when he wanted to come out and join you."

"It was probably smart to keep him in the truck. I'm okay," I called out to him.

"You're definitely wearing the bacon outfit tonight," he barked. "What do we do now?"

"Get Dani," I replied without hesitation. "We can't kill her. She's still a kid, and she was only peripherally involved in the deaths. There's still a chance we can … ." I trailed off, uncertain.

"What? Train her?" Aunt Tillie looked dubious. "Pulling her back won't be easy."

"But we have to try, right?"

Aunt Tillie held my gaze for a beat, her expression unreadable. Finally, she nodded. "We have to try."

"Fine. We'll take Dani," Landon volunteered. "What are you going to do to Diane?"

"What we have to do," I answered grimly. "She can't walk away from this."

"That's going to be hard to explain on a report," Chief Terry argued.

"Maybe not." I lifted my eyes to the ghosts again and focused on Viola. "Drive them toward their master," I suggested.

It took Viola a moment to realize what I meant before she brightened considerably. "Come on, guys," she encouraged. "Let's take this witch down."

Evie squawked as she turned to run, but there was nowhere for her to go. "Dani!" She screamed the girl's name. "You have to help protect me. It's the only way we'll survive this."

"No, Dani." I shook my head at the teenager's fearful expression as I called to her through the din of screeching birds and attacking ghosts. "This isn't your war. You have to let it go."

She looked uncertain. "But … ."

"You're done," Landon snapped, sliding up behind her and grabbing her arms, holding them tight as Chief Terry slapped cuffs on her. "You're so done, little girl."

"Dani!" Evie dropped to her knees and covered her head, screeching as the birds grew closer. With the ghosts directing them, there was no way for Evie to escape. She was fueling the fire in the birds – a tether she couldn't snap so late in the game – and they had to attack. Thanks to the ghosts cutting off the openings to other witches, there was only one available target.

I turned away when the birds reached her. I didn't need to see the final battle. It was over before it began, really, although Evie's screams would live with me for a very long time. That's how it should be, though, because light magic came with one other thing that dark magic didn't – a conscience.

TWENTY-NINE

Chief Terry called in Evie's death as a wild animal attack. The medical examiner was dubious, but there were no other marks on her body. He took her in and promised a full autopsy.

Lorna arrived to see about Dani. She didn't look happy – more resigned than anything else – but she didn't disavow her daughter. The disappointment on her face was obvious, but she was sober and aware ... something that she couldn't claim the last few days. Perhaps she realized she wasn't helping matters. That situation – however resolved – would take time to work out.

Dani struggled as she was led away in handcuffs. Once her aunt was gone, all that bluster she'd exhibited dried up. She looked like a frightened teenager.

"I don't know that this is a good idea," Landon intoned as he watched the girl being loaded into a cruiser. She looked forlorn, tears streaking down her cheeks. "She's dangerous, Bay."

I pressed the heel of my hand to my forehead and pressed hard. "So am I."

"You saved lives today. She wanted to take them."

"Maybe." It was possible he was right. "There's still a chance she can turn things around. She didn't murder her father and Masterson. She knew ... and maybe she helped a bit... but she wasn't the driving force behind those murders. That was Evie ... er, Diane ... or whatever her name was."

"She wasn't lying about having it legally changed. I checked. If we'd dug harder ... ."

"It doesn't matter now." I reached over and laced my fingers with his. "It's over. I don't think there ever was a way to save Diane. But Dani still has a chance."

"We're keeping her in jail overnight ... maybe several nights. After that, what do we do with her?"

"I don't know." That was the truth. I hadn't gotten that far in my planning. "Let's get through the wedding, give Clove the celebration she's always wanted, and figure out what to do with Dani tomorrow."

"That seems like the lazy way to do it."

I laughed. I couldn't help myself. "Well ... it has been a busy few days."

"It has," he agreed, leaning close so he could press a kiss to my forehead. "You know, before this I just assumed that any children we have would naturally be good because you're good. This makes me wonder. I mean ... was Dani born bad?"

"I don't think so. She had a temper as a child. She managed to set the drapes on fire when she was five. I told you how fire witches are rare. We'll have to rein her in quickly if there's any chance of saving her. Still ... *still* ... I don't know that I believe she was born bad. I prefer believing circumstances made her conflicted."

"You're going to try to save her." It was a statement rather than a question.

"I'll do what I can," I clarified. "That might well be nothing. I really can't say with any degree of certainty what I'm going to do. I couldn't kill her, though. I just ... couldn't."

He blew out a sigh and dragged a hand through his hair. "Fair enough," he said. "I couldn't have killed her either. And setting her loose to run amok doesn't seem like a good idea."

"Definitely not."

"So, we'll do things your way," he supplied. "I'll help you any way I can."

I already knew that, which was only one of the reasons I felt hopeful that we would be able to change Dani's life. Additional aid would come in the form of my mother and aunts … and maybe even Aunt Tillie.

"I should probably head upstairs." I turned to stare at the second-floor window. I could see Thistle standing on the other side, gesturing wildly as Twila approached her with what appeared to be a box of hair dye. "I think the adventures of the day are just beginning."

Landon followed my gaze, smiling. "That looks … fun."

"Then you're clearly not picturing it right."

"Oh, I have a fairly good idea how all of that is going to go." His grin widened and then he swooped in to give me a kiss. "It's going to be okay, Bay. Your instincts are rarely wrong. If you believe helping Dani is the way to go, then I'm with you."

"Thanks." I slid my arms around his neck and held tight. I needed the moment of healing, an instant of quiet before the family storm. Perhaps we both did. I didn't pull away until I heard someone clearing a throat behind us. When I turned, I wasn't surprised to find Hazel. "Do you need something?"

"I was going to ask you that," she replied, shooting Landon a smile. "I didn't mean to interrupt. I just wanted to catch you before you headed upstairs. I'm sure we'll see each other at the wedding and ritual later. We're doing a big blessing for Clove and the baby, so it should be a fun night."

"I'm sure Clove will be thankful for that," I said perfunctorily.

"You're not comfortable around me," Hazel deduced. "I wish it were different, but … you're leery."

"I don't know you," I corrected. "I'm leery around anyone who claims to know what's best for me."

"I don't believe I've ever done anything of the sort."

"No?" I arched a challenging eyebrow. I had one very specific memory of Hazel from before the coven split. "That wasn't you insisting to my mother that she should bind my powers because I was a threat to everyone around me?"

Hazel hesitated before answering. "I didn't know you overheard us that day."

Landon stirred. "I'm sorry, you did what?"

Hazel hung her head. "I wasn't trying to hurt Bay," she insisted. "That was never my intention. She's a very powerful witch, and I had the impression she wasn't getting the proper guidance under this roof. I see now that I was mistaken.

"You have to understand, back then I thought I knew what was best for everybody," she continued. "I wasn't trying to curtail magic, only regulate it. I see now that I should've kept my big nose out of your life. Your mother and aunts raised you exactly as they should have.

"You're still powerful, Bay, but because they let you grow at your own pace you didn't turn into a dark witch like Dani. You never believed you were better than anyone because you were stronger. You were never molded into a fierce warrior. All that strength you put on display today comes from inside."

"Not exactly," I countered, my eyes briefly drifting to Aunt Tillie, who was busy making faces at Dani through the cruiser window. "A lot of my strength comes from them. I have weaknesses. I never forgot what you said to my mother that day, though … and I never forgot the way Aunt Tillie reacted.

"She took responsibility for breaking us away from the coven, but in truth she did it for me," I continued. "She wanted to make sure you had no control over me. That's why things fell apart."

"And they came together because your mother realized you were safe from us and the coven could be reunited," Hazel offered. "I want to help you with Dani. In fact, I think I might move up here – if only temporarily – to offer her a home."

I was taken aback. "She has a home."

"With a mother who is terrified of her."

I hadn't really considered that. "So … what? You would rent a place and live here with Dani?"

"I know you plan to try to rehabilitate her. You're going to need help."

That was true. I couldn't do it on my own. "I don't think that's a terrible idea," I hedged. "I need time to think about it."

Hazel cracked a smile. "You also want to talk about it with your family. Tillie might not be happy with the prospect of me staying."

That was the understatement of the year. "She might surprise you." Probably not, but you never know.

"I think she might be softening toward me," Hazel offered brightly. "She promised me some special gummy bears with my ice cream once the cake is cut. She seemed to think it was a good thing."

I had news for her. Those gummy bears were tainted. Still … that was Aunt Tillie's business. "Tonight is for Clove," I insisted. "She's been dreaming about this day since we were kids. I want her to have everything she's ever wanted … and that means getting upstairs so they can poke and prod me for the next five hours. We can talk about the rest of it tomorrow."

Hazel let loose a low chuckle. "You're a good cousin, Bay, and we can indeed discuss the girl's fate in the morning. Clove isn't the only dreamer, though. You used to be one, too." Her gaze was heavy when it landed on Landon. "I think your dreams have come true as well."

At least that was something we could agree on. "They have. Now, if you'll excuse me, my witchy Bridezilla awaits."

LANDON

The revelry went late into the night. He danced, ate his weight in bacon, played with Peg and sat under the stars with his blond witch. It was the perfect evening, though she was starting to tire. He could read it in the slope of her shoulders.

The other witches got drunk, throwing bird seed with a little too much zest for his liking given everything that happened earlier in the day. They pelted Clove and Sam with it as they climbed in the back of the limo and left for their honeymoon. Clove stuck her head out the window to exuberantly say goodbye to Thistle and Bay, tears streaming down her cheeks. When he looked to Bay, she was crying, too. This time, however, he wasn't sure she could blame it on Clove's hormones.

When he recognized that she wouldn't be able to keep her eyes open much longer, Landon suggested she say goodbye to the remaining witches and meet him at the guesthouse. She agreed and trudged away in the darkness.

He'd looked everywhere for Winnie for the past hour and come up empty. He wasn't surprised to find her washing dishes in the kitchen.

"Can't that wait until tomorrow?" he asked, folding his arms across his chest and resting his hip against the cupboards.

Winnie's eyebrows hopped in surprise. "What are you doing here? I thought you would've passed out by now."

"Not quite. I had a few drinks, but I didn't want to be drunk in case Dani somehow managed to conjure a flock of birds from her jail cell."

"Ah." Winnie nodded, her expression caught between amusement and sadness. "Do you need something? I'm just putting a load of dishes in before heading back out. It's going to take about ten loads before we're finished, so I thought I'd get a jump on things before the naked dancing starts." Her smile was smug as she focused on Landon.

"I do need something." Landon's voice was soft, his nerves getting the better of him. Finally, he blurted it out. "I'm going to ask Bay to marry me."

If Winnie was surprised, she didn't show it. "Okay."

"I want your permission to do it … soon."

Now she was surprised. "Shouldn't you be asking her father?"

"She loves her father. But you're the one who matters. I want to make sure it's okay with you."

Winnie carefully dried her hands as she regarded him. "Before I answer, may I ask you a question?"

"Sure."

"Why did you wait so long?"

"Because … ." He cocked his head to the side, considering. "Because at first I was afraid she would say no. I know now that was irrational, but I felt real fear. Then Clove got engaged and I didn't want her to think it was a reaction to that. I want Bay to be the center of attention like Clove has been since she announced her engagement."

"I figured as much." Winnie's face split into a wide grin. "Of course you have my permission."

Even though he expected the answer, Landon exhaled heavily. "Thank you."

"It's not my place to grant permission, though. She's her own woman and you're all she wants. You don't have to be nervous about asking her. She'll say 'yes.'"

"I certainly hope so. I won't be able to stop myself from being nervous. It goes with the territory."

"Well … I think it's sweet you asked." She patted his shoulder. "When will you do it?"

"Soon. I want to plan something special. I need you to keep it a secret until then. I know that's not always easy for you given the way this family gossips, but I don't want her surprise ruined."

"I won't tell anyone. You have my word."

"Thank you." Landon leaned forward and gave her a hug. "I love her. You know that, right?" The question came out on a whisper.

Winnie briefly pressed her eyes shut. "I know." Her voice choked up. "I've never doubted that. If you need help setting up something special, I'm at your disposal."

"I just might take you up on that."

She gave him another squeeze and then released him. "Now, go dance with Bay. If you call it a night within the next hour, you'll probably miss the naked dancing."

"Thanks for the tip." He saluted and headed toward the door, slowing when his fingers wrapped around the handle. "Thank you for raising her to be what she is."

"Thank you for loving who and what she is."

"How could I not love her? She's … everything I never knew I wanted. We're going to be happy together. I promise."

"Oh, honey, I've always known that. You don't have to worry about me. Terry, however, might be a little angry about being cut out of the loop."

"He'll be fine." Landon smiled at the prospect. "It's going to be a great life."

"It certainly is."

CPSIA information can be obtained
at www.ICGtesting.com
Printed in the USA
LVHW110002191119
637663LV00006BA/2325/P